HONEYMOON COTTAGE

A PAJARO BAY MYSTERY

BARBARA COOL LEE

PAJARO BAY PUBLISHING

INTRODUCTION

Camilla Stewart's ex-fiancé ripped her off and disappeared, leaving her to care for his eight-year-old son alone. But when she arrives in Pajaro Bay, she finds a village full of cute cottages, quirky characters... and a killer on the loose who is somehow linked to her, the young boy, and the darling little house known as the *Honeymoon Cottage*.

Originally published: March 12, 2012

This edition published: April 20, 2018

2018-04-20-A

As always, for Mom,
my co-writer.

CHAPTER ONE

PAJARO BAY, CALIFORNIA
Monday, April 9, 4:35 p.m.

CAMILLA STEWART STARED AT THE RHINESTONE BROOCHES PINNED to a piece of blue velvet, but she was not really seeing them. All around her the dusty little junk shop was silent except for the incessant ticking of eighteen clocks on the wall. Eighteen. She'd had plenty of time to count them. She tried to keep her hands from shaking.

She moved on to a collection of old wooden chairs with peeling paint and missing rungs. What would she do if she couldn't sell the ring? She was completely out of money, out of gas, out of options. No. She always had options. She would find a way.

Little Oliver sat in the corner, his nose buried in a book. She would like to buy him the book. But she didn't have the money. That was the problem. She didn't have any money at all.

Correction. She had one dollar and thirty-seven cents.

She could strangle Dennis Hutchins! Or whoever he really

was. He had taken everything when he'd disappeared. Except his son. She watched eight-year-old Oliver Hutchins, so like his father in appearance, so unlike him in personality. The darling boy's dark brown hair fell across his forehead as he bent down to silently mouth the words of the book.

She knew he was sounding out the hard words—they practiced that every night, and he was getting better and better. Now he had actually picked up a book by himself and started reading. It was a breakthrough, and she should be thrilled for him. But the thrill was tempered by the sour-looking woman behind the shop's counter.

"It'll be a little while," the woman had said when Camilla had offered up the ring for sale. Now the woman just sat behind a glass display case, one hand on the cash register, one hand fingering the ring. She seemed to be waiting for something. Why was it taking so long?

Camilla sat down in a chair that looked sturdier than the rest and tapped her fingers on the arms, then jumped back up, too nervous to stay still.

She looked out the front window of the shop.

The stupid convertible sat parked out front, windows cracking, paint job rusting, and gas gauge on empty. "A convertible is perfect for the California sunshine," she had joked to Oliver. She had been doing a lot of joking lately, trying to make light of the terrible mess they were in.

She missed her sleek fern-green Prius hybrid. She missed swinging into the Starbucks parking lot every morning on her way to work, zipping in wearing her favorite lavender suit and pearls, buying a latté for herself and a hot chocolate for Oliver, then dropping him at the private school for his extra tutoring.

The rush of being in her first year out of college, with a great job in the accounting department of the hottest high-tech firm in Silicon Valley, had made her feel like she'd really made it in the big world. She had been in control of her life then. She had been successful. She had been happy. It had been nice while it lasted.

Now in two months it was all gone. From a whirlwind courtship to court dates and jail staring her in the face, all in two short months. Thanks to her despicable ex-fiancé, her life had been reduced to begging in a junk shop for her next meal.

She had to get gas, get food, get Oliver and herself to the house on the hill before this podunk little town rolled up its sidewalks at dusk. And it would be dusk soon. What was taking so long?

RYAN KNIGHT PULLED THE DEPARTMENT'S SUV INTO A PARKING slot in front of The Junque Shoppe. He parked next to a rusty red convertible that had seen better days. He got out and slammed the door shut. *To protect and to serve*, the logo on the door said.

Mabel Rutherford was a business owner in Pajaro Bay, so his job was to protect and to serve her. He sighed. Mabel Rutherford could make anyone wish he were a fisherman instead of the officer in charge of the Pajaro Bay Sheriff's Substation. But he was responsible for this sleepy little beach town and all its eccentric citizens. For two more weeks. Then he was out of here, and Mabel Rutherford and all the rest were on their own. They'd be better off that way—and so would he.

He stepped up onto the wooden sidewalk leading to the row of storefronts.

In the waning afternoon sun, the light glistened on the crystal and carnival glass in the junk store's windows. He remembered Angie explaining about carnival glass, her eyes lighting up as she went on about maker's marks and the hunt for particular pieces, and the giggle in her voice when she came home after finding that one weird-looking gravy boat she'd been so crazy about. He almost smiled at the memory from a year—a lifetime—ago. He

3

wondered if she'd ever laugh like that again. He knew he wouldn't.

He took a deep breath and let it out. He thought he'd be able to stay here after she left. But the past lurked all around him, haunting him with every step. He needed to let go. Let go of thinking about a past he couldn't change. Let go of caring. Stop thinking he could make a difference and just move on.

He pushed open the purple shop door and walked in, prepared for the worst Mabel Rutherford could conjure.

He automatically surveyed the premises: Mrs. Rutherford behind the counter, a little boy reading in the far corner, then he stopped. A curvy woman in a flowered shirt and jeans stood silently watching him. He scanned her figure automatically. She was not carrying a gun—no room to hide it under those clothes. But just the same, every nerve in his body came alive at the sight of her.

The window with the carnival glass was behind her. The sun slanted through the glass and turned her curly red hair into a halo around her round face. Her eyes were green, like fresh-mown grass in the springtime, and her skin was pale, with a blush of pink like the mother-of-pearl inside a shell. She had freckles on her nose. The freckles and wide eyes in the round face gave her an almost childlike look—lost and alone, even frightened. He felt the urge to take her in his arms and tell her it was going to be all right. He brushed that thought aside quickly, surprised at himself for the jolt of emotion the woman brought out in him.

He turned to Mrs. Rutherford, who sat behind the counter looking proud of herself. She motioned for him to come closer. He went around behind the counter and leaned down to her. She whispered: "She wanted to sell this ring." The sign in the front window said Jewelry Bought And Sold so he just waited.

She pushed the ring into his hand with a smirk.

He took it from her. It was obviously an engagement ring.

Platinum band, with a fat round diamond much bigger than the one he'd been able to give Angie two years ago. He remembered pricing rings, and the shock of finding out how much those little chips of stone and metal had cost. This one didn't look cheap. "You think it's counterfeit, Ma'am?" He always called Mabel Rutherford, "Ma'am." It was better than using the term that sprang to mind in her presence.

The shopkeeper shook her head. "Oh, no. The ring's real all right."

"Then what's the problem?"

"Did you see her car?"

"The junker by the curb? Yeah."

"Where'd she get the ring?"

"I have the certificate," the woman said. Her voice was not a child's voice. It was all woman: soft, throaty, but with an edge of nervousness that made sense under the circumstances.

He turned to her. "The certificate?"

Mrs. Rutherford picked up the paper from the counter and handed it to him. He examined it. The certification showed not only that the ring had been purchased by Dennis Hutchins and Camilla Stewart three weeks ago, but stated that the ring was worth—he choked. Yeah, he'd been right. It wasn't cheap.

"You're Camilla Stewart?" he asked. The woman nodded. Classy name. Classy woman.

He tried to focus. "You don't think you can sell it?" he asked Mrs. Rutherford.

She nodded. "Sure, I can sell it. I have a jeweler I pass on the more valuable pieces to."

"And this is valuable?"

"It's a five-figure ring."

"What?"

"Worth five figures, retail. That's what made me wonder. She was so anxious to get rid of it immediately. I knew you could handle it, Captain Ryan." She emphasized his title, glaring openly at the woman, who took the implied accusation silently, but with a hint on her face of the anger that must be bubbling under the surface. That restrained anger, even more than the certificate, reinforced his instinct that the redhead was telling the truth.

He'd seen so many liars in his life. Innocent people tended to seem confused, overwhelmed when confronted. Dishonest people had glib stories ready, and pat alibis that were always a little bit too perfect. They loudly proclaimed their innocence the moment they were accused. If he had a dollar for every time some scumbag had sworn an oath on his grandmother's sainted memory, with loud cries of moral outrage—and the murder weapon burning a hole in his pocket....

Honest people stood out amid the sea of lowlifes he'd encountered all his life. And the set of Camilla Stewart's jaw and the flush in her pale face as she stood there silently taking Mabel Rutherford's rudeness screamed the truth more loudly than any words.

"When I told her there were ways to get a higher sale price, she still wanted to sell it to me. I offered her rock-bottom wholesale and she said she'd take it."

"I need the money now," the redhead said with finality, as if she'd explained all. And perhaps she had. She walked over to the far corner of the shop. Her spine was very straight and she held her head up proudly, but it was obvious she was angry now. She stood by the little boy sitting on the floor. The boy seemed to be ignoring the whole conversation, absorbed in reading a book.

He turned back to the shopkeeper. "Let me see if I've got this straight, Ma'am: you tried to take advantage of her desperation and she said okay, so you called me?"

She smiled, oblivious to his sarcasm. "That's right, Sonny. I knew you could handle the problem."

He took a deep breath and counted to ten. "Do you want to buy the ring from her, Ma'am?"

She nodded. "I already made out the check."

6

"Then why exactly did you call me?"

She shrugged. "I just thought she was suspicious and you should check her out."

"Yeah, she looks really suspicious. Don't worry, I'll check her out." He was checking her out. He was checking out every inch of her as she bent over the little boy. He turned away to keep from staring any more. He was surprised at himself. It had been a long time since he'd noticed—really noticed—a woman like that. The last thing he needed in his life was some woman with a bunch of problems. This was work, he reminded himself. Just do the job and go home.

He watched as Camilla Stewart held out her hand and the boy reluctantly handed her the book. With a sigh, she returned it to the stack.

"Throw in the book," he said to Mrs. Rutherford.

"Huh?"

"The book the boy was reading. It's not worth much, is it? Add that to the sale."

She nodded. "Are you going to cuff her?" she whispered confidentially.

"I don't think that will be necessary," he whispered back.

He took the check from her and went over to the pair. He gave the intriguing Camilla Stewart the check.

"Which book were you reading?" he asked the little boy. The boy handed it to him. It was a repair manual for a '93 pickup truck. He handed it back to the little boy. "You can keep it," he said.

"I like trucks," the kid said with a grin.

"So do I," Ryan responded.

He let them go ahead of him out the door. Camilla wondered what the cop had said to the shopkeeper to convince her to buy the ring. She clutched the precious check in one hand like a lifeline. It wasn't nearly what the ring was worth, but it would tide them over until the house was sold.

She should be grateful that the cop had arrived to settle things, but she didn't feel the least bit grateful. A cop, of all the people to get mixed up with. She felt like a felon just looking at this officious man in the uniform. "Thank you, officer," she said briskly, hoping he'd go away. "Goodbye."

They stopped in the parking lot, between the dark green sheriff department SUV and her rusty red convertible. He watched her, not getting the message. She wondered what he wanted now.

"It's going to get cold once the fog rolls in," he said. "You might want to put up the top."

"The convertible doesn't have a top," Oliver piped up. "Camilla says it's good to have the wind in our hair."

She wanted to hush Oliver, but didn't want the cop to realize how nervous she was getting. Stay cool, as her dad always said. Don't let 'em know what you're thinking.

She took Oliver by the hand. "We need to get going," she said.

Oliver pulled back. He grinned and pointed at the rank insignia on the cop's uniform. "Are you a deputy?"

The officer pointed to his shoulder. Camilla couldn't help noticing how broad those shoulders were under the khaki uniform. "Those are captain's bars, son."

Oliver saluted him. "Aye, aye, Captain." He laughed, and the captain smiled back at him. The smile didn't quite reach his eyes, she noticed.

Oliver opened the driver's side door, scrambled between the front seats, and settled into the back.

"The seats don't move, either," the boy said. Camilla needed Oliver to stop talking to the man, but it was rare for Oliver to be so outgoing, so she just ignored it and turned to the man.

"Thank you for your help, Captain." She realized she was

thanking him for the third time in two minutes, and wondered if she was giving herself away.

He nodded briskly. "No problem, Ma'am." He added, as if it were an idle question: "May I see your license and car registration?"

She must have been too eager to get rid of him and it had tipped him off. She should have acted more nonchalant. She tried not to let her dismay show. He was being polite, but there was no getting out of this. She got the car registration and proof of insurance from the glove compartment, thinking frantically of her options.

A couple walked by on the wooden boardwalk in front of the shops. They stared at the woman being questioned by the police, and whispered to each other. She was used to that reaction, and ignored it.

She stepped away from her car, out of Oliver's earshot, and handed the officer the registration. Calm down, she told herself. You aren't in any trouble. Stop assuming this is going to be a problem.

She knew what the next question would be.

"I.D.?"

She gave him the driver's license from her purse.

He seemed to notice her reluctance. "Just want to make sure you're not a wanted jewel thief," he said lightly.

Terrific. She crossed her arms, trying to stop their shaking while he went and sat in his car with the door open. She was watching him push buttons on a little computer in the center of the dashboard when she caught a glimpse of her reflection in the window of the junk shop. She realized to her horror she looked exactly like her mother always looked around police—arms folded across her chest, jaw set in a stubborn line, resentful glare toward the cop. She carefully uncrossed her arms and unclenched her jaw.

She turned away from the window and gazed down the main street toward the bayfront in the distance.

The cop sat in his truck for a long time, punching buttons, waiting for information to come up on the screen. All the while the sun sank lower in the sky and, as he had predicted, the fog drifted in from the bay to surround them in the damp taste of the sea. The sight of the bay faded from view, obscured by the mask of gray. Soon the last warmth drained out of the day. Still she stood in the gray mist, waiting for this to be over, all the while very deliberately not standing like her mother.

She knew the computer had finally spit out the results when the man's expression went from neutral and professional to grim. She straightened up, prepared for an argument.

He got back out of the truck. "Does your bail bondsman know you're 90 miles from home?"

Home. She didn't have a home. "Yes. I told him exactly where I'd be," she said, lifting her chin defensively. Why did she feel so angry? He was just doing his job. "My file should show—does it show?" She took a breath and tried again. "The charges are going to be dropped next Monday," she said, trying to get the belligerent tone out of her voice. "Then I can get the bail money back. I—I just got caught short. That's why I had to sell the ring."

His eyes narrowed. "Why can't your fiancé help you out?"

She threw her shoulders back and glared up at the tall man. "My fiancé's the one who stole the money I'm accused of taking." She could see the doubt in his eyes. "So I don't give a rat's—" She glanced back toward Oliver. "I don't need his help, even if I could find him. I didn't do anything wrong. The charges will be dropped next Monday." She repeated it, praying it would be true.

A cop, she kept thinking. She'd been in town for twenty minutes and already she'd run into her worst nightmare. Well, he couldn't do anything to her.

Actually, he probably could haul her in. It all depended on how things looked on paper. She wished she knew what the police report on her said. Her public defender hadn't exactly been helpful, and she was assuming the lawyer had followed up on the paperwork. Probably shouldn't have assumed that. She tapped her foot on the pavement nervously.

His eyes swept over her again, shrewd and judging her, and she became suddenly aware of herself. Her skin tingled, her heart pulsing loudly in her chest. She felt like he was able to count her heartbeats, and she was naked before him—not physically bare, but even worse, emotionally. As if he were someone who could look into her very soul.

That was ridiculous. She was jumping to conclusions. He was a cop, and she was "a perp." She had been horrified the first time she heard herself called that. By now, it should feel less outrageous than it did.

He watched her face. She could see him reading her. She had no poker face. She knew that. Everything she was thinking was obvious, whether she spoke or not.

Her stupid blush betrayed her again and she had to look away. She had tried self-hypnosis once, just to see if she could learn to control her blushing. That and her Irish temper. Of course nothing worked. She was cursed to be an open book. No secrets. No defenses.

She couldn't change her face, but she could get stronger. She would get stronger. She had to. She was going to find a way to beat this, and get her life back. She looked back at him, defiant, trying to stare him down. Of course she lost.

He stood watching, one hand resting on his gun—probably unconsciously. She really hoped it was an unconscious thing, because she was definitely not interested in causing him the slightest bit of trouble.

"Sir, can we go now?" she asked tentatively, but he just held up a hand to her. She tried not to take offense at that.

He took out his cell phone and she watched him while he punched in a number. Firm jaw, just a trace of dark stubble showing at the jawline. He looked tired, she suddenly realized. He had circles under his dark blue eyes. His eyes would be a beautiful rich blue—if they belonged to a guy who wasn't holding her fate in his hands.

He looked beyond tired. Haunted. She'd seen that look in her own mirror lately. No sleep, worries tormenting every waking moment until it showed all over her face.

This man wasn't her enemy. He was a human being with problems of his own that were wearing him down. He was just a guy doing his job, and that thought made the anger drain from her body. She wondered if he was as tired as she was, and hoped for his sake he was going off duty soon. Surely there couldn't be much crime in a little town like this.

She turned away, and caught Oliver's worried look from the car. She smiled at him reassuringly. The poor kid. If she got hauled in to jail, where would he spend the night?

"Is this Al?" The man said. "This is Captain Ryan Knight at the Sheriff's Substation at Pajaro Bay."

She whipped around to face him. Al of Alfonzo's Bail Bonds. He was checking on her story? That seemed a little much. Stay away from small town cops, her father always reminded her. They have too much time on their hands.

"Yeah, the surfing was good over here today. Listen, I'm calling about—yeah. So you know? No, no problem."

She felt the blush start somewhere on her chest and rise to her neck, her chin, her cheeks, all the way to her forehead. All the while those cold blue eyes watched her, expressionless.

"Uh huh." He listened to Al on the phone, and then looked her up and down, assessing her, seeing her in a new light. She felt the blush fade again as she realized his view of her had changed. He no longer thought a criminal mastermind had invaded his town. She was no master thief, not even a normally intelligent woman who could handle her own life. He now believed she was a stupid, gullible twit of a girl who hadn't the wits to figure out she was being used by a con man until it was too late. She hated to see that truth reflected in his eyes, and turned away until he finished the call.

"So where's this cottage?" he said quietly.

She turned back to face him, holding her head high. She gave him the address, and he raised an eyebrow in surprise.

"The Honeymoon Cottage?"

She shook her head. "No. It's 43 Cliff Drive."

"I know where it is," he said. "Come on. We had better get you lost waifs off the street before dark."

CHAPTER TWO

LOST WAIFS. OUCH.

But unfortunately, the take-charge Captain Ryan Knight was right.

Somehow, everything went more smoothly after he showed up. The captain escorted them down the street to the bank and waited while she cashed the check, then escorted them to the gas station while she filled a gas can, then escorted them through the little general store where she bought coffee, milk, and boxed macaroni-and-cheese. She held Oliver's hand the whole time, and his warm little palm against hers kept her focused on what was important—getting him fed and somewhere safe to sleep for the night.

The cop said nothing the whole time. Just stood behind her, about as big and communicative as an oak tree, shadowing her every move, while she fumbled her way through all she needed to do. Why wouldn't he leave her alone? He'd obviously decided she wasn't going to cause trouble. Now he seemed convinced she was stupid and helpless. She didn't dare complain. She'd already tried brushing him off, and it had made him more curious about her.

She had to act as law-abiding and boring as possible and just hope he'd soon lose interest and go away.

They walked back to the car, still silently.

The only time he spoke was when she was twisting off the gas cap on the convertible and tipping in the new fuel. The gas fumes stung her throat and she coughed. "Does the gas gauge work on the car?" he asked, without a trace of sarcasm.

She swallowed the sharp answer she wanted to make. She wasn't a complete idiot, after all. "It's probably broken," she said. She didn't bother to explain that the gauge had said full 50 miles ago. She had excuses for everything, but nothing made sense anymore. Her world had stopped making sense two-and-a-half weeks ago.

Before long she was driving the car up a winding hill toward Cliff Drive, following in the wake of the very take-charge Captain Knight's car.

Ryan Knight. She rubbed her thumb over the raised lettering on the business card he'd given her. To protect and to serve, it said, with a symbol of a badge on it. Right. Like she bought that slogan. Captain Ryan, he'd told Oliver to call him. All confidence and big muscles and attitude was Captain Ryan.

She clutched the business card while she shifted gears and found her thumb kept coming back to rest on the gold embossed badge. She should be happy that he had solved all her immediate problems, but it didn't make her feel good at all. "Lost waifs" he had called them, and the truth of it stung. It was just more evidence that he—that anyone other than she—could handle this better than she was handling it.

She followed that perfectly polished green SUV until the road evened out and she found they were skirting the edge of the oceanside cliff. The expanse of the Pacific was somewhere below them, now seen only as a darker gray through the light gray wisps of fog. Then Cliff Drive turned slightly inland so there were houses on both the ocean side and the inland side of the road.

Small glimpses of sea were all she saw between hedges and high fences all along the cliff side of the road. The houses here guarded their privacy well. An expensive neighborhood, she guessed from the gated driveways and bits of towering rooflines occasionally visible. Expensive was good.

On the inland side of the road, the houses were multi-story, towering high behind their privacy walls and manicured trees, obviously designed to take in what must be an impressive view.

On the ocean side most of the houses were low-slung, invisible behind the shrubbery. She wondered which side her little house was on.

The real estate agent who contacted her with the key had warned her the place was small and not new. But even a little, old house here was apparently worth a lot of money. And she needed every one of those dollars to get herself out of the hole she was in.

She found herself praying: Please let the kitchen be up to date. It was hard to sell a house with old appliances. Please let there be a nice yard with good plantings. She didn't have time to grow a new lawn from seed. Let there be a modern bathroom, and please no 1950s pink tile and 1970s avocado green shag carpet like her last college rental. She didn't have money to pay for materials, so please let the house need only "minor cosmetic updates," as the real estate agent had told her when she'd handed over the key and the title to the house. Please let one thing go right, and let her get it sold quickly so she could pay down the massive debt hanging over her before her former boss's board of directors pushed forward with the lawsuit to recover their lost payroll.

The SUV in front of her finally pulled off the pavement onto the gravel shoulder. She pulled over behind it, and turned off the ignition.

The house, like the others, was invisible behind a high hedge, but the sign was posted: Cliff Front Home For Sale, with a phone number. Cliff front. That had to be a good sign.

This was it. This stupid house of Dennis's—of hers—had better be worth as much as the real estate agent had estimated.

Captain Ryan came back to the convertible. "Curb your wheels," he said calmly. She clenched her jaw in anger, but again said nothing to him. She was so flustered she couldn't even park correctly. She started up the car again and turned the wheels so if the emergency brake failed (a definite possibility with this old crate) the car wouldn't roll down the road into someone's perfect little hedge.

She felt herself flush with embarrassment, but he didn't seem to notice. He helped Oliver out of the car on the passenger side, easily lifting the boy out of the back seat and setting him on the pavement. Oliver looked up at him worshipfully. "You're strong."

She got out of the car before the big man got the idea to lift her out like a child, too, and grabbed her purse. He led the way down the path between the high hedges, holding Oliver's hand.

"My daddy bought the house for Camilla," Oliver was telling him. "Now we're going to sell it so we have money until he gets back."

"Back from where?" he asked.

Oliver shrugged. Good question, Captain Ryan.

At the bottom of the path they came to an imposing wooden gate—all iron hinges and dark-stained wood, about eight feet high. He checked the handle. Locked.

She forgot everything for a moment at the sight of the tall man in the sleek uniform standing before that medieval-looking gate. Some primal part of her wanted to go to the knight, ask him to take over and make everything okay again. She closed her eyes. That was the kind of thinking that had ruined her life—thinking some fairy-tale man would love her and care for her and not turn her life into a mess. She opened her eyes and he was just a cop holding her little boy's hand and waiting for her to unlock the gate.

She fished in her purse for the set of keys.

The path was narrow, so she had to brush past him to reach the gate. She ignored the sudden pound of her heart as she felt his body heat so close. Whoa. That rush of attraction wasn't something she'd expected. Sure, he had startling deep blue eyes and more muscles than he had a right to, but she wasn't in the mood for any man, especially not one who'd judged her a fool and didn't hide that opinion. She needed to turn off her hormones and get down to the business of salvaging what was left of her dignity. Now.

She unlocked the gate, then turned to face him. "Thank you for your help, Captain Ryan. I can handle it from here."

"I'd better see you inside safely."

She wondered at what point his obvious impression that she was incompetent would make her either lose her temper—or fall all over him in relief. But since she knew he was right about her, she just shrugged and went through the gate, Oliver and the man trailing behind her.

As soon as the house came into view she realized her prayers for a quick sale had not been answered.

She stopped in her tracks. It was a monstrosity. No. That wasn't the word. At least a monstrosity would have adequate square footage. This was... it was indescribable.

It was tiny—all of two and a half stories high and still probably smaller than her one-bedroom condo had been.

It had obviously been built without a blueprint. It was crooked. She didn't see a straight line anywhere in sight. The roofline was pitched at an angle that defied gravity, with one side climbing toward the sky at a steep slope, and the other side swooping down practically to the ground.

"The roof...," she muttered.

"Cat slide," Captain Ryan said. "That's what they call that steep, one-sided pitch," he explained to Oliver.

Oliver stood, as wide-eyed as she herself must appear, trying to take it all in. "Yeah," he muttered. "A cat would slide right off, huh?"

"The Honeymoon Cottage was the first Stockdale," Captain Ryan said.

She didn't have time to ask him what the heck a "stockdale" was, because she was busy walking around the front of the cottage, trying to make sense of it.

The walls appeared to be made of stucco in a charming shade of cream-and-mildew, interspersed with huge, rough-hewn beams of what she imagined was ancient redwood. The beams appeared to be barely holding up the walls. Iron sconces framed the door.

And the door, a round-topped slab of redwood, obviously hand-carved by a carpenter who didn't own a level, stood proudly off-center in the front wall, flanked by not only the gargoyle-shaped sconces, but also by heavy-framed, diamond-paned windows that arched into unbelievable shapes never imagined by the folks at Home Depot.

"Oh, no," she muttered.

"Haven't you been to the Honeymoon Cottage before?" he asked.

"Stop calling it that!" she snapped. "Honeymoon cottage—like it's some cozy little getaway for a newlywed couple. Divorce cottage, more like it. One look and the marriage broke up."

"The house then. You haven't seen the house."

"House? This isn't a house. It's—it's—" She was at a loss. A complete loss. All her plans for a quick sale and a getaway to a new life were shot in this one, first glimpse of—

"—It looks like it was built by a drunken leprechaun," she finally said.

Unexpectedly, the taciturn captain chuckled. "I think that's the best description of a Stockdale cottage I've ever heard."

He pushed open the door, which wasn't even locked. Why would it be? Who would want to break in? The iron hinges on the door gave way with a creak straight out of an old horror movie. He ushered them inside. "We might as well see the rest."

She went in.

It was a mess. The walls were as crooked inside as they had appeared from the outside, the diamond-pane windows were missing glass in several spots, and there was ample evidence that something—she prayed it wasn't raccoons—had taken up residence in the middle of the living room floor.

"I think it's neat," said Oliver. He ran over to the fireplace. "See all the different pictures!" He started tracing out patterns in the ceramic tiles framing the fireplace. "This one's a squirrel!"

Numb, Camilla followed him over to the fireplace. He was right. It was beautiful. Under the grime and slime, the fireplace was covered in handmade embossed tiles. There were trees and starfish and suns, all in rich browns and golds and greens—many greens, from pale moss to deep forest. More and more came to light with every sweep of Oliver's hands against the dirty surface.

It smelled of mold.

"This cottage is worth a lot of money," the man behind her said.

"Why?" she said sarcastically. "You get a lot of drunken leprechauns around here needing housing?"

"You don't know? It's a Stockdale. Built by Jefferson Stockdale. The architect."

"Using the term loosely," she muttered.

"The village is littered with them. People come from all over the place just to see them. Postcards, walking tours, they even filmed an old TV series here years ago. You know—about that old lady who solved mysteries."

"I don't think this place is on the tourist maps."

"Not now. But a little repair, a little spit and polish—"

She pulled at a loose tile on the hearth and it came off in a cascade of decayed grout and mouse droppings.

"—Okay, a lot of spit and polish. But this place is full of history. If you own it, you're sitting on a gold mine."

He was talking a lot. The silent captain had become very chatty all of a sudden.

"How do you know?"

He froze, as if he realized he was revealing too much, and then said, "Um, I know somebody who inherited one."

"How nice for them," she said. Then the words "gold mine" sunk in. "You think I can get a good price for it? The real estate agent told me it just needed a bit of fixing up."

He looked around the room. "Your real estate agent is an optimist. I imagine it'll take some money to hire the team of specialists...."

"I'm doing the work myself. Yes," she added at his skeptical look. "I have experience with—well, not with this sort of house, but with normal houses."

He looked down at her from his six-foot-two. "Really?"

"Yes, really. My father did construction." When he wasn't in jail. She looked him in the eye, glad she hadn't said that last part aloud. "I am capable of taking care of myself, Captain Knight."

"I don't doubt you," he said, but she didn't believe him.

She went to the front door, and held it open.

He still stood in the middle of the room, as if he wanted to say something more.

"Thank you for your help, Captain." She looked at him pointedly and he finally came over to where she stood. Again she felt that surge of adrenalin as he invaded her personal space. She had no room to step back, with the redwood door behind her and the tree of a man only a foot in front of her.

He stood there for another few seconds while she held her breath. Some insane part of her wanted to ask him to stay: Don't go. It's all too much for me. I want you to help. But luckily her mind was stronger than that idiotic thought. She stood silently and finally he stepped through the door and walked up the path to the street.

She watched him go. At last he was out of her life. But long after the gate creaked shut, and the SUV's engine roared to life, and the sound of the tires crunching on the gravel faded in the distance, she still stood there, her thumb rubbing over the gold embossed badge on the business card.

"What's for dinner?" Oliver's voice cut into her swirling thoughts. She realized her face was damp with evening fog, and the sun was almost completely gone. It would be dark soon, and she didn't even know if the place had working lights.

She turned to Oliver. "Macaroni and cheese for dinner. Assuming there's a stove. Let's find out." She held out her hand to him and they went to find the kitchen.

CHAPTER THREE

On the way down from Cliff Drive Ryan checked in with his deputy.

"I'm done with that call."

"Mabel Rutherford?" The smile in Joe Serrano's voice came in clearly over the speaker.

"Yeah. It was nothing, of course. Stranded tourists out of gas. Got them to their house. Any other calls come in?"

He slowed down near the corner of Cliff Drive and Calle Principal.

"None."

"Then I'll sign out. You can take off, too. Tell the switchboard to forward calls to me overnight."

"Got it," Joe responded. After a pause, "you want to stop by for dinner? I'm grilling my famous California turkey burgers. Avocado and jack with a grilled poblano on top. Cold cerveza. Maria and Marisol would love to see you."

"No thanks, Joe. See you tomorrow." He hung up.

Ryan pulled over and parked right before Cliff dead-ended at Calle Principal. He looked over at the house proudly perched at an angle on the corner, noticing the cat slide roof and lopsided windows as if for the first time. "Drunken leprechauns," he muttered, and felt himself smile. And then the smile faded. FOR SALE, the sign said, with the local real estate agent's smiling mug beneath it. Angie had loved her family's old vacation cottage at the beach. Now he couldn't stand the sight of it, a barren reminder of the life that had been lost in a split second. She had insisted he take it in the divorce. But he couldn't keep it. Once it was sold, it would sever the last tie between them. If only he could sever the memories that easily.

He went inside, and felt the silence surround him.

The house, as always, was so still. The mantel clock ticked softly, loudly echoing the emptiness. There was nothing alive here, except him. And he was barely alive.

He carefully took off his jacket, putting it over the back of one of the dinette chairs. He removed his holster and gun, setting them on the top of the refrigerator, out of sight but within easy reach, as always.

The feel of the gun in his hand still brought back the memories of the first days. In the first few terrible days after it happened, he had sat up alone far into the night, just wondering if it would be better to end it all. He was past that part, thank God. He knew that wasn't the answer. He had to face his guilt, find a way to live with it, and go on with what was left of his life.

He went into the living room and turned on the TV. Some random cop show was on, with pretty people in a shiny lab solving elaborate crimes in 45 minutes. He sat on the sofa and watched, not really paying much attention. His days were running together. Go to work, do the job, come home, lose himself in a TV show or a book until he finally got tired enough to sleep. Get up. Run on the beach. Go to work. Come home.

He knew it was unhealthy. He knew he had to break the cycle. So in two weeks it would be over. He would leave his job for the last time and take off on the cross-country trip he and Angie had planned before things fell apart. After that? Who knew, but it would give him the break he needed to start fresh somewhere new. All he needed was to make it through the next two weeks without any complications.

The last thing he needed was a woman wearing freckles and a halo, a little boy who loved trucks, a glimpse of goodness and honesty that was impossible for him to ever know again.

It was a vision of something beyond this empty, echoing life. Something he had forgotten even existed.

And now these innocents walked into his life and tempted him to see goodness and forget the horrors that lurked just beneath the surface.

For the tiniest span of time, he had forgotten the grief, had forgotten Angie and little Sara. And now, remembering, he felt even worse.

He would keep his distance from the likes of Camilla Stewart. Knowing her could only cause more grief.

The ringing cell phone pulled him away from those thoughts. "Knight," he answered, expecting the department's answering service with a call about a lost cat or a loud party.

"Ryan?" His sister's voice sounded stressed.

"What's wrong, Leah? Are you okay?"

"That's what I was calling to ask you."

He muted the TV. "I'm fine. Do you need anything? You're not having any trouble with Pop, are you?"

He heard her sigh. "No more than usual. He keeps trying to leave the nursing home to go to the liquor store. Nothing new."

He stifled a curse. She shouldn't be stuck dealing with that crap from the old man. "You can just ignore it, you know. Those nurses are getting paid big money to deal with him."

"He's my father, Ryan." He noticed she didn't call him "their" father. She knew better than to drag him into it. He sent his money for the old man's care, and that was it. He didn't owe the S.O.B. any more. And neither did she.

"How are you doing, Ryan?"

She sounded really worried, so he gave her the standard line. "Fine, just fine. Everything's going great here."

"Don't give me that standard line, Ryan. You've been using it since you were six years old. It would help if you'd talk about it. Please talk to me."

He looked around at the dead cottage. "Life's just a blast here, Sis. Now stop worrying about me. I'm the big brother. I'm supposed to take care of you, not the other way around."

"Your friends here in Sacramento ask about you all the time. But you never talk about anyone down there in that little town."

He flashed to an image of Camilla and Oliver and the broken-down Stockdale cottage just up the hill from where he now sat. "Nothing to talk about," he said. "What are you expecting, Leah? That I'll go out partying every night?"

"But you're so—"

Alone, he knew she wanted to say. "I'm fine, sis. Hector's fixing up my Mustang, and when it's ready I'll be ready for my big trip."

"This isn't about that stupid car, Ryan!"

"It's not a stupid car. It's a '66 Mustang, Sis. I always wanted a car like that."

"When you were 16, sure. But I'm talking about your life here, not things. You remember how you used to be? You knew everyone in the neighborhood, were connected to everyone...."

"I'm not that person anymore." It was closer than he'd ever gotten to telling the truth. Which was, what exactly? That he had once been arrogant enough to think he could make a difference in people's lives? That he had thought his life had some meaning? That his own ego made him think he could do good when his mistakes cost people their lives? That caring about people just led to disaster?

"But, Ryan—"

"Hey, I've gotta go, Leah. I'll call you in a couple of days. You take care crossing the street now."

"Ryan, please—"

"Bye now, Sis." He hung up the phone. The last thing he needed right now was his baby sister ragging on him.

Leah would just spout a bunch of platitudes about how he needed to move on, forgive himself, and find happiness.

He looked at the photograph on the fireplace mantle: a smiling blonde California girl, all grown up into a confident woman. Smiling, that was Angie. Always smiling. And in the picture next to her, a young spitting image of her. Little Sara, forever ten years old.

He glared at the TV, where the cops were triumphantly handcuffing the bad guy without breaking a sweat.

Gone. In one stupid day. It had taken one day to go from "Daddy Ryan? Can we go get ice cream?" to telling Angie that he'd broken his promise to honor and protect his family.

One moment he'd been opening the door to the convenience store for little Sara, the next moment he'd glimpsed the drug-addled teenager pressing a gun to the sobbing clerk's temple.

It was too late to get Sara outside, so he'd pushed her behind him and pulled his own gun, telling the perp he was a cop and ordering him to put down his weapon.

It was a split-second he'd replayed a million times, that one moment when Ryan had looked into the kid's eyes and seen the shrewd, calculated decision, the kid realizing the child peeking out from behind Ryan was his weak spot, the perp's gun firing, not at him but at Sara, and then the gunman laughing—laughing! —as Ryan's aim had faltered, he'd turned to catch Sara and ignored the creep dashing out the door as his step-daughter crumpled lifelessly to the floor.

Sara had died because she was with him. And Angie had died inside that day, too. How could he explain that he'd blown it? That he'd made a mistake that cost her daughter her life?

He had tried to stay on the job this last year, tried to function in the way he used to. But it hadn't worked. People kept telling him he just needed time, he needed to get over Sara's death, get over the divorce. Get over feeling guilty. But nothing was working.

He couldn't do the job anymore. He couldn't be there when people needed him, not like he used to do. He'd lost the illusion of invincibility he'd had. He now knew how fallible he was. So it was best for him to leave before he made a mistake that cost someone else's life. Leave before it was too late.

Two more weeks.

Two more weeks of keeping the peace in this dinky little town. Nothing much ever happened here, so he couldn't screw anything up. He went to work. He came home. He did it again. Day after day. He didn't get involved. He didn't care. That was the way it had to be.

Two more weeks and it would be over.

RYAN FELT THE HARD-PACKED SAND BENEATH HIS THIN RUNNING shoes. He pounded out the miles, ignoring the warmth of the morning sun beating down on his bare back, ignoring the sweat gathering between his shoulder blades. He ran faster, as if he could outrun the thoughts crowding his mind.

Why was she here? She was carrying secrets, she and the little boy who called her Camilla, not mom. His "daddy" was missing. His daddy was her fiancé—the creep who'd ripped her off. But she was taking care of the boy, the child of the man who'd gotten her arrested. That didn't make sense. And he tried to tell himself that was the only reason he wondered. He didn't like things that didn't add up. He needed to solve the riddle.

Though Camilla and Oliver had no business being together, they matched, the two lost waifs. The sadness in the child's eyes when he talked about his jerk of a "daddy." It matched some lostness deep inside the woman. They were alike, woman and child. Both strong, self-contained, but needing help they weren't prepared to ask for.

He passed an elderly couple doing tai chi on the beach. Their matching steel gray hair shone in the sunlight, and their matching workout clothes—blue today, green yesterday, no doubt red tomorrow—made them look almost like twins. They moved as one, in the slow forms of the ancient exercise, just as they did every morning when he passed them at this spot. He briefly wondered what it would be like to be part of a matched set, but knew it wasn't for him.

He resisted the urge to glance up at the steep cliff face that overlooked the beach. He was right below the Cliff Drive cottages now, and he would be able to see their back yards if he just looked up. He didn't look up.

There was no reason to believe she was up there. She had looked tired last night, and was probably still fast asleep on her first morning in town. When he got to work he would call the San Jose PD, ask for a copy of the report on the embezzlement case. He tried to tell himself it was just part of his job, but he knew it was a lie. He was just plain curious about her. He hated that. He hadn't been curious about anything for months, and he needed it to stay that way.

He ran faster.

———

CAMILLA SAT AT THE KITCHEN TABLE, ENJOYING THE RICH SCENT OF the coffee wafting from the chipped ceramic mug in front of her.

From drinking Starbucks in a Cordova Computing staff cup to generic instant in an old mug she'd found in the cupboard. Quite a come-down. She should at least have kept the company mug. They sold for quite a bit on Ebay. And she could use the money.

But it was hard to feel down about that with the sun shining in the windows and the fresh ocean air coming in the back door.

She looked fondly at the old gas stove hunkered in along one wall. 1930s, she guessed. She remembered one remodel her dad had worked on where the owners had remodeled their house in period style. Their stove had been a reproduction, but it looked a lot like this one.

The stove dominated the little kitchen, its chunky cream-enameled body still radiating leftover warmth from her morning cooking, adding to the cheeriness of the tiny space.

She'd carefully checked out the gas lines before starting the stove last night. Oliver had thought it was pretty funny seeing her on her hands and knees with a dish of soapy water, sponging down the line to check for tell-tale bubbling leaks. But she knew the rules. Never trust the electrical or gas in an old house. Check everything for safety. Her dad had given her some good advice over the years.

Well, the stove had been safe, surprisingly. And they had eaten a cozy dinner of mac and cheese and instant coffee and hot cocoa. Maybe the rest of the house would turn out to be okay, too.

Actually, she had to admit the kitchen was more than okay—it was adorable. She'd given it a pretty good scrubbing last night, and underneath the grime, it was not bad at all.

The Honeymoon Cottage. On a sunny spring day the name fit a bit better than it had last night.

The old hardwood cabinets had once been painted a cream that matched the stove. The paint was worn, but with the soft color, and the faded little hearts someone had painted free-hand on the doors in a pale blue that matched the stove's trim, it was clear the cottage had once been loved.

She could picture children tumbling indoors after playing on the beach, and a mother out of a commercial holding a tray of cookies for them.

She shook her head. It was out of a commercial. People didn't really live like that.

She took another sip of the bitter coffee. She'd forgotten to buy sugar. She hated black coffee. But even that was okay today. Things were looking up. They were going to make it through this.

She ignored the little pang of longing that the old-fashioned kitchen brought out in her. She'd never lived in a house like this —a house with a history, and a sense that it could really be a home, not just a place to sleep.

She stopped daydreaming and looked around objectively. The cottage was a far cry from her upscale condo in the city, but it had a certain appeal that should attract a buyer looking for nostalgia. If she really cleaned it up, and did all the little repairs, it might just sell to someone dumb enough to want charm over practicality.

She'd find a scrap of blue fabric at one of the used clothing stores in town and make a little curtain for the kitchen window. That would appeal to someone gullible enough to like that kind of thing. Not her. She wouldn't like that at all.

The blue trim on the stove was more aqua than true blue, she decided. Darker than the glimpse of ocean out the window, but not as deep a blue as Captain Ryan's eyes.

Enough of that. But even as she scolded herself she had to smile. She was feeling so much better after a good sleep that even the thought of the overbearing cop couldn't dampen her spirits.

Oddly, crashing in a sleeping bag on the floor of this tiny cottage had given her the best night's sleep she'd had in weeks. Outside the diamond-pane windows, the sea had whispered all night, and the fog had cocooned Oliver and her from the outside world. All had felt warm and cozy inside. She'd finally gotten the deep restful sleep she had so desperately needed. It was as if the cottage was holding them safe in its arms. Nice feeling, even if it was merely a result of exhaustion and stress.

Now the fog had burned off, the sun was shining, and she could face what was to come.

And the first thing to come was getting Oliver back in school ASAP.

"Oliver? Where are you, hon?"

"Come look, Camilla!"

His voice came from the back yard.

She got up and went to the heavy dutch door that was half-open to the ocean air. The morning breeze was repeatedly banging the top half of the door against the outside wall. The bottom was still latched closed by its iron handle.

"What is it, Oliver? You should be getting ready for school."

"Come see!" he said.

"We don't have time for this. We've got to get you to school by nine."

"Come look, Camilla," he shouted gleefully from outside.

She opened the door and went out.

He was standing in the back yard—a sweep of overgrown grass leading to the cliff. A riot of rhododendrons and stubby, twisted pines hid the houses to either side of them. Behind her was the little cottage, and in front of her at the cliff's edge was a low stone wall.

"Don't lean on that wall, Oliver! It might not be stable."

He stopped leaning. "But come see!"

She did.

The silky sand of the bayshore lay a hundred feet below the cliff where they stood—from this angle it seemed as if they were standing above a golden crescent curving outward on both sides below them.

A working wharf was off to the right in the distance, fishing boats bustling. The seagulls swarmed around the boats in clouds of gray and white, small as flies from this far away. The sea glistened out to the horizon, shining beneath the clear blue morning sky. In the middle of the bay, a tiny island could be seen, frothy waves crashing on its rocks, the tower of a lighthouse rising up high.

Closer, she watched a small, black, duck-like bird circle toward the cliff in a soaring dance, bright white patches flickering on its wings as it came in for a landing somewhere on the cliff face. She leaned forward on the crumbling stone wall that defined the cliff edge, but couldn't see where the bird had landed.

"There are a lot of birds," she said.

"Pajaro. That means bird," Oliver said. Interesting. Where'd he picked up Spanish? But before she could question him further she spotted a movement below.

A man was running on the beach, wearing shorts and no shirt, the ripple of muscles across his back visible even from this distance. He was a big guy, but lean and moving with a mesmerizing grace. She watched, entranced, as his long legs ate up the distance and he got farther and farther away. He had dark hair, kind of wavy with the sweat, and she couldn't see his face, but something about his arms pumping—

She quickly looked away. It was him. She felt stupid, realizing she'd been ogling that cop from last night. He was not the kind of man she found attractive. She liked low-key guys, the mild-mannered nerdy type. Definitely not some big, brutish guy with tanned arms big as tree branches and the bossy personality to match.

Camilla took Oliver by the arm and pulled him back from the edge. "It's a bit dangerous, I think, young man. We can bird-watch some other time."

"Birds? Why would I look at birds?"

He pointed off to the left.

About a half-mile down the beach she was surprised to see an old-fashioned amusement park—a Ferris wheel and great red-and-white towers of a wooden roller coaster jutted up into the clear sky, and other brightly colored buildings hinted of summer fun.

"It's heaven," Oliver said. "Let's stay here forever."

"It's heaven," she whispered, watching the tiny figure of the cop far off down the beach. This place felt far apart from the harsh world outside. It was as if here was a place she could start over, be whoever she wanted to be, dream any dream and make it come true. She briefly considered what it would be like to live permanently in a little cottage, in a cute village surrounded by sand and sea and cotton candy, with the chance to just be herself and have nothing to hide. Then she quickly dismissed it. Ridiculous. She couldn't do that. Even if she didn't need to sell the cottage to pay off her debt to Cordova Computing, she wasn't staying here.

She needed to find a job somewhere no one had heard about her arrest. She needed a new city big enough to get lost in, somewhere she could be anonymous. Pajaro Bay was most definitely not that place. She was pretty sure the natives wouldn't accept having a criminal as a neighbor, and by now, everyone in town had probably heard about her arrest record.

"Let's go!" Oliver said excitedly. "Right now!"

"To the amusement park? Not today. Come on. We've got to get you enrolled in school." She led him inside, shutting out the distractions behind them and returning to reality. "You don't even have your shoes on."

He shrugged. "Can't find 'em."

They spent several minutes looking for the shoes, which turned out to have been conveniently lost under a pile of clothes. Oliver put them on v-e-r-y slowly. The more she tried to rush him, the slower his movements got. She kept scolding him, but he tuned her out. Well, she wasn't going to smack him. That had never worked on her and she wasn't about to try it on him.

"I'm going in the bathroom, kid. Be ready when I get out."

She sat in the bathroom for a while, wondering if she was

really up to being a mom to this little boy. She had no clue how to take care of a child. Why had Dennis done this to her? But she had to make this work. There was no one else to do it. If she didn't take responsibility for Oliver, he'd be put in emergency foster care. She'd been told that when she was arrested and asked what would happen if she didn't make bail by the end of the day. The thought of Oliver sitting at school waiting for someone who never came had lit a fire under her. She'd pulled together every penny she could scrounge to make bail by the time his school let out that afternoon.

How could she live with herself if she let him down now? So, it was her lousy parenting skills or nothing. She gave her hair a quick brush, pulled her sweatshirt straight, and came out of the bathroom.

Oliver's shoes were tied and he was standing there, kicking at the floor with one foot.

"Get your backpack, kid, it's time to go."

"No." He crossed his arms and stood there, looking so much like Dennis for a minute that she had to swallow the angry response she wanted to make. Amazing how the kid could go from buoyant to bratty in two seconds.

She took a deep breath. "Yes. Now." She said it calmly.

He walked to the door with her as slowly as humanly possible, dragging his worn backpack by one ripped shoulder strap.

"That won't work," she said matter-of-factly. "No matter how slow you are, you'll still end up in school. Might as well go now."

The set of his jaw said he was spoiling for a fight, but she wasn't going to let him win. He took one look at her expression and picked up his pack and slung it over one shoulder. He glared defiantly at her. "Dad wouldn't make me go on the first day in town. He'd take me to the amusement park."

He probably would. Creep. "Well, I'm not your dad," she said coolly. "And you are going to school. No discussion, young man." She assumed that the firm tone in her voice was a good imitation

37

of how caring mothers all over the world sounded on weekday mornings, but since she had no personal experience to go by, she was winging it.

She took him by the hand and led him out the door. "You need to go to school every day. So you don't fall behind." And so you don't end up a criminal bum like your father. She was careful not to say that last part out loud. She didn't know why Dennis had dumped Oliver on her, but as long as she had him, she was going to treat him the way she thought a child should be treated, not the way Dennis—or her own father—had done it.

She locked the cottage gate, then pushed him ahead of her in the direction of the car.

He scrambled into the back seat and threw down his pack next to him. "Maybe the car won't start," he mumbled.

It didn't.

Camilla sat there in the old convertible, staring at the dashboard. Nothing happened when she turned the key in the ignition.

"Maybe we'll be too late to go to school today," Oliver said hopefully.

"No chance. We're going even if we have to walk."

"I ain't walkin' that whole way."

"Don't say ain't."

"Why not?"

"It ain't polite," she said, and winked at him.

She turned the key again. Still nothing. That didn't make sense.

"Maybe it's out of gas," Oliver said eagerly.

"Of course it's not. I just put gas in—" She looked at the gas gauge. Empty. Okay. There was definitely something wrong with this piece of junk.

"What are we going to do?"

She took the key out of the ignition. "I guess we're going to walk."

CHAPTER FOUR

SHE WAS AS CUTE AS BEFORE. RYAN GOT OUT OF HIS TRUCK, annoyed by her cuteness, annoyed by how it made him feel. Camilla stood by the convertible. Little Oliver sat in the back seat, a big grin on his face.

Well, it was his fault for driving by here to check things out on his way to work. Now he was stuck.

He had been hoping that when he saw her again, the effect would have worn off, but it hadn't. She still unsettled him in some fundamental way.

She looked at him, confused. "Why are you here?—I mean," she quickly added, "it's actually good that you are, but—I mean—" Her voice was still smooth and soft. He really wished he didn't notice these things about her.

He found himself smiling at her, the blush and the stammer seeming really cute to him for some reason. Cute. He didn't want her to be cute. He didn't need cute in his life.

"Just passing this way," he explained.

Right. His office was in the other direction, but she didn't need to know that. "Is there a problem?"

"We're out of gas," Oliver piped up.

She spun around and shushed him.

"Well, we are," Oliver said. "Now I don't have to go to school."

Ryan leaned into the driver's side and checked the gas gauge. Empty. He took out his cell phone and dialed. "Hector? Can you get a tow up here on Cliff Drive right away? No, not for me. There's a lady here. Something's wrong with her car. I need you to take a look ASAP. Yeah. The Honeymoon Cottage."

She started to protest even before he hung up the phone.

"But—" she started.

"He'll give you a free estimate," Ryan told her. "I know you don't have much money. But something's obviously wrong. He'll see if he can figure out what it is so you don't keep getting stranded."

She still looked doubtful. "You know, I can handle this myself."

"Didn't you want me to help?"

She blushed. Why was that cute, too? She hesitated, then said, grudgingly, "thank you for your help, Captain Ryan. But I can't afford a mechanic."

"Hector's Garage is not only reasonably priced, it also has the advantage of being the only mechanic in Pajaro Bay."

"Oh. I guess unless I want to spend the rest of my life in Pajaro Bay, I'll have to get the car fixed." She wasn't planning to spend the rest of her life here? He wondered what she was planning— not that it was any of his business.

She got her purse out of the car and helped Oliver out of the back seat. "I did put gas in the car," she said defensively.

"I know. I watched you."

"Right," she said. "So you know it's not my fault."

"Your fault?" He raised an eyebrow.

She shook her head. "Never mind. Come on Oliver. And stop kicking up dust in the road," she added as he shuffled toward her, dragging his backpack.

"No school today," Oliver said hopefully.

"Yes, school today," she said firmly.

She turned back to face Ryan. "I really appreciate this, Captain—"

The tow truck from Hector's Garage pulled in behind him, belching exhaust, with a blare of its horn for welcome. Hector, all tie-dyed and bleary eyed, got out. He appeared reasonably alert, but it was only 8:30 in the morning. Looked like he was living up to their agreement: stay clean and sober during business hours and while driving, and Ryan wouldn't go out of his way to investigate his after-hours hobbies.

"Sheriff dude! The lady needs a tow?"

Ryan pointed at the little car, and they all got out of Hector's way.

With a quick glance and a grin at Camilla, Hector got to work.

They all stood silently watching while he expertly swung his tow truck around and hooked up Camilla's convertible. Once he had the car rigged, he drove off with a cheerful wave and another toot of the horn that Ryan just knew would lead to at least one noise complaint call from the old ladies on Cliff Drive.

They stood in the street in his dusty wake. "Thank you, Captain Ryan," she finally said.

"—Just Ryan is fine."

"—Okay, Ryan. I'm Camilla. And I really do appreciate it." She put her purse strap over her shoulder. "It's not much of a walk to the elementary school, is it?"

"It's on the other side of town." He neglected to mention that "the other side of town" meant it was about four blocks away. "I'll give you a lift."

Oliver was scuffing his feet on the gravel. Definitely not a happy camper this morning.

"Ever ridden in a police car, Oliver?" Ryan asked him.

"Yeah," the boy said forlornly, and Ryan was startled. That

wasn't the usual response, but he'd forgotten what the kid must've been through.

"Well, have you ever ridden in a specially equipped sheriff's department SUV?"

Oliver looked up with a sudden grin. "Does it have four-wheel drive?"

"You bet it does. Come on." He escorted them to his car.

"We could do something fun instead of going to school," the boy said to Camilla, obviously continuing an argument they'd started earlier. "Don't you think so, Captain Ryan?"

"There's nothing fun to do in this little town, Oliver," she said.

"There's an amusement park down at the beach," Ryan said, then wished he hadn't. The look Camilla shot him was not exactly cheery. So she had a temper along with the soft demeanor. Why did he find that intriguing?

"It's only open on the weekends until summer starts," he added, and her expression softened.

"Gee," she said with a sudden grin that lit up her face and sent a jolt through his gut. "That sounds like a great incentive for a little boy to go to school every day this week and do all his homework."

"Can we? Really?"

She looked a little nervous at what he'd just cornered her into promising.

"My treat," he found himself saying. "Saturday."

She started to protest, but he added, "It's not expensive. Rides for a dollar from now until summer. It's a great amusement park. You'll enjoy it." Why did he end up chattering so much every time he got near her? And now look what he'd done. He had roped himself into seeing her again. By the weekend he should have satisfied his curiosity about her case, and would have absolutely no reason to see her again. But there were still several days before the weekend. By then he'd find a way to back out of this.

From the glum look on her face, she might be the one backing out. He didn't let her dismay at being stuck with him wound his ego. He was way past the stage of wanting women to like him.

Oliver was still pouting at the thought of all the schoolwork standing between him and the amusement park, so Ryan talked a mile a minute about engine capacities and off-road capabilities, trying to distract the boy from the fact that he was being put in the back of a police vehicle. He needn't have worried about traumatizing him.

"Can I pretend I'm being hauled off to the slammer?" the kid asked as Camilla buckled him in to the back seat.

"Sure," Ryan said. "If you give me any guff, outlaw, I'll run you in with lights and sirens blazing."

"Yeah!" Oliver said. "Do that."

Ryan closed the door on the boy with a reassuring smile, then opened the front passenger door for Camilla.

"I can sit in the back with Oliver," she said gruffly.

"That's not necessary." He held out his hand to help her step up into the high SUV, and she reluctantly put her hand in his.

He very determinedly didn't notice how soft and warm her hand was. He didn't notice how nice she looked as she settled into the seat, either. He closed the passenger door with a scowl, not thinking about how green her eyes looked this morning and how nice the pale pink sweatshirt she wore looked against her skin. He didn't notice anything at all, he grumbled to himself as he went around to the driver's side and got in.

What was it about her? Pajaro Bay was always full of tourists in bikinis spoiling for a good time. He was used to ignoring the drunken overtures of women on vacation who were just dying to act out their fantasies about men in uniforms. Why did this woman—who seemed to have no interest in him at all—get under his skin?

She was pretty. No doubt about it. But she was wearing a

sweatshirt, not a swimsuit. His reaction to her made no sense. It wasn't about looks, somehow.

Maybe it was just his cop's curiosity. Her situation didn't make sense. So he felt a need to investigate until he got all the answers.

He wished that were all, but he knew it wasn't.

There was something about the way she looked at him. She wasn't going to take life's problems lying down. She was facing her troubles with that cute little button nose up and a stubborn set to her jaw. There was something admirable about her. The awareness that she was alone in the world, without a penny to her name, but she wasn't going to stop trying until she found a way out of the mess in which she found herself.

He wished he had her faith that everything would work out, if one only kept trying. But he knew too much about the world to have her optimism. It wasn't attraction, he told himself firmly. It was just her innocence he envied.

He got in the truck.

He glanced over at her and noticed she didn't have her seat belt on.

"I can't find the latch," she said when he asked. "It must have slipped down behind the seat."

"Here." He leaned across her body and pulled the shoulder belt across her, then reached in the crevice next to her left thigh and found the missing seat latch. He pulled the seat belt taut across her chest and fastened it. She smelled like flowers. She wouldn't meet his eyes.

"How would it look for me to be driving around violating the seat-belt law," he whispered, his mouth only inches from her ear.

"We can't have that," she whispered back, her voice husky.

He pulled away, fastened his own seat belt, and started up the car.

"Lights and sirens. You promised," came from the back seat.

"Yup," he said, not looking at anything but the road in front of him. "I promised. Here we go."

THE SCHOOL PRINCIPAL'S OFFICE WAS SMALL BUT CHEERFUL, WITH big posters on the walls and a window overlooking the playground. Ryan hadn't set foot in a school since his step-daughter was murdered, and he found his palms sweating at the sight of all the kids—the kids Sara's age—playing in the yard outside the window.

He stood back as Val DiPietro, the principal, motioned for Camilla and Oliver to take seats by her desk.

"Hey, Captain Ryan. It's good to see you out and about," Val said, giving him a big smile. He mumbled something polite. Why did everyone talk to him like he was a recluse?

Because he was. They never saw him except on duty. At least she hadn't commented on his resignation. The grapevine must not have picked up on it yet, 'cause Val, with two gossipy sisters, was at the top of the gossip food chain in town.

"So how are you, Ryan?"

He shrugged, his usual answer to that constant question. "Fine," he muttered.

"This won't take long," Val added with another smile in his direction. She turned to Camilla and Oliver.

"And how are you, young man?"

"Fine," Oliver mumbled in a perfect imitation of Ryan's attitude, and he felt himself smile.

Camilla introduced Oliver, and then handed over a folder. "His school records and a copy of the adoption papers giving me authority to sign him up for school," she said. She'd adopted the boy even before marrying his father? Add that to his mental list of things that didn't make sense about them.

45

Val took the folder, glanced through it, then turned back to Oliver.

"So, you're eight—"

"—and a quarter," he quickly corrected.

"I'll make a note of that." She wrote something on a pad of paper.

Ryan went over to a bulletin board to read the notices. He listened closely as Val tried and failed to draw Oliver out of his shell.

"Do you like school, Oliver?" she finally asked after "how was your trip here?" and "what's your favorite subject?" drew no answers.

Shrug. Still no response.

"I see." Val looked through the papers. "I see we have some attendance and grade issues. Has Oliver been evaluated for learning disabilities?"

"He's been tested. There's nothing wrong with him that a steady home life and doing his homework won't cure," Camilla said firmly.

Ryan turned to watch her. She looked like a momma tiger, eyes flashing a warning. Val may have met her match.

The principal looked a bit skeptically from Camilla to the silent, pouting boy.

"Tell her about your new book, Oliver," Camilla said.

He shrugged.

"You know," Camilla continued unfazed, "I'm not sure you really understood all those diagrams about engines in that last chapter you read...."

"I did so!" The boy sat up straight in the chair. "The truck's fuel injectors could get clogged, and that would impede its performance, so it's important to periodically use a fuel injector cleaner." He sat back triumphantly. "I do so understand it."

"What's a fuel injector, Oliver?" Val asked.

"It mixes air and gas in the engine to make it more fuel-efficient. It makes the car work better 'cause it doesn't waste gas."

Camilla turned to Val. "Like I said, he's a very smart boy, but he's moved around too much, and no one has been supervising him when he does his homework. That's changed now."

Period. End of sentence. Round one to Camilla. He felt himself liking her more and more, and had to remind himself that liking her was not on his agenda. He was just here to do his job—help her get around until her car was fixed. And, though he had no intention of telling her, his investigative instincts went on high alert every time he saw her, and he wanted to figure out what was going on. It was just part of his job, he told himself again. The sooner he satisfied his curiosity, the sooner he could retreat back into his shell and ignore these two.

Val sat back in her chair. "So will you do your homework if your mom helps you, Oliver?" she asked him.

"Not my mom."

"Joyce Hutchins passed away some time ago," Camilla said quickly.

"Camilla's my adopted mom." Oliver looked down at the floor again.

"Of course. Thank you for straightening me out. And your dad...?"

"He had to go away. He travels a lot on business. He said he'd come back after he finished his latest job." Ryan watched Camilla's jaw clench, but she kept a neutral expression on her face.

"I see." Val looked skeptical.

Oliver looked up at Val, obviously catching her expression. "He wouldn't stay away. After Mommy died he promised he'd always take care of me."

"That's good. And your last school was in San Jose?"

Oliver crossed his arms and pressed his lips together.

"It's okay to say yes, Oliver," Camilla said softly. "I knew you in San Jose, so it's not giving anything away."

San Jose. Heart of Silicon Valley. Ryan could picture Camilla there, working at some high-tech company. He wondered again about Dennis Hutchins, about how he'd fooled this obviously intelligent woman into letting him have access to her computer— and to her. He felt his own jaw clench in imitation of Camilla's, and wondered if he could control it as well as she did. He hated the thought of her with that con man. Her ex-fiancé she had called him, sounding disgusted. He had given her a ring— probably bought with her own money. They had been engaged. Ryan wasn't naive enough to think they had waited for marriage to get together. How could she have allowed a con man to touch her? Whoa. There he went again. It was totally irrelevant to the case how much physical contact she'd had with the jerk. Dennis was out of her life.

And now she sat in this tiny office with the frightened boy next to her, lost and alone and trying to start over. He realized Oliver was still talking and tuned back in to the conversation to catch the end of what he was saying.

"Sacramento with Mommy, then Fresno, Salinas, San Jose," Oliver ticked off on his fingers.

"You've lived in all those places, young man? My, you're a real traveler."

Up and down the state of California in eight years. Probably one jump ahead of the law. Ryan felt the urge to wring Dennis Hutchins' neck for what he'd done to his own son.

"I didn't know about Fresno," Camilla said quietly. "Why didn't you tell me about it?"

"Daddy always says it's best not to chatter too much about the past."

Camilla blushed, which Ryan had noticed happened whenever she was upset. She always showed just what she was thinking, and right now she was clearly thinking some not-so-polite thoughts about Oliver's "daddy."

"I think it's important for us to know all the schools you went to so we can help you do better," she said patiently. The gentleness in her voice was surprising, given how mad she obviously was at Oliver's father. She was very good at separating her feelings about Dennis Hutchins from her feelings toward his son. The boy was in good hands.

"Are those the only cities you lived in?" Camilla asked.

Oliver pressed his lips tightly together again and nodded.

"You sure?"

"I'm not a stool pigeon." That wasn't an answer, but it sure said a lot about his life with his father. Ryan began to get a picture of the mess Camilla was in, and apparently so did Val.

"Well," the principal said breezily while standing up from the desk. "I'll have a chat with your adopted mom about your lesson plans later. For now, let's get you to class. Ms. Gonzalez is a wonderful teacher. I'm sure you'll like her." She came around the desk.

Both Oliver and Camilla stood, too.

Val followed them all out into the hallway. "I'll take Oliver to class and get him settled. Let's arrange a time to talk later, Ms. Stewart?"

Camilla nodded.

"Goodbye, Captain Ryan," Val said. "It's really nice to see you. Will you be there tonight? I know a lot of people are looking forward to saying hello to you."

"No," he said automatically before he even knew what she was talking about. Right. The school fundraiser tonight. They were raising money for gym equipment or library books or something. Whatever. He hadn't attended one of those things for months, but people never gave up trying to convince him to go. He bought tickets, donated his money. They should be glad he wasn't showing up to eat enchiladas and take up space. But they still bugged him about it every time. "Can't make it, I'm afraid," he added gruffly.

"Are you ready to go, Ms. Stewart?" he added.

"Thank you, Captain Knight," she answered, gathering her things. "You be good, Oliver."

"I will," he promised.

Ryan escorted her out.

CAMILLA PUT THE ADOPTION PAPERS BACK IN HER PURSE AS THEY left the building. She was disturbed by Oliver's latest revelations, but hoped it didn't show. There was still so much she didn't understand about Dennis Hutchins. But she knew that teaching his son to lie was wrong, as wrong as ripping her off had been. But who could she talk to about this? Not Ryan. The less he knew, the better.

Ryan held open the car door for her.

"I appreciate your help, Captain Knight, but I can walk home. It's only a few blocks."

"Ryan, not Captain Knight. And it's no problem. You're going to be living here in town, and it's my job to help Pajaro Bay's citizens."

She didn't want to correct him, but she was definitely not going to be a "Pajaro Bay citizen" for long. The sooner she got that silly cottage sold and moved on to some place no one knew the truth about her, the better.

"Did I say something wrong?" he asked.

"I'm leaving town as soon as I sell the cottage," she said firmly, hoping to end the conversation there. "Thanks for the offer of a ride, but I could use a chance to walk and clear my head before I get to work on the house."

He still held the car door open. "Why get tired out before you even start? Come on. I won't bite."

He smiled, and the warmth for the first time reached his eyes, lighting up their cold depths and transforming him from an imposing figure into something warm and accessible. She felt a tightness in her throat. Again, like the first time she'd met him, she felt that moment of recognition—he wasn't just a cop, and she wasn't just a perp. He was a human being just like her, and he was more than that—kind and concerned, and genuinely a nice guy.

She took a step toward him, then stopped. She looked away quickly. What was she thinking? This was the last thing she needed. She wasn't going to find him attractive. She just wasn't. The last thing she needed in her life right now was a man.

But she wasn't thinking, she was feeling. That was the problem. She wasn't making lists, or rationally crunching numbers pro and con. She was feeling. Feeling something she really didn't want to ever feel again.

He cleared his throat, and she looked at him again. He was watching her with that assessing look. "Let's go before Val calls her sisters and we become topic number one in the town's gossip mill."

She looked around the parking lot anxiously, then quickly got in the car.

He smiled faintly at her as he shut the door, then leaned in the open window.

She still looked around. She didn't see anyone watching. "Where is she?"

"Who? Oh, Val? I was kidding—well, half-kidding. This is a small town, and if you are here for more than a day everyone will know everything about you."

Her dismay must have shown on her face, because he added, "Don't worry about it. As long as you don't break any laws, there won't be any problem."

"I have no intention of breaking any laws," she said. She could hear the stiffness in her voice, and he looked taken aback by her

51

reaction. What had he expected? She hated being reminded of her criminal record. She stared out the window while he walked around the SUV and got in the driver's side.

"I'm sorry, Camilla," he said quietly. "I meant it as a joke."

She turned to face him, watched his sheepish expression as he buckled his seat belt. She pulled in her claws, forcing herself to let go of the sense of shame he brought out from somewhere deep inside of her. "I'm sorry—Ryan," she said. She added, trying to make it light: "I know you're used to dealing with criminal types. I shouldn't overreact."

He laughed out loud, a warm, rumbling sound that seemed to surprise him as much as it did her. "You couldn't be a 'criminal type' if you tried." He glanced her way quickly before starting the car. "I really do believe you're innocent, you know."

She felt such a surge of relief it surprised her. Why did his opinion matter so much? Because the shame felt too familiar, too much like something she'd been running from all her life.

He still watched her, looking a bit wary at the fleeting emotions that must—as always—be obvious on her face. She smiled at him, forcing herself to stop thinking about herself. "So, I suppose you've seen a lot of criminals. How long have you been a cop?"

"Ten years in major crime with the Sacramento PD before I came here two years ago. Homicide, drugs, pretty much everything. Listen—" He shot her another quick glance. "You're holding up just fine." He seemed to want to say something more, but just pulled the car out of the parking lot.

"What? What do you want to say?" she asked.

"I wanted to ask...."

Her expression must have been transparent, because he added, almost reluctantly, "I'm not asking officially. What happened in San Jose is out of my jurisdiction. I'd just like to hear your story. Maybe I can help."

Maybe he could help. She was so tired of dealing with this on her own. But she knew she couldn't really open up to him. Still, maybe telling him about Dennis would get him off her back. Maybe saying it all out loud would answer all his questions and then he wouldn't bother her anymore. "It's all right," she finally said, making up her mind. "I've told the story so many times, what's one more?"

She leaned back against the vinyl seat. "Where can I start? Let's see. I worked for Felix Cordova."

Ryan whistled. "Cordova Computing? The big high-tech firm? I guess it didn't register just how big a company you'd been part of."

That was the reaction everyone had when she said it. She used to be so proud when she announced where she worked. The cutting-edge biotech firm run by the brilliant ex-astronaut supposedly hired only the best graduates from top universities.

"Yeah. It was a lucky break. I interned in their payroll department when I was earning my accounting degree from San Jose State." She skipped everything that happened before college. He didn't need to know any of that.

"It doesn't sound like luck. You must be pretty good at your job to get hired while still in college."

She sighed. She used to think she was. "Like I said, it was a lucky break. Anyway. I used to eat lunch in a park next to the company grounds—a lot of employees took their lunches there. Oh, no," she added as it struck her. "Dennis must have known that. He was staking out the park looking for—"

"—Somebody from the payroll department. Probably." Ryan pulled the SUV to a stop and turned to her. "So you met him in the park?"

"Right. He was there with Oliver. It was really Oliver I noticed first. The little boy, so closed-in, needing something—"

"—Someone," he said softly.

She didn't know how to explain it. The feeling that had come over her when she'd seen Oliver. It had been almost like seeing herself as a child. Almost like recognizing something familiar in him, something deep inside of her that she'd been avoiding all her life.

She tried to figure out how to explain how her life had turned upside down so suddenly without revealing too much about herself. "It was almost like Dennis was looking for a woman who liked his son, more than him." She was talking almost to herself, remembering, trying to put it together. "They were there many times during my lunch hour, and we got to talking, and I heard his story."

"Which was?"

"He was a single father. Oliver's mother had died in a car accident. I think I wouldn't have been so quick to trust him if he was just some guy hitting on me in the park. It was the picture of them, a father and son trying to rebuild their lives after Oliver's mother died. They were so alone. I knew what that felt like."

"Being alone?"

She hurried on with the story, afraid she had said too much. "So anyway, that's why I fell for him. He was so...."

"Vulnerable?"

"Yeah."

"So what does Dennis look like?"

"Look like? That's funny. I don't even have a photograph of him, of us together, or even of Oliver with him. I guess I'd describe him as average. Really average. Brown hair and eyes, medium height, medium build, no particular habits that stand out." She might have been more wary if Dennis had been more handsome, more flashy. "He was just average, in a non-threatening way. He looked so nice."

"Of course."

"What do you mean, of course?"

"He's a con man. He's going to be easy to like, easy to get along with, agreeable and, yeah, 'nice.'"

"But I should have realized." She found she was wringing her hands, and deliberately unclasped them. "Looking back, there were red flags everywhere. His interest in my job, in how I handled my money, my computer. His vague explanations about his own job and where he went all day while I was at work."

She sighed. "I was an idiot. I was on my way to meet him to elope and go to Hawaii—I had my wedding dress on a hanger in my cubicle—the day the police came. They had thrown me a party. I was sitting at my desk finishing up some work on the quarterly report. I remember I was stuffed full of pineapple cake and wearing a pink lei around my neck and... was happy." It had seemed like her life was falling into place so easily. Everything was so effortless.

She shook her head. "And then the police appeared at my desk and hauled me away in handcuffs in front of everyone. The head of the department had discovered the theft. Someone using my computer codes had transferred over a million dollars to a bogus account in the middle of the night. Then the account was closed and cashed out before I got to work that morning. I worked on those computers and I still don't know how he pulled it off. He might have used a worm," she muttered, going over the details in her mind again. "Something to track my keystrokes. But how he got it on the computer at work I can't imagine."

She pulled her mind back to the facts. "I should have known. Should have seen it coming. But he just seemed so... comfortable. He made me feel relaxed."

Unlike the man sitting next to her, prickly and overbearing. It wasn't just his uniform—the constant reminder that he had the authority to check into her background, to dig up every bit of dirt from her past. The problem was more than that. It was him. His presence making the car feel too small, too close. She looked out the window and realized they were parked in front of the cottage.

"I'm sorry you have to go through all this, Camilla. If there's anything I can do to help you, I will." His intense gaze pinned her to the seat, but finally she forced herself to turn away.

She unfastened her seat belt as nonchalantly as possible and opened the door to get out, then hesitated. "Coffee?" she asked tentatively, wondering if she was nuts to actually invite him in. "It's instant, but it's drinkable."

He nodded and got out of the car, too. He seemed hesitant, too, and that relaxed her for some reason. He wasn't as cold as he seemed, maybe. Maybe that was what was drawing her to him. That almost-hidden vulnerability peeking through his armor.

He came around the front of the car to meet her.

"Why me?" she asked. "That's what I keep asking myself. Why did he pick me? It's almost like he planned to leave Oliver with me, like he planned to leave me alone with this junky cottage and his son. Why would he do that?" On a roll, she recklessly voiced her real fear: "Was he able to see something in me that made me deserve this?"

He smiled. "You sound like one of our town's aging hippies. Do you really believe you have some kind of karma that attracts trouble to you?"

"Maybe I deserve trouble," she mumbled, then wished she could take it back.

He leaned in closer, and those eyes glinted as he picked up on the importance of what she'd said. "Why would you deserve trouble?" he asked, his voice so soft she felt herself leaning closer to him to catch the words.

She shrank back. Oh, Captain Knight was a good interrogator, wasn't he? That's the way these cops were. They always found a way to mess up your story. Picking away at you endlessly until you slipped up. She took a step back and straightened up. She turned away from the dangerous subject of her own past and said, "I just mean that out of all the people in the world, he did this to me. I guess it just seems so weird to be targeted like this."

Ryan pulled back, too, and seemed to relax. "I don't know the answers, Camilla. But maybe we can figure it out. Every criminal has an M.O. We can find Dennis Hutchins's. So, has he left his son with other women?"

She was glad to move back onto safer territory. Ryan was a cop. He could help figure this out. He wasn't investigating her, but just curious about Dennis, so she needed to get herself under control and focus on the problem in front of her. "I'm pretty sure Dennis never had any other woman legally adopt Oliver," she said matter-of-factly. "At least, not as far as I know. That's part of the problem. I don't know much. Half of what Oliver said today was news to me. He thinks telling me about his father would be snitching, and the police don't seem to know much about any of this. They're more focused on the missing money than on Oliver being abandoned."

"Oliver isn't abandoned." He was smiling that tentative smile at her again.

"No," she agreed. "I'll never abandon him. He's safe with me."

"Yes, he is." Ryan leaned against the side of the SUV. "So go over the story again."

She quickly went through the timeline again. She tried to skip over her shame and embarrassment. Her love of Oliver. How she got swept up in the suddenness of it all and lost her sense. How it all came crashing down. But somehow she felt he saw all of it through those cold blue eyes of his.

When she stopped he said, "Well at least I can understand why he picked you."

She froze. So he did believe she deserved this? "You think he likes redheads?" she said sarcastically.

"I'm serious."

"So am I," she said defensively. "I have no idea what made him target me, except my complete gullibility."

"No. He trusted you."

"Trusted me?" Of all the things he might have said, that was the most ridiculous. "He knew I was an idiot he could scam, you mean."

"No, that's not what I mean." He looked at her very seriously. "I mean he trusted you with his son's life. He trusted you not to take out your anger—your very understandable anger toward him—on his son."

"What are you talking about? Of course I would never blame Oliver."

"Exactly. There are women who would."

"Who would hurt a little child like him? He's darling. Give me a break."

"You don't think anyone ever hurts darling, innocent children?"

She took a deep breath, letting it out slowly. She was wringing her hands again, and this time he definitely noticed.

He covered her hands with his own. The touch of those large, rough hands was surprisingly warm, and she felt her clenched fingers relax in his palms. "You're a decent person, Camilla." He let go of her suddenly, and she missed the warmth. "You would never hurt Oliver."

"I wouldn't do that, no matter what."

Ryan nodded. "And he could read you, 'like a book' you said. He knew you had a compassionate heart."

"You don't even know me." But she worried that he did know too much about her, and she didn't like how it made her feel.

He continued on calmly, in that cool way of his. "I know you are broke, out of work, and struggling to get on your feet, but you took time out of your first day in town to enroll Oliver in school."

"He'll get behind if I don't."

"Right."

She felt uncomfortable, like he too could read her like a book. That sensation made her feel unsafe. She wished she hadn't invited him in for coffee, and wondered how to brush him off.

"Why do you feel guilty?" he asked. "You're the victim, not the criminal."

"Haven't you ever made a single mistake and had it snowball into something awful?"

He stepped back like she'd stabbed him in the heart.

What had she said?

"Let's take a rain check on the coffee," he said stiffly. "I'd better be getting to work. Good day, Ma'am." He got back into the SUV and pulled away, leaving her standing there in the road.

CHAPTER FIVE

THE COUNTY SHERIFF DEPARTMENT'S SUBSTATION WAS JUST A LITTLE place in the center of town, tucked between Santos' Market and the modern art gallery. This month Santos' front window was advertising red fishing worms on sale, and the gallery, appropriately enough, had their front window full of abstract sculptures made from sinewy curves of copper pipe.

Ryan felt he should find that amusing, but he was in a foul mood. Ever do something small that changes everything? Camilla had said. Why was this woman getting to him? She was simply saying what he'd thought a million times himself. So why did it sound like an accusation coming from her? The weird part was, after seeing her with Oliver, after seeing the softness that sometimes came through in her eyes when she wasn't on her guard, he felt like she was one of the few people he could talk to about why he couldn't be a cop anymore....

There was a deep compassion in her, something rare. She was brave, and honest, and whip-smart, but the thing that made her different from everyone else he'd ever met was that unwavering kindness. She treated Oliver like her own child, though she could have dumped him into the system without a backward glance.

The boy was difficult and moody, and he knew how to push her buttons, but she still treated him with that compassionate, gentle kindness. She was a rare person.

So why did that make him so uncomfortable?

He slammed the car door and stalked into the building.

The substation was already open. Ryan's deputy, Joe Serrano, always started his shift at eight.

Ryan hung up his hat next to Joe's on the coat rack by the door. There was a small waiting area, then four desks—Joe was on the phone at his, Ryan's own desk was piled with papers, and the two other desks sat pristinely empty, waiting for the reserve deputies who'd be assigned here from the county seat in June.

Ryan went to his own desk and looked over the stack of messages. Nothing important.

He listened to Joe on the phone trying to get a word in edgewise with whoever he had on the line. His deputy was going to be a good cop. He was young, and the substation was his first assignment, but he had good instincts. Ryan felt a deep responsibility to him. He had been brought up in the ranks by older officers who'd trained him well, going out of their way to make sure he kept safe and learned what he needed. He had wanted to pass that on to Joe. But he couldn't teach Joe everything he needed to know in the next two weeks.

He continued to watch Joe, noting that he wasn't being assertive enough with the caller. He would have to work with him about that. Being too polite could get him killed. He had to be able to take charge of a situation, especially with a belligerent suspect. Otherwise things could get out of hand quickly.

Joe hung up the phone after promising the person on the other end of the line that he'd get there ASAP.

"Farmer up on Pajaro Ridge," Joe quickly explained.

"What's his problem?"

"Some of his chickens have disappeared. He thinks it's a conspiracy. Wants me to come see the evidence."

Ryan nodded.

"I told him someone would be right out."

A drive to the top of Pajaro Ridge and back would take an hour over heavily rutted mountain roads.

"If you'd like to take it, Sir, I wouldn't want to overstep my authority." Joe's expression was angelic.

Ryan laughed out loud. Joe looked really surprised at that, and Ryan felt the surprise, too. Suddenly his emotions seemed to be closer to the surface than they'd been in a long time. He seemed to be smiling, laughing—and getting angry—in ways he hadn't for a very long time.

"I think I can trust you to handle it, Serrano. That's how you get the experience to make detective—working the tough cases."

Joe grabbed his hat and headed for the door.

"Deputy?"

Joe stopped and looked back. Ryan was tempted to go with him to make sure he handled things properly.

"Yeah?"

"Nothing, Joe. Radio me if you have any problems."

Joe nodded. He paused in the open doorway. "Um." Another pause. Ryan raised an eyebrow and Joe said, "I heard about your resignation."

He nodded. "You'll be working with a new guy after I'm gone. I'm sure it'll be fine."

Joe nodded. Paused again. "Hey," he said.

"Yeah?"

"You coming tonight?"

"To the school fundraiser?" Ryan shook his head.

"I'm cooking enchiladas for 200 people. Don't you want to see me sweat?"

"You never sweat, Joe."

"You haven't seen me playing Monopoly with Marisol. You haven't sweated till you owe your life savings to an eight-year-old. Now, how about dinner, Captain? The family would love to see you."

"Some other time," Ryan said. There would be no other time, and they both knew it. He knew Joe meant well, but there was no way he was going to one of the town gabfests once word got out that he was resigning. Mabel Rutherford alone would be more than he could take.

Joe shrugged and left.

Ryan watched him go, then his mind shifted back to what was really bothering him. Camilla, Oliver, and the mysterious Dennis Hutchins.

As soon as Joe was gone Ryan fired up his computer. While it was booting up, he opened up his notebook to a new page. He wrote down a list of names: Dennis Hutchins, Oliver Hutchins, Joyce Hutchins, Camilla Stewart. None of what he'd learned about them in the last day made any sense. He hated unsolved mysteries.

He tore out the page. This wasn't his case—in fact, there was no case related to Pajaro Bay at all. The only crime was embezzlement, and he didn't have jurisdiction over that.

He crumpled up the paper and threw it in the trash. Read through his phone messages, read a brochure on some optional training available and made some notes for Joe on courses he should take. He was leaving, he reminded himself. Coasting through his final work days until he could hit the open road.

He dug the crumpled page out of the trash. Dennis Hutchins was a fugitive with a felony warrant. He might be in this area. It was entirely appropriate for him to do a bit of background checking on the situation. He ignored the voice asking him why he needed to stick his nose into this, and got to work.

He tried the official databases, looking for the missing Dennis Hutchins. Nothing. No criminal record under that name. A warrant out of San Jose on suspicion of grand theft. No details in that other than what he'd already learned from Camilla. Dead end.

He didn't have enough of a detailed description to do a more general search, and he saw the warrant was not detailed either. San Jose P.D. didn't have anything more than he did, at least in this database. He should call San Jose and get the details before he went much further with this.

He called, got shuffled around a bit and ended up leaving a message for the detective on the case. He looked up at the clock. Still before 10 a.m. He had a little more time before he headed out on his mid-day tour of the village. A visible police presence helped keep things running smoothly, and with Joe gone it would be his turn to make the daily stops—coffee shop, fishermen at the wharf, a swing past the school and a stop at the fish shack for a cup of coffee and an update on the town news from Mel, the crotchety old guy who ran the place.

He had a little more time. He looked at his crumpled page again.

All right. He'd go at this another way. He'd learned over the years that the info was usually out there. He just had to be creative to get it.

He googled the name Dennis Hutchins. Hutchins was too common a name. He got hundreds of hits.

He tried again, looking for the names Dennis, Oliver and Joyce Hutchins all together.

Still nothing.

So probably Hutchins wasn't his real name. What had Oliver said? First in Sacramento with Mommy.

He tried the names Dennis, Oliver, and Joyce, with Sacramento.

He got an immediate hit.

The Sacramento Bee had a funeral notice for a Joyce Ashford Henning.

He clicked on the article.

A car accident. Two years ago, March the 9th. So Oliver had lived with his mother until two years ago?

The woman in the picture was darkly beautiful, with a warm smile. She had left behind Dennis, her "loving husband," and her beloved six-year-old son, Oliver.

Poor kid. And now his father was gone, too. At least Oliver was in good hands with Camilla.

He read the article over again, more slowly. Something was off, but he couldn't pin it down.

He picked up the phone.

"Sacramento Investigations," the voice on the phone said.

"Paul?"

Detective Paul Graham dropped the official neutrality from his voice. "Hey! Ryan. You really going through with your plan?"

"Yup."

The answer was clipped, but Paul kept pushing. "If you're sick of living at the beach, you could come back to work with us. You know how much it would mean to the squad. I owe you my own life twice over, Ryan—"

"—Listen, partner," Ryan cut in before Paul started making a big deal about their old times together. "I'm actually calling you for a favor."

"Anything, man. Say the word."

"I'm working a case here." That sounded more professional than saying he was playing a hunch, so he went with it. "I've got a fugitive I'm trying to trace, wanted for larceny."

"Ooh, a big case out there at the beach," Paul said. "What did he steal? A pair of flip-flops?"

"Fairly big," Ryan said calmly. "Payroll worth more than a mil."

Paul whistled. "Oh. That big."

"Yeah. He has family in my jurisdiction. I'm doing some background on him, see if I can get a lead."

"Anything I can help with, just ask."

"A car accident, two years ago. March the 9th. Joyce Ashford Henning."

Ryan heard the computer keys clicking. "How's this related to your perp?"

"He was husband of the dead woman."

"Think it's a homicide?"

As soon as Paul said it, Ryan knew that was exactly what he was thinking. But he had no logical reason for believing that. Just something that didn't add up about Camilla, and little Oliver, and the missing Dennis. "Not necessarily. Just checking."

"No murder here. Single car accident. Late at night on a wet road. She hit a guardrail and gas tank punctured. Explosion rocked two city blocks."

"Autopsy?"

"Let me check." A pause, then he was back on the line. "What was left of her. Identified through dental records. No sign of drugs or alcohol. No suspicion of foul play in the report. Just one of those things."

"Thanks. Gotta go."

"Ryan—wait." Ryan waited for it, knowing what was coming. "You know you're welcome to come for a visit anytime—or, hey. I can take a couple of days off and drive over to the coast. We can go fishing or something."

Right. And he could spend a couple of days being told what a "hero" he was and how he was such a "good cop," and how he shouldn't give up his "life's work." No, thanks. "That's a great idea, Paul. But not right now. I've got some stuff to take care of. I'll call you soon. Bye."

He hung up before Paul could start in again. He didn't need anyone trying to get him to talk about it. He was so sick of that phrase. There was nothing to talk about.

Joyce Henning's funeral notice was still up on his computer screen. Ryan almost hit the button to close the screen, but hesitated. The smiling woman with short dark hair and Oliver's eyes stared back at him from the computer. His gut was telling him something and he couldn't let it go, not quite yet.

He picked up the phone again. "Hector?" There were sounds of a car revving in the background.

"Hey, Dude," came Hector's voice over the phone. "Your car's almost ready. The new muffler came in yesterday, and I got the pony seats installed and—"

"I'm calling about the car from this morning."

"Oh, yeah. I was just going to call the lady. Manuel, knock off the noise—I'm on the phone with the fuzz." The engine sound died off in the background.

"Hector?"

"Yeah, I'm here, sheriff dude."

"You found out what's wrong with Ms. Stewart's car?"

"The pretty lady's car? Did I ever."

"Yeah?" Ryan prompted patiently. Hector was a good mechanic, but not the best conversationalist. Too many wipeouts while surfing had made him a little fuzzy, and his heavy marijuana use fell more into the recreational than the medicinal category....

When Ryan heard only silence on the line, he prompted again: "Hector? What did you find out?"

"Huh?"

"The car. Camilla's—Ms. Stewart's—car. What's wrong with it?"

Somehow, Ryan knew what was coming, but it still hit him in the stomach like a meatball hero and two beers on a hot day.

"Punctured gas tank."

He hated being right. Ryan reached in his desk for some antacid.

"Sheriff dude? You there?"

"Yeah. I'm still here, Hector."

"She probably didn't smell the gas 'cause it's a convertible. Glad we caught it. I'll call the lady and tell her."

"I'll do it, Hector. Thanks. Can you tell how they punctured the tank?"

"They? You think it's a 'they'?"

Ryan swallowed the antacid. "I'm just asking. You're the expert."

"Doesn't have to be a they. Could be an it. A nail on the road. She goes through a construction zone and something pops up and hits the tank. She runs over a curb with that low-slung convertible chassis. Could be a lot of things. Doesn't have to be a 'they.'"

"Got it. What do you think it was?"

"It?"

"The thing that punctured the gas tank, Hector. Stay with me."

"Oh, yeah. Well, it's a round hole, not too big. Made a real slow leak. Probably a nail."

"Okay. Can you fix it?"

"Sure. Easy fix. Not too expensive. Have it done by tomorrow. Not tonight. Going to the fundraiser tonight. Craving for enchiladas. Chips and salsa. Chiles rellenos. You know how it is."

Ryan was only half-listening now. "Yeah, I'm sure those munchies are something."

"Yeah, dude. You know it. So, you gonna be there?"

"I don't usually get the munchies, Hector."

"But the food, sheriff dude. You gotta eat." He was the third person to ask him about this stupid fundraiser. Did people think he couldn't feed himself? On the other hand, Camilla needed to eat. And he'd like to find out more about Oliver's life in Sacramento—what was going on between his parents before his mother died. The fundraiser would be a good chance to grill her and Oliver about this whole weird case. A good chance to find out if what he was thinking could actually be true: that Dennis Hutchins/Henning/whatever was not just a thief, but a killer. And that she and Oliver were next on his list.

"Sheriff Dude?"

He started at the sound in his ear. "Thanks, Hector. I'll tell Ms. Stewart her car will be ready tomorrow."

"You tell the lady she's got some good karma."

"What do you mean?"

"Puncture like that. Gas leaking all over the undercarriage. One spark, thing blows up like a bottle rocket. No more pretty lady."

"Yeah." Ryan looked at the picture of Oliver's mother on the screen in front of him. "No more pretty lady."

"WHERE AM I GOING TO FIND A WINDOW LIKE THAT?"

Camilla stood in front of the cottage, gazing up (and up) to the tip of the pointy roof, where, just under the eaves, a crooked window with a broken pane stared mournfully back at her. The poor thing looked sad up there with its glass missing and one foot-long section of wooden muntin dangling dangerously, just waiting for the next breeze to knock it down.

She had ventured up to the third floor inside and counted all the missing panes of glass. The whole third floor, all eight by ten feet of it, was full of pine needles from the trees leaning over the cottage, and the signs of visiting animals were even stronger than in the living room. Fixing that window was a good place to start the reclaiming of the cottage.

She stared for a bit, trying to think. There was no way she could buy a piece of glass to match. She didn't have the money, for one thing. The cash she'd gotten for the engagement ring had to last them for a while. And the kind of old-fashioned wavy glass she'd need to match the rest of the windows wouldn't be cheap.

She wished her dad was around to give her advice. She doubted even he had seen a house quite like this one, but he knew all about repairing old houses, and she sure could use some help. But he was out of reach. Her family members were all out of reach now, either physically like her father, or emotionally like her mother.

Best not to think about Mother. Not Mom, Mama, or Ma, but Mother. That voice that echoed in her head, telling her she was sure to screw things up, she was her father's daughter and so she must end up being a loser and a failure like him. Maybe if someone had believed in her—

No, she refused to go there. She wasn't going to use her mother as an excuse for her mistakes. She was an adult and this was her life. She would take responsibility for both the good and the bad. The mistakes she'd made and the successes she'd had. She was on her own in this, and she'd better stop staring blankly at the cottage and figure out a solution.

She went around to the back yard, picking her way through the overgrown hydrangeas and bits of trash. Why on earth had Dennis dumped this place on her? It seemed like the last bit of cruelty, to take her boss's money, ruin her job and destroy her reputation, abandon Oliver, and then top it off by giving her this charming little junk pile.

"What are you doing?"

She turned at the voice. "Oh, Thea." Thea Paris, her real estate agent, was staring at her. "I guess I do look like a mess, don't I." She ran her hand through her curls self-consciously.

Thea, as always, looked perfect. Teetering on three-inch heels ($500 from a San Francisco boutique, Thea had previously informed her), her hair a glossy sheet of ebony perfection (a $300 keratin treatment would even be able to 'salvage' Camilla's hair, Thea had helpfully explained), and Thea's essential accessory, that slightly snooty air she'd apparently been born with. Camilla wondered if it was too late to switch agents to someone a little less annoying.

Camilla pulled her pink sweatshirt straight and wiped her hands on her dirty jeans.

"What are you doing?" Thea repeated.

"Oh. Sorry. I'm looking for building supplies." She started to turn back toward the front of the house when she spotted something—"Hey! A shed."

"What about it?"

"Have you looked in here?" The little garden shed was pretty good-sized, at least as big as the kitchen in the house. "It might have old tools, junk, even a few pieces of wood." Camilla put one hand on the rusty door handle. "It might be a gold mine."

Thea shook her head, looking offended by the thought of touching the handle. "Get away from that place, Camilla. It's probably disgusting inside."

"That's okay; I can handle a little dirt." She pulled the door open. It took her eyes a moment to adjust to the gloom, but then she squealed in glee. It was a gold mine. She could see discarded beams of old-growth redwood against one wall, a bookcase of solid oak in the corner, and, leaning against an old freezer in the back of the shed, "Yes!"

"What?" said Thea's voice right behind her.

"Look—this is great." Camilla picked her way through the stuff, climbing over a stack of wood and pushing aside a moldy cardboard box. The box fell open and out tumbled—"Diamonds!" Camilla said with a laugh. Gorgeous old glass doorknobs in a rainbow of colors spilled across the floor, catching the light from the doorway. Replacing some of the rusty doorknobs in the house with these would really dress up the place.

"Get out of there, Camilla," Thea warned.

"It's okay, I'm already dirty. But stay back or you'll wreck your shoes." Over Thea's continued protests she continued on until she got to her target: a stack of old window frames. The frames leaned up against the freezer, covered in a thick layer of grime. She pulled them out, one by one. Some were missing glass, some missing muntins, but add them all together, and she'd have enough parts to bring every window in the house back to perfection—or perfect lopsidedness, as the case may be.

She pulled one likely suspect out of the stack and made her way back to the doorway, where Thea stood, looking relieved.

"Thought I'd break my neck, huh?"

"You looked like you'd gone nuts. Is that thing what you wanted?" She eyed the broken window in distaste.

"Original wavy glass." She leaned the window against the side of the shed, while Thea shut the door.

"You should keep this locked. Oliver could get hurt if he went messing around in there."

"You're right. I'll pick up a lock next time I'm in town." She headed back toward the front of the cottage, Thea alongside her.

They stopped at the front door.

"How about a cup of coffee?"

"I can't stay. I just brought you some flyers." She pulled them out, and Camilla felt an odd lurch in her stomach at the sight of the flyer: FOR SALE in big print over a picture of her silly crooked cottage. "Now that you've seen the place, you understand why I had to fudge the details a bit."

"Yeah, I see." Camilla read the description: "Cozy, charming— all the usual code words for a tiny piece of junk." She said it with a laugh, but it made her feel almost disloyal to the little house. But that was ridiculous.

"I have to go now, so I'll leave some of these with you."

Camilla set the window down and took the flyers.

She waved goodbye to Thea, and watched her walk away. Then she turned back to the house. The place was a piece of junk. She did want to sell it. This wasn't her home, it was just a stop along the way toward where she wanted to be.

And where was that? she asked herself.

She picked up the window frame and carried it inside. She could think about that while she worked.

"THANK YOU FOR BRINGING OLIVER HOME FROM SCHOOL, CAPTAIN Ryan." Oliver slipped past Camilla through the cottage door to run into the house.

"What's for dinner?" Oliver called out from inside.

Captain Ryan still stood in the doorway, his hat in his hands.

"Well," she said awkwardly, wondering when—or if—he would explain about his abrupt departure earlier. "Um, thanks again."

"No problem. And Hector said your car will be fixed tomorrow." He looked almost sheepish about that, and she waited for the explanation.

"Bye," he finally said, and turned to go.

With a shrug, she shut the door. What had all that been about? It was for the best. She didn't want to get to know him any better, anyway. So if he was going to act like he hated her, that was just fine with her.

"What about dinner?" Oliver repeated.

"Mac and cheese again."

Oliver wrinkled his nose.

"Sorry, kid, but that's the way it is for now." She didn't like it any more than he did, but they weren't exactly rolling in dough. "Get cleaned up and I'll start cooking."

A minute later, she heard a knock on the door.

When she opened the old redwood door on its melodramatically creaking hinges, there Ryan stood, all six feet-plus of muscle, with a hesitant look on his face.

"Yes, Captain Ryan?" she prompted when he didn't say anything.

"Dinner?" He said the one word and then just stood there.

She smothered a grin. So he wasn't as tough as he acted. She felt her back straighten as she realized he actually was, just maybe, attracted to her a little bit. "Yes, we do eat dinner every night when we can get it. Is that your question?"

He looked down. All the confidence gone, like a small boy,

lost and very alone, and her heart melted. She couldn't stay mad at him when he looked like that. "I'd love to have dinner with you, Ryan."

"Great." He twirled his hat between his fingers. "Great. Um, now? You and Oliver? Tonight?"

She looked around at the empty house with its mile-long to-do list, and at Oliver standing there. Macaroni and cheese from a box, or dinner out with a hunk of a guy? Tough choice. "Yes, now would be terrific. Let me grab my purse. Come on, Oliver. We're going out to dinner."

They got in his SUV.

"This is great," she said. "We really didn't want to have mac and cheese again."

"What kind of food are we having?" asked Oliver from the back seat as Ryan started the car.

"What kind do you want?" she asked him.

"Thai food. Chicken with peanut goop on it and that weird tea with coconut milk in it."

"Sounds tasty," she said. "How's Thai food sound to you, Ryan?"

Ryan laughed. "Um, how about Mexican food?"

"Why is it funny?"

"Did you even look at the town when you came through, Camilla?"

"No, I was kind of busy dealing with the car stalling. By the way, you haven't told me what the mechanic found."

"I'll explain over dinner," he said somberly. Then he nodded out the window. "Don't blink or you'll miss downtown Pajaro Bay."

He turned down onto the main street through town. "This is Calle Principal." As they drove slowly down the street, he pointed out Santos' Market (the little grocer where she'd bought food the previous day), Treasures From the Sea (a gift shop selling nautical relics), a coffee shop (closed) that looked like they'd never heard of an espresso machine, a dry cleaner, an Art Deco movie theater that advertised live theater instead of the latest double feature, the sheriff's substation, a snooty-looking art gallery with a bunch of copper pipes in its front window, a darling little pet store called, appropriately enough, The Surfing Puggle, the Junque Shoppe that now owned her diamond ring, and then the street dead-ended at the high school.

"Oh," she said.

"Oh what?" said Oliver.

"Oh, there aren't any restaurants."

Ryan laughed. "Actually, there are a bunch of restaurants in town. It is a tourist town, after all."

"Where are they?"

"Well, there's a nice French restaurant in Torres Alley downtown, the coffee shop's not as bad as it looks, and there are a half-dozen places down by the wharf. You just have to know where to look. But no Thai food. Sorry."

"That's okay," she said. "Mexican food sounds good." She looked back over her shoulder. "But didn't we just pass Wharf Road?"

"Yup."

"But isn't that where the other restaurants are?"

"Yup." He turned those deep blue eyes in her direction and her breath caught in her throat. "Trust me."

Oddly, she did, though until he looked away, she couldn't have spoken to save her life.

He turned away and faced the windshield again. She let out a ragged breath. This man was so confusing, one moment cold and distant and the next searing straight into her with those sad, soulful eyes.

She turned to look out the window in time to see that they were entering the parking lot by the high school gym. There were about 40 cars all parked in the lot, and families heading into the gym. So much for a date with a hunk in some romantic hideaway. Since thinking of Captain Ryan as anything other than the local cop was dangerous, she should be thrilled instead of disappointed. Right?

"I hope at least it's edible," she said doubtfully, looking at the kids running into the old gym.

He raised an eyebrow. "Just wait."

CHAPTER SIX

THE GYM WAS PACKED, AND THE SMELLS COMING FROM A LONG ROW of tables along the wall were intoxicating—cilantro, meat, chili peppers, cheese. A Hispanic man in a sheriff's department uniform and a white apron grinned widely at Ryan and gave her a quick wave. Camilla hesitantly waved back.

She noticed that a lot of the people in the gym were looking in their direction, most friendly, a few frowning, but all downright curious.

"Why are they staring? You bring a lot of women to this romantic hideaway?"

He shook his head.

A little girl came running up. "Uncle Ryan! You came!"

"Hi, Marisol. This is my friend Oliver."

"My daddy's cooking," Marisol informed Oliver. "Come on." She took Oliver by the hand and started him down the food line in front of them.

The deputy sauntered over, clapped Ryan on the shoulder. "I'm Joe Serrano," he told Camilla with another big grin. "You can call me Deputy Joe." He was looking way-too happy for a casual meeting. "You came," he stated the obvious to Ryan.

"They needed dinner."

"I'm glad," Joe said.

"This is Camilla Stewart."

"And who's my daughter's new boyfriend?" he asked, leaning down to the two kids.

"This is Oliver Hen—Hutchins," Ryan said.

"We're going to eat some of everything," Marisol said gleefully.

Oliver looked at Ryan warily, but seemed to relax when Joe grinned at them again. "Nice to meet you both. Hope you're hungry." He turned back to Camilla. "I'm glad you brought our resident recluse out on a date."

"It's not a date," Ryan said, a bit too quickly.

"No, it isn't," she confirmed, also too quickly. They both sounded like awkward teenagers, and Joe grinned again. She wanted to ask Joe about the "resident recluse" comment, but Oliver interrupted.

"Yes it is a date," said Oliver. "We're having Mexican food."

Ryan handed Camilla a plate and they started down the line after Marisol and Oliver.

"Do you like rellenos?" Marisol asked Oliver.

"Yup," Oliver said with authority.

"My daddy's the best cook," Marisol said.

Oliver nodded. "Yeah. It smells just like Olvera Street."

"Why thank you, Oliver," Joe said.

"What's Olvera Street?" Camilla asked.

"It's in L.A.," Joe answered over his shoulder. "You from Southern Cali, kid?"

From the back Camilla watched Oliver shrink down and hunch his shoulders in what she had come to call his No Snitching look. Southern California. None of the cities he'd mentioned at school this morning were near L.A. Another mystery. She was getting really sick of all these secrets.

Deputy Joe didn't seem to notice Oliver's reaction. He led

them all down the line, piling their plates ridiculously high with food.

"What's the matter, Buddy?" Ryan said when they got to the end of the line.

Oliver was frowning at the trays of cookies and slices of chocolate cake.

"Can't make up your mind?"

Oliver nodded.

"Why don't you wait until you've eaten all your supper first," Camilla said. "Then maybe you won't have room for dessert."

Oliver looked like he was heading into another pout when Ryan said, "It might be gone by then. You probably should take some now."

Oliver grabbed a plate with a huge slice of chocolate cake. "Okay, Camilla?"

She nodded. She wasn't about to deprive Oliver of chocolate cake—especially if it brought him out of his pout.

"After all," Oliver said. "Daddy always says it's better to be safe than sorry."

"Does he?" Ryan said, perking up. "That's very wise. What else does he say?"

What was Ryan up to?

Oliver bit his lip and said nothing.

Ryan put a hand on Oliver's shoulder. "So, kid, when you used to eat at Olvera Street, did your dad take you there?"

Definitely not casual, and even Oliver could see it. He wiggled away from Ryan's hand and shrugged.

Camilla stepped in between them. She wasn't going to let this big cop bully her kid.

Camilla bent down to Oliver. "It's okay. You don't have to snitch on your dad. I understand."

"Whatever." He shrugged as if it meant nothing to him, but she noticed he stopped hunching his shoulders.

"Come on," said Marisol, and she ran off to sit at one of the tables.

Oliver turned to Camilla. "Can I eat with my friends?"

"Sure," she said, "but be sure to stay in the building."

He ran off to join them.

Wow. That hadn't taken long. She didn't know a soul in town —except Ryan. Oliver already had friends to eat dinner with. She felt conspicuous standing at the end of the food line with a big plate and no idea where to turn. It was like the first day at a new high school—everybody seemed to know everyone, and she was the odd one out.

"I wasn't going to interrogate him," Ryan said. He looked a bit sheepish, though, and she didn't believe him.

"It's fine," she said, realizing she sounded kind-of stiff. She couldn't help it. She hated that whole "cop thing," where they wouldn't let go of something and just leave people in peace.

"Why don't we sit over here," he said. Then Ryan put an arm around her shoulder and guided her to one of the tables, and she felt all the eyes in the gym turn to her. She wasn't sure being "friends" with Captain Ryan was going to help her blend in.

Ryan set their plates on the table and pulled out the squeaky folding chair for Camilla. She sat down and set her purse on the floor.

Across from her sat a gorgeous woman with toffee-colored skin and a stunning mane of glossy streaked hair—another woman who was obviously no stranger to expensive salons.

Camilla self-consciously patted her messy curls and pulled her sweatshirt straight. She was sure the woman was looking down on her. She hated that.

"Camilla, Robin. Robin, Camilla," said Ryan. "I've gotta touch base with Joe. Be right back." He bent down toward her, almost as if he was going to kiss her goodbye, then straightened up and was gone. She let out her breath and turned to the woman seated across from her.

Robin stretched one hand across the table. "Nice to meet you, Camilla. I'm Robin Brenham of Robin's Nest."

They shook hands, Camilla noticing how her own now-ragged nails looked compared to Robin's perfectly gleaming red ones.

Camilla sighed. "I remember nail polish."

Robin laughed. "This is just because I have out-of-town clients coming in tomorrow. I've got to get the Nest ready."

"Robin's Nest?"

"The real estate office near Santos'. Anything you need, from a cottage to a mansion, all at post-recession prices." She took a bite of her enchilada. "End of sales pitch. So, you've come from the land of manicures and designer clothes?"

She nodded.

"Me, too."

Camilla smiled. "It seems a long way from here. Where are you from?"

"San Francisco. And you?"

"San Jose."

"So what brought you here?"

Camilla shrugged. She didn't want to go into it. "Long story. Why did you move here?"

"That's a long story, too. We'll have to do lunch and I can give you all the boring details."

Camilla wanted to say yes. It would be nice to have a friend. But she didn't think it was smart to start opening up to people in town, so she changed the subject. "You're in real estate? Then maybe you can explain to me why 'near Santos' Market,' or 'down Torres Alley' instead of just giving the address?"

"Because we don't really have street addresses here. The only time you use an address is when you're getting a package delivered. We don't have home mail delivery, so people just say the names of the places, 'Cat Slide Cottage'—that's Ryan's ex's place at the corner of Cliff and Principal, or they give the location, like "the place with the green door in Torres Alley." It's easy once you get used to it. You'll get used to our quirks soon enough."

"Ryan's ex?"

Robin's smiled vanished. "Ah. You noticed that. He'll tell you when he's ready, I'm sure. Nothing stays a secret for long in this town. You'll get hooked into the grapevine."

"I'm just here temporarily. I'm fixing up a place to sell."

Robin's eyes lit up. "Ooh, potential customer? Wanna borrow my nail polish? Or would that be considered a bribe?"

Camilla smiled. As hard as she was trying to keep her distance, it was impossible not to like Robin. She looked like any high-powered executive from Camilla's old life, but the warmth in her eyes took away any sense of intimidation. "I already have the place listed," she explained, "but my agent thought doing some improvements would give me a better chance at top dollar."

"Good idea. Putting in a little sweat equity can pay off big-time. Who's your agent?"

She told her.

Robin shrugged. "She's not local—but that's okay. There's enough business to go around." She grinned again. "So, my incoming clients are looking for something ocean view, low maintenance for weekends and summers. Where's your place?"

"It's 43 Cliff Drive. It's uh—-I don't know if you'd call it a low-maintenance kind of place—"

Ryan sat down next to Camilla in time to catch the last of the conversation. "It's the Honeymoon Cottage next to Ms. Zelda's, Robin." He grinned mischievously. "Or, as it's been called, the Drunken Leprechaun House."

"Great name. You should put that in the advertising. Wait—you're the one selling the Honeymoon Cottage?"

"I guess. Is that what it's called?"

"Yeah. Wow. That's the very first Stockdale. Ms. Zelda will give you the info. I'm dying to get inside that one. I bet I could get it sold for you in days. I'll tell my clients. I'm already taking them to the Turret Cottage and Ryan's place, but yours has so much more history behind it."

"It might not be quite ready for visitors yet, right, Camilla? She hasn't even had a chance to talk to Ms. Zelda."

Camilla nodded again. This was all going so fast. Sell it in days? She hadn't even had a chance to finish fixing all the windows.

Who was she kidding? She wasn't thinking about windows. She was thinking about leaving town before getting to know the guy sitting next to her. She hadn't even known he was divorced. They hadn't taken Oliver to the amusement park yet.

"I—I'm not quite ready to show the place yet. But I'll let you know when it's ready. And who's Ms. Zelda, and why do I need to talk to her before I sell the place?"

"Oh, you are new here," said Robin. "Ryan'll get you up to speed." She stood up. "But if you want any good gossip—or just a cup of genuine espresso—give me a ring." She handed Camilla a business card. "I mean it. Coffee, soon?"

It did feel like the first day in a new school, and one of the popular kids had asked her to play. She grinned at Robin. "Yeah. I'd like that."

"Now, I've got to make an appearance at the grown-up's table. I see the Madrigals are holding court." With another friendly smile, she walked away.

Camilla looked over her shoulder to see what she was talking about. At the far end of the gym, one table was crowded with people sitting shoulder to shoulder. At the head of the table, a pair of tall, noble-looking people sat—a young man and a teenage girl, obviously related, both with dark, curly hair and the aristocratic bone structure of Spanish conquistadors.

"Descendants of Pajaro Bay's founders," Ryan whispered in her ear. "He's the mayor and she's the homecoming queen." Wow. She so didn't care. His warm breath against her neck made her completely uninterested in whether he'd said they were the town's founders or a pair of guinea pigs. She just wanted him to say something else.

Without moving, she whispered, "So who's Ms. Zelda?"

"Zelda Potter. Former movie star, head of the Historical Preservation Committee, and your next-door neighbor. You can't remodel a Stockdale cottage without the Committee's approval."

He nodded toward another table, where several well-preserved ladies chattered and picked over their plates of beans and rice. One of them, her white hair only partially concealed by a vibrant orange hat, nodded back at them.

Next to her sat the junk shop woman. She didn't smile or nod, but she seemed exceedingly interested in the fact that Ryan and Camilla were sitting so close together. Camilla scooted away from Ryan and bent her head over her plate.

They ate in silence for a while. Camilla was trying to make sense of all the names and intertwined relationships in this town. Coming here to dinner with Ryan had been a big mistake. She'd bet everyone in town would know her name and where she lived before the morning. Not the way to keep a low profile. But if all they learned was where she lived, she'd be okay.

"What's up?" Ryan finally asked.

"What do you mean?"

"I mean, you've gone silent. That's usually my thing."

She laughed out loud. "You know you're like that?"

"Sure. My—" he paused. "My ex-wife used to call me the clam when I'd get like that. Sorry."

"Is that why she's your ex?"

"No." He stared down at his plate for a minute.

She leaned over and whispered. "You're doing it."

He looked up, smiled. "Yes, I am. I'm not ready to talk about it yet. Is that better?"

"Why, yes. It is. Almost like a grown-up."

He put his arm around her, then quickly withdrew it. "That's probably not the best thing to do while everyone's watching us like hawks."

"So why are they watching? Or is that part of what you aren't ready to talk about?"

"It is."

"So, let's talk about something else. Um, tell me why people sit at the tables they do."

"Okay," he said, relaxing his shoulders and leaning in closer. "I think you're ready for the truth. In a small town like this there are serious issues that divide people."

"Politics? Religion?"

He shook his head. "Clam chowder."

She laughed out loud.

"You think I'm joking."

"You're not?"

He whispered, "See Mama Thu? The petite lady on the left?" At the next table sat a lovely Asian woman with her graying hair in braids. She was enveloped in flowing layers of tie-dye.

"Yup," she whispered back.

"She owns the French-Vietnamese café in Torres Alley. Her organic clam chowder is made with tiny new potatoes, a delicate broth, and a hint of organic cream—"

"—from cheerful free-range cows."

"You've got the picture. It's served to you in a little hole-in-the-wall place overlooking the sea, where they have white lace curtains on the windows. Every bowl of chowder comes garnished with a sprig of parsley, and they offer free refills on organic herbal tea—"

"—from cheerful free-range herbs."

"Exactly." He nodded toward another table. "Now, see this dude?" A wiry old guy in faded overalls lorded over another table, wearing his fisherman's cap like a badge of honor.

"Let me guess—his chowder isn't served with a sprig of parsley."

"Mel's Fish Shack is down on the wharf, where the view is of the fishing boats unloading, and the sea lions bark so loudly outside the windows you can't hear yourself think. Mel's chowder is made with a pound of russet potatoes per serving, and so much heavy cream your arteries start clogging at the sight of the bowl—which, by the way, is not only bigger than a dinner plate, but come to the table with a hunk of butter melting on top and a platter of clam fritters and deep-fried onion rings on the side."

"Sounds wonderful."

"Careful, Miss," he drawled. "Them's fightin' words in this town."

"Well, then I think I'll have to try both before deciding."

"That might be arranged," he whispered, and then suddenly they both pulled away. That was unmistakably an invitation. And they both didn't want that. Right?

"Having fun?"

Camilla cringed at that unmistakable voice.

"Hello, Mrs. Rutherford," Ryan said cheerily. It sounded so unlike him Camilla realized what he was doing—it was the same overly polite tone he'd had the first time she'd heard him talk to the junk shop woman. Now she saw it was how he covered his annoyance when dealing with jerks. She stifled a chuckle.

But Mrs. Rutherford had apparently never figured Ryan out—or just didn't care. She smiled viciously at Camilla. "I don't know what you have to smile about, young lady. But I see you're making some important friends. That's fortunate for you." She sat down at the table uninvited and looked Camilla over with that same malicious grin.

"Did you need something, Ma'am?" Ryan asked, again in that oh-so patient tone.

She ignored him, and kept staring at Camilla. "I know where I've seen you before."

Camilla felt her stomach drop like the floor gave way beneath her. "I have no idea what you're talking about." She looked away, and saw that the entire contingent of preservation committee ladies were avidly watching this exchange.

"Of course you do. I subscribe to the out-of-town edition of the San Jose Mercury."

Oh, crap.

"You're the woman who stole the payroll from that computer company," she said, loud enough for the nearest few hundred people to hear. "So why aren't you in jail?"

Camilla looked around the table. Everyone was staring at her. Everyone in the whole high school gym was staring.

Robin came up quietly and sat down across from her again.

Camilla saw the question in Robin's eyes, and realized she was about to lose a potential friend—or any chance of finding a friend in this town.

She just sat there, frozen. The embarrassment of a high school gym full of staring people was just too much. She'd been in another gym, another time, when the shame of crime had touched her—

How had she so miscalculated? She had thought she could stay anonymous here. For a short time, she'd even entertained the idea—face it, she'd dreamed it—that she might even be able to stay here, start over, leave the past behind. Maybe settle down with a cute cop and little Oliver....

But no. She pushed the plate of food away from her, no longer hungry.

Ryan stood up to face Mrs. Rutherford, but when he leaned down to help her to her feet, she shook off his hand. She kept her eyes down, on the plate. She was not going to argue with all these people. They had made up their minds about her, and she didn't care what they thought. She felt around on the floor, trying to find her purse. She was getting out of here, ASAP. Where was her purse?!

"Here it is," Robin said, pulling her purse up on the other side of the table. "I must have snagged it with my foot. Ooh, Ralph Lauren. We were born to be soul mates." She handed it to Camilla across the table.

"I just got it on Ebay," Camilla mumbled.

"Fabulous."

Camilla stared at her, and Robin winked back.

Did she think this was a joke?

"Camilla?" Ryan said, luckily interrupting her before she said something stupid.

"I'm fine," she whispered.

"What's the matter, little Missy? Thought you were fooling people?" That voice could shatter glass, and not in a melodic, Mariah Carey kind of way.

"That's enough, Ma'am."

"No, it isn't."

"Yes, it is. You're out of line."

Camilla looked up at Ryan, shocked.

"Captain Knight!" Mrs. Rutherford said, just as shocked. "You're defending this woman?"

"People are innocent until proven guilty," Ryan said firmly, not backing down. "Maybe you haven't been reading your newspapers thoroughly enough. The real embezzler was identified. Ms. Stewart has not been convicted of any crimes. And attempting to ruin her reputation in town is not okay. That's not how we treat people in Pajaro Bay."

Camilla heard a few mutters of "no, it's not," and wondered if they'd still agree if they really knew the whole story.

"I guess if you make friends in the right places..." Mrs. Rutherford said, eyeing Captain Knight significantly.

"That's out of line, Ma'am," he said again. Camilla watched him stare her down without blinking. Oh, if she could only be that brave. "Are you accusing me of not doing my job?" He handed her a card. "That's the sheriff's number. Feel free to use it."

"You think I won't? You think because you're quitting your job —" There were a few gasps from the onlookers—"you can say whatever you want?"

"Oh, give it a rest, Mabel." Camilla stared at the new speaker. The arrogant-looking old lady with the orange hat gazed back at her with what Camilla would swear was a twinkle in her eye. Then the woman turned back to Mrs. Rutherford. "Mabel, you've committed a few crimes yourself in your day...."

"What?! Why, Zelda, I never—"

"Honey, if that pie you donated to the last bake sale doesn't qualify as a felony, I don't know what would."

That finally broke the tension. Everyone laughed, and people began to drift back to their own dinners and their own conversations.

Mrs. Rutherford stalked away, and Camilla turned to Ryan.

"I'm so sorry," she said as he helped her to her feet. She clutched her purse and made a beeline for where the kids were playing.

"Slow down, Camilla." It took him only a few long strides to catch up to her.

Oliver was with a couple of kids his age, all apparently taking a turn at some game on a phone. Thank God for that—the old battle-axe's insults apparently hadn't carried this far. "Come on, hon. We're going."

She held out her hand to him, and he reluctantly took it. "But my turn's next. I'm winning."

"I'm sorry, but we've gotta go."

"Why?" Ryan stepped in front of them. "Slow down."

"I'm sorry, Ryan."

"For what? For being targeted by that old witch? Everybody in town's been on the receiving end of her jabs. Don't let it bother you. I know you. You don't associate with criminals. You're the victim. Don't forget that—Why are you blushing? What did I say?"

He was just making it worse. He didn't know her. His defense of her was wrong. She wasn't the innocent little flower he seemed to think she was, and the more he insisted on it the worse she felt. Why had she thought this was a good idea? He had a completely wrong impression of her, and he'd just be furious if he found out how mistaken he was about her.

She shook her head at him. "I'm just embarrassed. I want to go now." She tried to brush past him, but just bumped into someone else. Her purse went flying, but Ryan's arm quickly came around her waist, keeping her from falling. His hand felt good there, natural, and she hated that, knowing how un-natural it was.

The older woman she'd bumped into handed back her purse. "Robin was right. It is a nice Ralph Lauren. Introduce us, Captain Ryan." It was not a request.

Ryan kept his arm around Camilla's waist. "Ms. Potter, this is Camilla Stewart. Camilla, this is Ms. Zelda Potter."

Camilla looked—really looked—at the elderly woman. She saw sparkling blue eyes with a perpetually amused twinkle in the pale, heavily lined face. The arched brows, distinctive features—something seemed familiar about her, but she couldn't place it.

"Hello," she muttered. She tried to pull away from Ryan, but he held her tightly. At another time, that might have felt nice, but now she just wanted to run, and he was stopping her.

"Let go, Ryan," she growled.

He dropped his arm and she took one step.

"Now that's how you should have talked to Mabel, young lady."

Camilla started to walk away.

"We haven't talked, Camilla." Ms. Zelda's voice stopped her. The woman sure could command a room.

"Talked about what?"

"About the Honeymoon Cottage, of course." She pulled out a tiny notebook with an orange suede cover. "I have time tomorrow morning. I will see you at 11 a.m." She wrote a note with a gold pen and then closed the notebook. "We will discuss your remodeling then."

"Will you be bringing the whole committee?"

Zelda laughed. "No. Mabel is busy with her little tschotscke shop. She wouldn't be invited anyway, dear. She doesn't have the sensitivity it takes to remodel old homes."

"But she's on the preservation committee."

Zelda laughed again. "Pajaro Bay is a small town. We have to live with each other here. We don't cut people off no matter how annoying they are, or we'd have no one to bring pies to the bake sales."

"Even lousy pies."

"Exactly." She smiled. "You'll get used to us, after a while."

"I'm not staying," she said firmly. "I'm just remodeling the cottage so I can sell it and move on."

For the first time Ms. Zelda looked unsure. "But the boy's father said you were coming to stay...?"

Ryan jumped on that. "The boy's father, Ms. Z?"

"We'll discuss it tomorrow, dear," she said to Camilla.

"But Ms. Z—" Ryan started, but she raised a hand. He immediately fell silent, and Camilla wished she could capture whatever it was that made her so good at dealing with people.

"That's not for you, Captain Ryan," Ms. Zelda continued. "This is a matter for your young friend and me to discuss."

"Yes, Ma'am," Ryan said meekly, and Camilla almost laughed. Ms. Zelda was a powerful presence if she could make this oak tree of a man meekly obey. But she wasn't done with him:

"And now, Ryan. About Mabel."

"Yes, Ma'am?"

"As satisfying as your little take-down was, I would advise you not to repeat it. You have always behaved impeccably, and it would not do to change now."

He responded with a shrug. He looked a lot like Oliver at that moment, and Camilla almost laughed.

"Don't burn your bridges, young man. No man is an island. You need people more than you think you do. Two weeks is a long time." She glanced at Camilla. "A lot can change before you get that car from Hector."

Before Camilla had a chance to digest any of that, the imperious old lady added, "And as for you, young lady."

"Yes—Ma'am?" Somehow ma'am seemed appropriate with this person.

"We will be at the cottage at eleven o'clock."

"We? I thought—" but that thought was swept aside with a wave of Ms. Zelda's manicured hand.

"You will be there." It wasn't a question. "We will discuss the cottage and what you plan to do with it."

"Yes, Ma'am," Camilla said meekly.

Ms. Z took a step closer, then bent that arrogant head down until the brim of her orange hat brushed against Camilla's curls. "And if you allow a jerk like Mabel Rutherford to run you off, you're not worthy of the Honeymoon Cottage, young lady."

She swept out, and Camilla stared after her, openmouthed. She wasn't sure if she was thrilled to have a woman more imposing than the Queen of England offering her advice. Now she found herself half fascinated, half dreading the royal audience tomorrow, "promptly at eleven o'clock."

She shook off the lingering unrealness of that strange conversation, and looked around for Oliver. He was still hanging out with the deputy's daughter, Marisol. "Come along, kid. We're going."

He reluctantly came over.

"It's still early," Ryan said.

"I'm leaving, Ryan." She still felt like everyone was staring, and she hated that sensation.

"No one believes a word that old battle-axe says. All she does is gossip and bad-mouth everyone."

"But they don't know I'm innocent."

"But you know. So why do you care what others think?"

She didn't have an answer for that, so she just said, "I'm leaving. Now. Stop pushing me to stay where I'm not wanted."

He looked confused at her, but if he didn't get it, that was too bad. She wasn't hanging around here for one more minute.

She stalked to the door, Oliver in tow, hoping at least Ryan would have the courtesy to follow and drive them home.

"Wait up!" Robin came up in a clatter of high heels. "I can't run in these things."

"What do you want?" she snapped. That's all she needed was one more person criticizing her.

"Wow, Camilla. I guess you're not all sweetness and light after all."

"Sorry," she mumbled.

"Don't be. It's nice to see you've got a backbone under all that goody-goodyness."

Was she making fun of her? "What do you want, Robin?"

"I just wanted to tell you that I don't get into the office before ten."

"So?" She crossed her arms in front of her. "Why do I need to know this?"

"Because when you come by for coffee, you should wait until after ten, because I am *definitely* not a morning person."

"Oh. Okay." What was this? She still wanted to have coffee after what she'd heard?

"Tomorrow?"

"Yeah. Tomorrow. After I drop off Oliver at school, maybe."

"No maybe. I'll see you tomorrow sometime after ten. Will you teach me how to buy Ralph Lauren stuff on Ebay?"

"Um, sure." Was that why she was being friendly? She had an appointment with Ms. Zelda, but maybe she would stop by Robin's briefly before that. What could it hurt? "Yeah. I'll do that."

She walked away toward the door, where Ryan and Oliver stood waiting.

"What did Robin want?" Ryan asked.

"For me to teach her how to buy stuff on Ebay. What's that got to do with anything?"

"You think that's why she wants to be friends with you? For you to teach her something? People are trying to be nice to you. Why aren't you giving them a chance?"

"I—I don't know." How could she explain? "It's just better if I don't drag other people into my problems."

"Why? Isn't that what friends are for? To get dragged into your problems, and then they drag you into theirs, and then you realize your problems aren't all that bad after all?"

He made it all sound so easy. But it never was. She knew that. Why did Robin and Ms. Zelda and even Ryan keep trying to get to know her? She didn't like to open up.

"Maybe I like my shell. It's cozy inside."

"Cozy or suffocating?"

"Who are you to talk, aren't you 'the clam' yourself? When were you going to tell me you were leaving town?"

Wow. That was completely out of line. She didn't even know him. She had no right to expect him to share his personal life with her. It was none of her business.

He obviously thought so too, because they drove home in silence.

AT THE COTTAGE, RYAN PULLED TO A STOP. WHEN SHE STARTED TO get out, Ryan put his hand on her arm. She felt so warm and alive —and so distant. She tried to pull away from him again, but he couldn't let her go yet.

"Send Oliver inside. I need to talk to you about the car."

"Okay." She gave Oliver the gate keys and he ran down the path to the cottage.

She crossed her arms and stared at him. "What's wrong with the car and how much is it gonna cost?"

"Not much. It had a puncture in the gas tank and Hector can repair it tomorrow. Won't cost more than you can afford."

She uncrossed her arms and reached for the door handle. "Thanks for telling me."

"My stepdaughter was murdered a year ago," he blurted out.

She froze, then turned to him, her eyes so wide and stricken.

"I didn't mean to say it like that. It just came out. You wanted to know about me leaving town."

She slid over closer on the seat and put a hand on his arm. "I'm so sorry, Ryan. I didn't know."

"I know. You asked why." He turned away to look out the windshield. "I had been married to Angela about two years. We moved here, to her hometown, and I took the job with the sheriff's department." He recited the sentences matter-of-factly, trying to keep all trace of emotion out of his voice.

Camilla's hand moved to cover his. He realized he was holding the steering wheel in a death grip. He let go and let her put her hand in his, palm to palm. She felt warm and alive, and he realized how cold he was.

"What happened?" she whispered.

"Sara wanted to go to the market downtown. It's about two blocks away." He paused, drawing strength from the warmth of her hand. "I took her, because I didn't think she should walk there by herself. We walked in on a robbery in progress. I was off-duty, of course, but I pushed her behind me and drew my gun."

"uh huh."

"The perp and I stared each other down for a—for I don't know how long—it seemed like an hour but was about ten seconds according to the witnesses."

He was saying too much, trying to excuse his mistakes, trying to make sense of something completely senseless.

"He fired. She was killed instantly." He said it flatly, not mentioning his growing horror as he had winged the creep, ran after him as he escaped, been stopped by the screams of witnesses—and then turned back to see something he'd seen so many other times, but never with someone he was responsible for: the empty eyes staring, the blood everywhere, the sure knowledge that he'd failed to keep the promise he'd made to Angela, to Honor and Protect her and Sara till death did them part.

How could he explain the betrayal he saw in Angie's eyes when he told her. The look on her face reflecting the guilt on his own, the keening cry that tore out of her throat echoing the emptiness in his own soul. None of that.

"What happened to the man who shot her?"

"He's spending life at San Quentin. He said it flatly. "With the trash just like him."

She started at that. "San Quentin?" she said in a strangled voice.

He kept staring out the windshield, only her warm hand anchoring him to the present, keeping him from cracking as he told Camilla about the awful year that had just ended: the obsessive tracking of every clue to the perp until the answer had come together like the shaking of puzzle pieces into place. The arrest of the man, long-gone to some other town. The plea bargain where the killer avoided the death penalty in exchange for a life sentence. The press. The decision to stay on the job here. Then the realization that he couldn't do it. Couldn't be in a position to ever make a fatal mistake again. The realization that he didn't want to ever be responsible for other people's lives again.

When he'd finished he realized he was leaning forward, his forehead resting against the steering wheel, and Camilla had her hand on his back, and she was saying, "I'm so sorry, I'm so sorry," over and over.

CHAPTER SEVEN

RYAN SAT BACK IN THE CAR SEAT. HE TWISTED AROUND SO SHE took her hand off of him.

"I'm so sorry, Ryan. I know saying that doesn't help."

"Sure it does. It's over. It's just part of the past."

But Camilla didn't look like she believed him. "It must be hard to think about." Obviously she was thinking about how he'd lost it just a few minutes ago, acting like a fool and spilling the whole thing to her.

He shrugged. "It's better not to talk about it. Sorry I brought it up."

She put her hand on his again, and he saw she was about to go all sympathetic on him. He needed to change the subject, fast, before he ended up losing it again.

"So, about Oliver," he said.

She pulled her hand back. "We don't have to talk about it now. I know you're having a hard day."

"No, I'm not. And we need to talk about it."

"Okay. You asked for it." She said it like she was mad. And apparently she was. "Don't ever do that again."

"Do what?"

"Try to grill him about his father."

"I wasn't grilling him," he started, but she raised an eyebrow at him. "Okay, but it wasn't grilling. I was just taking the opportunity to ask him questions."

"Well, don't."

His eyes narrowed. "Why not, Camilla?"

"Don't look at me like that. I'm not protecting Dennis. I'm protecting Oliver. I'll get more info out of him in time, but I'm not going to have you putting him in some police interrogation room, with cops staring him down and trying to trip up his story."

"You've seen too much TV."

She looked really mad at that. "I'm not as young as you seem to think I am, Ryan. I know how the world works."

He must have grinned, because she said, spitting mad, "How old do you think I am? Twelve? I'm an adult."

"You're only 24." Those big eyes widened, so he added, "I saw your driver's license, remember?"

"Oh, yeah. Well, that's not young. I know how the world works."

He knew exactly how young and helpless that was. "My baby sister's 24," he explained. "That's awfully young for the amount of responsibility you have."

"What, is your sister still in diapers, Ryan?"

"No. But she's still in Sacramento, and I'm her only family."

"Oh. What does she do up there?"

"She runs a restaurant," he said, and Camilla laughed.

"Doesn't sound exactly helpless, Ryan. What are you, some kind of sexist? You think a woman can't take care of herself?"

"Of course not. That's not what I mean." He felt as protective of Joe Serrano as he did of anyone. It wasn't sexist. The fact was, he knew most people had no clue how tough it could be out there.

"You've got a strange way of looking at things, Ryan. How old are you, anyway, old timer?"

"34."

She laughed even harder, but he didn't see anything funny about it. He was a lifetime older than Camilla, or Leah, or Joe Serrano, or anybody else he was responsible for. She just didn't get it.

"Well, old man, I can see you've got a lot of experience and wisdom we don't have."

"Listen, Camilla. There's a lot you don't know."

"Oh, I'm sure." She was still smiling, but he wasn't kidding. The dumb kid was going to get herself killed, and he was rattling on about his life story. Why did he keep telling her things that were irrelevant to the job he was here to do? He needed to get her to pay attention to what he needed to say.

"Stop laughing and listen to me!" It came out sounding pretty harsh, and Camilla jerked her head back like he'd really offended her.

She stuck out that stubborn little jaw at him, folded her arms across her chest, and glared.

"I'm sorry," he said, seeing her ready to get all pigheaded on him. "I'm just trying to tell you something, and I need you to listen."

She unclenched her jaw, but kept her arms crossed protectively. "All right, Captain Ryan. I'm listening."

"Do you park your car out on the street at night?"

"Well, I don't think I can fit it in the garden shed." She glared at him. "So?"

"Did you park it on the street before you came to town yesterday?"

"No. My apartment in San Jose had a parking garage."

"And you ran out of gas on your way to Pajaro Bay."

"Yeah. I practically coasted off the highway onto Calle Principal. You know that. You were there. That's when you went

101

all white knight on me and got me home last night. And I did fill it up only 50 miles earlier. I'm not stupid."

"I never said you were."

"So what difference does it make where I parked?" Her eyes lit up. "Oh! You think someone's siphoning off my gas. That makes sense—no, wait. It doesn't. I ran out of gas on the way into town, and then again this morning. If you're trying to convince me someone's trailing me around, siphoning gas out of my car, that's ridiculous. That's a dumb idea."

She still didn't get what he was trying to say—what he was avoiding saying, because the thought of someone trying to harm this wide-eyed innocent made him sick. "I didn't say someone was siphoning of your gas."

"Then what are you saying, Ryan? Get to the point."

"Your car has a hole in the gas tank."

"Oh." She relaxed her shoulders. "Oh, it makes sense now." She uncrossed her arms and rested her palms against the dashboard. She seemed relieved. He watched her small, pale hands on the dash. They looked fragile, and he wanted to cover them with his own hands, feel their warmth against him again.

"So that's not too expensive to fix, I hope." She was smiling again, seeming really relieved that it was "only" a punctured tank. Then she frowned again. "Then why are you asking all these questions about where I park? What difference does it make?"

"I'm trying to figure out when it happened."

"Yeah," she said, perking up. "Hey, yeah. I mean, if I bought a car with a hole in the tank the seller should pay for it, not me."

Ryan jumped on that. "Who sold you the car?"

"A used car dealer in the city. I got the car about a week ago when I couldn't make payments on my other car. But, you know, I didn't have this problem until yesterday."

"Yesterday?" He resisted the urge to get out his notebook and write this down. He could compile the info later. Keep her talking. "So that's the first time you noticed the problem?"

She nodded. "In fact yesterday was only the second time I filled the tank. The gas lasted a long time after the first fill-up. So I don't think there was a hole in it before."

"What the name of the dealer?"

"Why? It's not your problem. I'll call him once I get the repair bill and I can argue with him about who's responsible."

"I need the name of the dealer."

"Why?"

How was he going to explain this to her? "Did Dennis ever threaten you in any way?"

"What? Are you kidding? I told you. He was always nice to me. You think I would've agreed to—well, everything, him and Oliver and the whole thing—if he was abusive? How dumb do you think I am?"

"I didn't say you were dumb." Naive, maybe, but not dumb. "I just wondered if you had any idea where Dennis has been since the arrest warrant came out."

She was all tensed up again. Her arms were crossed, and she was spitting mad. "If I knew where Dennis was, he'd be cooling his heels in jail and I'd be home free."

Ryan tried to find the right way to say it. He didn't want her to shut him out, but he seemed to be blowing this.

"Just spit it out, Captain Ryan. This is not the time to be a clam."

"Is it possible Dennis wants you out of the way for some reason—maybe to keep you from testifying against him in the embezzlement case?"

"Wait a minute here. He wouldn't sabotage the car to get to me—Oliver could get hurt."

He just watched her. Waited for it to sink in.

"Are you out of your freaking mind? He would never, ever hurt Oliver."

"We already talked about this, Camilla. People do hurt children. Even though it's wrong. Even though it's unthinkable."

"Why? Because Sara was shot, now you think everyone's a killer?" She threw open the car door and jumped out. "You're paranoid. Get some therapy, Captain Ryan." The car door slammed.

He realized two things. She was a strong door slammer for such a little thing. And he'd totally blown that conversation.

He sat there watching her stomp down the path to the garden gate, swing it open, then slam it shut behind her with a thud. A minute later, he heard the cottage door creak open on those protesting hinges, then another loud crash as the door slammed shut.

He shook his head. "Brilliant, Knight. Just brilliant police work."

He started up the SUV and pulled a U-turn to head back down Cliff toward town.

At the corner he stopped.

He flicked on the turn signal.

Get some therapy, Captain Ryan. Maybe. Maybe that's what he needed. Maybe he saw demons in every innocent accident now.

He listened to the turn signal's rhythmic click, and watched the green arrow on the dashboard flash on and off, pointing him down Calle Principal toward the Substation.

I don't want to be responsible for other people anymore. That's what he'd said, and that's what he believed.

But what had Oliver said? Daddy always says it's better to be safe than sorry.

He turned off the turn signal. Then pulled another U-turn and headed back up Cliff. He pulled the SUV onto the gravel next to Ms. Zelda's driveway and shut off the engine. From here he could get a peek through the trees at the little Honeymoon Cottage.

No street lights out here, and the fog blocked the moon now. The cottage was just a ghostly shadow beyond the trees.

104

He settled in to wait.

CAMILLA FOUND OLIVER ALREADY IN HIS PAJAMAS HUDDLED DOWN in his sleeping bag on the living room floor. "Cold," he said. It did feel cold in here. There was a meager-looking space heater in the hallway upstairs, and the old fireplace down here, but she wasn't sure either of them was safe to use. Getting someone to inspect the heater and the chimney would have to eat up a portion of her cash soon.

"Maybe tomorrow we'll get some firewood and get this old fireplace going," she said. Tomorrow she'd get some sort of heat for this place, and maybe even talk to Robin about bringing in those potential buyers, since her own out-of-town real estate agent didn't seem to be doing much.

She had to let go of Ryan's awful accusations about Dennis and focus on taking care of Oliver and herself. Poor kid. He had enough problems without a nosy cop trying to get him to betray his father. She should have known better than to trust a big, sexy guy with piercing eyes that saw right through her. Just because he sent her body into overdrive every time she saw him was no reason to let down her guard around him. She had been right about him—he was just using her and Oliver to try to catch Dennis.

Well fine. She wanted Dennis caught, too. But not at the expense of Oliver's peace of mind. Dennis wasn't trying to hurt his son. She was pretty sure that had just been Ryan's justification for pushing Oliver so hard and upsetting him. He was trying to make excuses because he knew how mad she was. Well it hadn't worked. Sure, she felt bad about his family. That was a horrible thing. But that didn't give him freedom to tear Oliver and her apart in his quest to catch Dennis.

She knelt down next to Oliver and brushed his hair back from his forehead. He was safe. She was going to make sure he stayed safe. She'd get them out of here soon.

She glanced at her watch. "It's late now, Sweetie. Go to sleep. You have another school day tomorrow."

"I'm not sleepy yet." She could tell he was lying, since he could barely keep his eyes open, but she just sat with him, to reassure him that it was okay to relax.

She wanted so much to ask him about Dennis, find out if she had totally misjudged Oliver's relationship with his father. She just knew in her gut that Dennis loved his son. Could his father really be the kind of monster who would hurt his own son? No. She didn't believe that, and she wasn't going to turn Oliver against his father with any crazy accusations. He'd had enough of people prodding him for information today. She had to do this her own way. Give him time to relax, to trust. If he said anything that could lead to his father, she'd turn it over to Ryan. But she wasn't going to pump him for information—it would just make him shut down even more.

So instead she just asked Oliver about his day at school, and, maybe because he was sleepy, he chattered some instead of clamming up. He told about his new teacher, about one kid who had a sneezing fit in class that set everyone off into giggles, about all the mundane details of his day. He was going to be fine. He was an incredibly resilient kid. He was already finding his way in this new school, this new town. He was going to be fine.

And then she was going to uproot him again, make him do it all over again. Was she as bad as his father, taking him away from this place? No. Her motives were good. She needed to find a place she could start over anonymously, without being judged. She needed to be able to get a job, an apartment, a new life, without everyone knowing she was the woman accused in large point type on the front page of the San Jose paper. She couldn't make a home for them in Pajaro Bay.

Even if Dennis was around—and she doubted it—it wouldn't

change anything with Oliver. If Dennis came back he would go to prison and she'd still have Oliver. This little boy was not a responsibility she would have chosen. But she couldn't regret it. She watched his dark eyes close and waited until his chatter slowed down to a murmur. She loved this kid.

She smiled down at him. "We make a good team, don't we, honey?"

"Yeah. But I miss daddy."

She felt guilty for wishing the guy was in jail. "I know," she said, choosing her words carefully. "It's natural to miss him. But you need to remember that his being gone isn't about you. It's about his own problems in his life, and his love for you is always there, even when he can't be." She wasn't sure how much that was true, but she wanted so badly for Oliver to believe in the fairy tale. It killed her to see the guilt and shame that flickered in his eyes when he wasn't pretending everything was okay.

"He never left me like this before."

She wanted to ask him about the past, but this wasn't the time. "It'll be okay, I promise." She brushed away the lock of dark hair. "He left you with me because he trusted me to take care of you. And I'm doing okay, aren't I?"

"Yeah." It was practically a whisper. His eyes were starting to droop.

She rubbed his head gently, and spoke extra-softly. "We can have lots of fun before your dad gets back. We'll walk on the beach and look for shells. We'll ride the rides at the amusement park."

"With Captain Ryan," he mumbled, eyes closed.

"Sure we will." Another lie. Maybe that was the secret of effective parenting: good lying.

"You're safe here in the cottage, and the ocean is whispering good night to you."

His breathing grew slower, more steady, and soon he was deeply asleep.

She wished it would be as easy for her.

She got to her feet. Her legs had cramped up from kneeling on the oak floor. She would have to get them real beds soon. This sleeping on the floor was a pain.

She watched Oliver sleep, the worried pucker in his little forehead finally gone. She could just strangle that Dennis Hutchins. But it wouldn't do any good. She had to find a way to help Oliver now, and forget about what an idiot his father was.

How could a man cause such pain to such a sweet, innocent child? That just didn't make sense. She wouldn't—couldn't—accept Ryan's accusation that Dennis would harm his son. If that were true, it would mean her own instincts were completely out of whack. She couldn't believe that the love she'd seen in Dennis whenever he looked at his son was an act.

So much of his behavior had been false, she could see that now. But not his love of Oliver. Not that. He was a lying, manipulative creep, but he loved his son.

Was that possible? Could a person separate out parts of himself like that? Could he be cruel to one person, lie, cheat and steal, but then truly, sincerely love his own child? She had to believe that was true, because the alternative was that Ryan was right, and Dennis actually would kill his own child.

"Sleep easy," she whispered to Oliver. "Everything's going to be all right." She went to the bathroom to change into her pajamas.

A LIGHT FLICKERED ON IN THE COTTAGE. THE KITCHEN. RYAN could see the old enamel stove. Camilla came into view, and his heart thumped in his chest. Why? Why should he react so strongly to the simple sight of this woman?

She had changed clothes. She was wearing something soft and pink. It looked like a pair of men's silk pajamas, tailored and sleek and masculine except for the shell pink color and the hint of curves he could see every time she moved.

She put an enameled kettle on the stove, turned on the flame. He could see the blue of the gas flame from here. The homey scene bothered him for some reason. The innocent woman in pink silk, her red curls loose around her face, the kettle on the stove in the cozy kitchen.

He felt uncomfortable. Like a peeping tom.

He should leave.

Camilla was pouring herself a cup of tea or something. Sat down at the kitchen table. Started to write something. He wondered what it was—shopping list, love letter?

She looked incredibly sad. He hoped he wasn't the one who made her so sad. He wondered what he could say to make her not look so sad. Nothing. There was nothing he could say. He wasn't responsible for her.

Right. That's why he was parked outside her house in the middle of the night like some voyeur. He might not be responsible for making her happy, but he was not going to let anything happen to her on his watch.

Ryan raised his wrist up until he caught the blue glow of his watch face. 11:23 p.m.

He settled back in the seat. It wasn't like he had anyone waiting for him at home. He'd hang around until morning.

Better safe than sorry.

CAMILLA PICKED UP THE PEN AGAIN, THEN HURRIED TO FINISH THE letter so she could mail it in the morning.

Dear Daddy,

This is my new address, so you can write to me here until I tell you differently: Camilla Stewart, at the Honeymoon Cottage, Pajaro Bay, California. Yes, really, Dad. That's the address.

I wish you could see the cottage. I told you in my last letter that I would be at this new address until I could get the place fixed up and sold. Well, I've now seen the place, and it's really strange. I doubt even in all your years working on houses you ever saw something like this. It was built by some eccentric old guy who didn't own a level. Now I've got to figure out how to fix it up so somebody will take it off my hands.

I'd love to have your help on this project, but since I can't, I'll just try to remember all the things you taught me about carpentry.

She paused, pen still poised over the paper. There wasn't any point in asking about Ryan's stepdaughter's killer. There was no reason her father would know about the case, about that kind of man.

She started writing again, in that same artificially cheery way she always did with Dad:

About visiting you—I checked, and I can't visit until the charges against me are dropped officially. It's against the rules, apparently. But I sure do miss you, and maybe I'll see you again before the summer is over.

In the meantime, I'm sending you another book of stamps so you can write to me. I appreciate the letters, even if I don't always write back as much as I should.

When I get a chance, I'll tell you all about the legal mess I'm in, but for now, just know that I'm working hard and I miss you.

Stay safe and out of trouble.

Love,

Your little apprentice.

She folded the letter and put it in the envelope, then addressed it:

From: Camilla Stewart, The Honeymoon Cottage, Pajaro Bay, CA 95000

To: Clifton Stewart, UA9911100, San Quentin State Prison, San Quentin, CA 94974.

———

CAMILLA LAY BACK IN HER SLEEPING BAG IN THE DARK LIVING room. Outside, she could hear the constant whisper of the waves far below them, and the old shrubs in the yard tapped against the windows. Next to her, Oliver was already asleep in his sleeping bag, the top of his head barely showing above the zipper. She listened to his steady breathing and felt more sure than ever of what she had to do.

In the morning she would get back to work on the cottage. No more goofing around, going to dinners with Ryan or trying to make friends with people in town. The awful scene with Mrs. Rutherford showed her that it had been wrong to get complacent. She needed the anonymity of a big city for herself and Oliver. And Ryan? He wasn't the man for her. He was a nice-enough guy (okay, he was a really nice guy), but they didn't have anything in common. The attraction she felt for him was hormonal. She needed to use her head and be reasonable about it. She was leaving town, and so was he. Their lives were headed in different directions. She was the daughter of a criminal, and he would be disgusted if he ever found out the way she'd lived as a kid. She would never, ever be able to let down her guard around him.

She needed to go back to her original plan: get the cottage sold, pay off her ex-boss, and start over somewhere else. There was a lot of work to do around the place, but she wasn't afraid of hard work. She'd get it all done, and fast.

She drifted off to sleep to images of little elves teetering on crooked little ladders busily polishing the fireplace tiles, fixing broken windows, and painting the eaves of the cottage.

The paint they were using smelled really bad. "Stinky elves," she muttered.

She was almost completely asleep when something crashed down right next to her. She sat up suddenly and felt around in the dark, trying to figure out what had happened. She felt something smooth and square on top of her sleeping bag. One of the fireplace tiles had fallen, right onto her. Wow. She picked it up, her hands making out the shape of an oak tree embossed on the face. That would have hurt if it had hit her in the head—or even worse, Oliver.

She could still hear his soft breathing. He hadn't woken up.

The stinky paint smell from the elves was still there, she thought groggily. Wait a minute. It wasn't paint. It was rotten eggs. She knew that smell.

"Oliver! Honey, wake up."

He didn't respond. The smell of natural gas shouldn't be this bad if the pilot light on the kitchen stove had gone out. Hadn't she just made a cup of tea a little while ago? She sat there with the tile in her hand, trying to remember when she'd had her tea.

Wait a minute. She wasn't making sense. She was too sleepy, too groggy to think straight.

"Oliver!" She shouted it, but it came out in a croak. She coughed to clear her throat, realizing that Oliver still wasn't moving. He was sound asleep.

She fumbled for the zipper on her sleeping bag. It seemed to take her a long time to unzip it, but finally it came open. She tried to stand up, but wobbled in the dark and couldn't stay upright.

On her hands and knees she crawled to Oliver's sleeping bag. He was still sound asleep. She shook him, shouted at him.

Finally, he mumbled, "Mama?"

She tried to get his sleeping bag unzipped, but didn't have any better luck with it than she'd had with her own.

"Oliver! Don't go back to sleep!"

He pulled the sleeping bag up over his face. "Not mornin'."

"No. It's not morning. But we have to get up. We have a problem." She tried really hard to speak clearly, all the while fumbling with the zipper.

Finally it came free and she dragged Oliver's sleepy little body out of its warm nest. He mumbled a protest and then curled up again.

"Help me, Oliver. We've got to go outside."

"Sleepin'." He rolled over and ignored her.

"No, Oliver. Now. We've got to go now." She shook him, hard. Then she slapped him on the shoulder.

"Ow!"

"Sorry. You've got to wake up. Come on."

He rolled away from her and started fumbling around in the dark.

"What are you doing?"

"Getting dressed."

"No. We don't have time. There's a gas leak."

"Smells bad," he said. She could see him standing in front of the fireplace, his eyes glowing in the dim light coming through the window. He swayed on his feet.

"No, son!"

She crawled over to him and grabbed him around the waist.

"Gotta headache," he mumbled.

"I know. Me, too. We have to go outside."

"Can't see. Turn on the switch."

"No! A spark could set off the gas."

"You yelling like Dora."

She didn't have time to grill him about who the heck Dora was. "Come on." She tried again to stand, but couldn't seem to get her feet to work right.

She let go of Oliver and then pushed him forward in front of her. "Go ahead, Oliver. Go out the kitchen door. I'm right behind you."

"You, too?"

"Yes. I'm coming. Don't wait for me. Go outside and leave the door open."

She tried to watch him, but had to put her head down because of the headache.

When she looked up she couldn't see straight. Which way was the kitchen? She felt around on the floor and felt something smooth. A square with an oak tree. The fireplace tile.

She reached out and felt a wall of smooth squares. The fireplace tiles. She pulled herself up, digging her fingernails into the old grout, using everything she had to get to her feet.

She felt the little acorns and squirrels, trees and leaves, trying to picture each tile, desperate to keep herself fixed here, in the real world. The shadows in her head receded, and she pulled again. She made it to her feet.

She turned her back to the fireplace. The kitchen was straight ahead of her. She pushed away from the fireplace, launching herself toward the open doorway in front of her. She took a few steps forward and saw a dark lump on the kitchen's checkerboard floor.

She wasn't much for praying, but she knew if she didn't get them out, they were done for. No one would notice until—when? Until Ms. Zelda came for her appointment? That was hours away.

"Oliver!"

No answer. She got to him, grabbed him by his pajama top—his favorite flannel race cars—and pulled. He slid across the smooth floor. She opened the bottom half of the dutch door and heard it bang against the cottage's wall. The outside air slapped her face—cold and wet and fresh.

She grabbed onto Oliver again. She pulled him closer to the door. She had to make it. She had to.

Then the top of the door banged open and something warm and hard was there. A person—not just any person, but Ryan. She had never felt so relieved at someone's presence in her whole life. He picked Oliver up in one swift movement, grabbed her with his other arm and propelled them out the door.

She felt cool grass wet beneath her. The air cold, wet, and so fresh and clean. She thought she heard Ryan saying something about backup and emergency, but she couldn't make it out.

She coughed and coughed. Ryan was bending over Oliver. She tried to ask if Oliver was okay, but it came out as a small squeak.

"He's alive," Ryan said briskly. "Come on, son, wake up!"

She crawled over to Oliver and started rubbing his face. "Honey, wake up. Wake up, please." His breathing was steady, the flannel race cars rising and falling with each breath. "Please, sweetheart."

He opened his eyes. "Mama?"

"It's Camilla, honey. You're okay. You're going to be okay."

"You're both going to be okay," Ryan said, sitting back on his heels.

CHAPTER EIGHT

"AND HOW ARE YOU DOING, YOUNG MAN?"

Dr. Lil had short gray hair, a no-nonsense bedside manner, and an air of competence that had put Camilla at ease from the moment they'd burst through the doors of the Pajaro Bay Medical Clinic at 2:15 a.m.

Now it was several hours later, the light was shining in the window of the little room, and she watched as the doc checked Oliver over again, re-testing all his reflexes.

Oliver looked over at Camilla. "I'm sorry."

"It's okay, Oliver. Don't you worry about anything."

"I just turned on the heater upstairs...."

"I know. You were cold."

Such a simple mistake. He had gone into the house ahead of her last night, and, feeling cold, had turned the knob on the heater in the upstairs hallway. The heater she hadn't yet checked for safety.

"You mad?"

"Of course not." She smiled at him. "Really. Not mad at all. You were very brave last night."

He stopped hunching over in the bed, and she relaxed. Oliver had enough on his small shoulders. The last thing the kid needed was to feel he'd done something wrong. It was an innocent mistake.

She gave him another big smile. "Now listen to Dr. Lil. She's still checking you out."

Dr. Lil straightened up. "I'm done checking. He's doing fine. His oxygen saturation levels are normal, and he's alert and responsive."

"I'm not brain dead?" he asked.

"Definitely not brain dead, young man." She winked at him.

"And you're not either, young lady," Dr. Lil said, turning to Camilla. "But you should get back to your bed." After assuring Oliver that he wasn't going to miss any exciting procedures if they left him alone for a few minutes, Dr. Lil helped Camilla back to her room.

"He still has a headache," Camilla said when she was being helped into her bed.

"That's normal. Your headache is, too. You had a close call."

"But he's okay?" She allowed the doc to pull the covers up over her and leaned back against the pillows.

"You're both completely okay. There's no permanent damage. A few more minutes and brain dead might not have been a joke." The doc looked over her clipboard. "These readings are very good. Oxygen content good. You got out very quickly. If you hadn't woken up so quickly, you could have died in your sleep."

She shuddered at the thought.

"But luckily the gas levels are pretty low. You hadn't breathed in too much before you got away from the source. It could have been much worse. Particularly in a child, it doesn't take much to cause serious problems."

"But he's okay." She needed to hear it again to be reassured.

"He's fine. You did the right thing getting out immediately. If you had slept until morning, you might never have woken up."

"The elves woke us up," she muttered.

"Elves?" Dr. Lil raised an eyebrow at her.

"No, I'm not hallucinating, Doc. I'm just joking. One of the old fireplace tiles fell on me and woke me up. It was almost like the cottage itself warned me."

"Ah. You're in a Stockdale," Dr. Lil said, deadpan.

Camilla looked incredulously at the no-nonsense doctor. "You believe in elves?"

She laughed and shook her head. "Not quite. Some of the old timers believe the cottages are haunted—enchanted, more accurately. They believe Stockdales have personalities, and individual presences."

Camilla must have looked shocked, because Doc clarified: "I'm not saying I believe that. But a lot of people here do. But whatever the reason, you and Oliver are very lucky—both that you woke up and that Captain Ryan was there to rush you to the clinic."

"Yeah." She frowned, which made her head hurt worse, so she tried to stop. She hadn't had a chance to discuss Ryan's sudden arrival with him. That couldn't have been coincidence. She didn't believe in little elves, and she didn't believe Captain Ryan Knight was just "passing by" her cottage at two a.m. either.

"DON'T SIT DOWN, RYAN. YOU'RE NOT STAYING." CAMILLA SAT UP in the hospital bed and scowled at him.

Ryan stood up quickly from the chair he had been about to plop down in. "So we're back to Captain Ryan. After I dragged you out of there?"

She realized she was feeling really angry with him, and it wasn't fair. "I'm sorry," she mumbled.

He leaned over so his face was inches away from hers. "It's okay," he whispered. His hand brushed across the top of her head, just barely touching her curls, but she felt the tingle across her scalp. "I was afraid you were going to die," he whispered.

She pulled back from him, and he straightened up. "Can I sit down? I've been up all night rescuing damsels in distress."

She motioned to the chair by the bed and he plopped down in it. He looked exhausted.

He seemed to have trouble figuring out where to put his hands, eventually resting his palms on his knees. He cleared his throat. "This is a nice room."

"Yup. If I can figure out how to pay for it, it'll be even nicer."

He nodded. "I can talk to Dr. Lil. I'm sure something can be worked out."

There he went again, trying to run things. How had she gone from avoiding him, to having him controlling her? "Thank you for saving my life," she said, very formally.

"You're welcome, Ma'am," he said, equally stiffly. But there was a ghost of a smile on his face and the skin around his eyes crinkled up, making him look tired and charming and quite adorable.

She tried to stay mad. Mad was good, because it protected her from the feelings she felt every time she was around him. Anger protected her from noticing how his big hands looked all strong and tanned, and about how his blue eyes seemed warm and friendly today, not intimidating and piercing, and how she really wanted him to brush his hand across her head again, and maybe even touch her somewhere other than the top of her head....

"About how you saved us, though," she said, trying not to smile in response to his little grin. "Maybe you can explain how you happened to know we needed help?" She crossed her arms across her chest and glared at him.

She was pretty sure her glare wasn't effective, though, because his smile just got bigger. "Isn't there some old saying about not looking a gift horse in the mouth?"

"Don't get evasive with me, Ryan. You haven't answered my question. What were you doing outside my house at two in the morning?" Maybe she owed him something for saving them. Maybe she wanted to just lay back in the hospital bed and relish the warmth of him being here next to her, the feeling of him protecting her, sharing some of the burden of this strange situation she was in. Maybe she did, but she just knew that would be a mistake. She had tried to keep her distance from him, and yet she kept ending up spending time with him. She kept feeling an attraction that was going to lead to disaster when he, a do-gooder cop, found out she was a criminal's daughter, with secrets of her own. When he found out she wasn't "good," and "honest," and "smart," and "kind," and all the other words he kept calling her that she knew were part of the act she was putting on for him.

"Nope," he said, the grin vanishing at her expression. "You're definitely a gift-horse-looker."

"I just want an answer."

"Nice pink pajamas."

"Leftovers from my old life. I paid cash for them, so nobody could repossess them when I went bankrupt."

"That's good. Those pajama repo men can be brutal."

She laughed in spite of herself. She watched those hands of his, and told herself again not to fall. "You're not answering my question," she said stiffly.

He smiled weakly. "I'd say you look cute when you're angry, but that wouldn't help, would it?"

"Don't joke with me. My head hurts."

"Sorry. Should I call Doc to get you an aspirin?"

"Stop trying to take care of me, and explain what you were doing there."

"We do patrol the streets of Pajaro Bay, you know."

"I'm not stupid."

"I would never suggest you were stupid."

"You did last night, when you told me Dennis could be a murderer."

"Yeah. About what I said last night..."

"Wait. I first want to know what you were doing there."

"Same question." He looked at her pointedly.

She sat there rubbing her aching forehead until she got it. "You mean you're stalking us because you think Dennis is trying to kill us?"

"I would think you might take me a little more seriously after last night."

"After last night? Oh. You mean the heater? Oliver turned on a heater without checking with me. It was old and cracked—the fire department investigator was here an hour ago to explain how it was broken—which you should know if you're stalking me."

"I'm not stalking you. Stop being melodramatic."

"Then stop being crazy!" But he didn't look like a crazy man. He looked like he was tired, and worried. "Okay, Ryan. Let's assume for the moment that you're not insane."

"That sounds good."

"What were you doing outside the house?"

"Waiting for Dennis. No, wait," he said when she started to interrupt. "I'm not sure he's a murderer. I'm not sure which one of us is right. Yes, I talked to the fire investigator, too. It looks like an accident, and—" he paused, and she wondered if he was trying to appease her when he added: "and it probably was."

"So, you agree that maybe I do know what I'm talking about when it comes to Dennis's relationship with his son?"

"If you're right—okay, you're probably right—if you are, then I have even more reason to be outside the cottage."

She nodded. "You want to catch him."

"Don't you?"

"Yes! That's the only way to completely clear my name." She thought back to what she'd been thinking last night when putting

Oliver to bed. "And it's the only way to settle things for Oliver, to give him stability. But that doesn't mean you have to stalk me."

"It's not stalking."

"Okay, follow closely with the intent of tracking my every move."

He smiled. "You're cute when you're being impossible."

"I warned you about teasing me when my head hurts."

"Yes, you did. I'm sorry."

She plucked at the bedcovers for a minute. "You don't have to wait outside. I would call you if Dennis showed up."

"Maybe."

"Maybe! You think I'm hiding Dennis? You think I'm still seeing him?"

"Of course not. But I think he might come for Oliver. And if he does, he'll probably want to make sure you don't call the police."

"By blowing me up in the car?"

"I didn't say that."

"What are you saying? That Dennis snuck into the house last night, sabotaged the gas heater so it would leak when it was turned on, then snuck out without taking his son? You're not making any sense."

"No. I'm not," he conceded. He sat back in the chair. "I'm not making sense. But that's because nothing is making sense. You've got to admit this is a weird situation."

"I am the first to admit this is a weird situation." She paused, and looked across the room at a stand full of medical supplies. She made up her mind. "It doesn't make any sense," she said. "But the bottom line is, I don't want you hanging around us. I'm grateful you saved us, but I don't want you following us around any more." It's too dangerous to my heart, she added silently.

"I might have to follow you around," he said quietly.

She stared at him, and saw the determination in his eyes. "Even if I don't want you to?"

He nodded. "If I have to follow you to keep you safe, I will. Ma'am. It's my job."

He stood up. "Now, I'm going to have a talk with Oliver." He headed for the door.

She threw back the bedcovers and put her legs over the side. "Oh, no you're not. Not without me there. I know my legal rights. If you even think of interrogating Oliver about this without his legal guardian present, I'll"—

He turned back. "What will you do, Camilla?"

"I'll"—tell your boss, she started to say. "I'll never speak to you again, Captain Knight."

He took a step closer to the bed, his expression hard. "That would be a terrible thing," he said quietly.

He leaned down, and put a hand around that back of her neck and then he was kissing her. His lips were surprisingly soft, and gentle. He smelled of the ocean and warm skin and something distinctively him.

She should pull away and tell him to knock it off, but her arms were around his shoulders and it took at least five more seconds before she pushed him away.

He immediately pulled back and stood up straight, but his eyes looking down at her were no longer icy. The blue looked like the blue light of a gas flame and that thought brought her crashing back to reality. She looked down at her hands, now folded in her lap.

"I'm sorry," he said.

"I'm not," she said. "I think you're slightly nuts. But I don't want to never see you again. That was a stupid thing to say. But what happened at the house was an accident. It's an old house. I should have checked out the heater upstairs, or at least told Oliver not to touch it. It was careless of me. I was tired the first night, and just so glad things were working I didn't worry about it, and then didn't follow up yesterday. It was a rookie mistake, and I know more about remodeling houses than that. I was an idiot."

"Now you're kicking yourself."

"No. I admit it when I'm wrong. I will have all the gas lines in the house checked first thing. But that's all it was. A simple accident that could have been a disaster, but luckily wasn't."

"You're welcome."

She smiled up at him. "You're right. I haven't really said how grateful I am to you. Thank you for pulling us out of there."

"You probably would have made it out on your own," he said grudgingly.

"Thanks. I'm glad you acknowledge that someone other than you just might be able to do something. But you did save us."

"Or at least helped." He smiled tentatively.

"Thank you." She smiled back. "We both deserve some credit. So let's not argue. I'm not going to throw some childish fit and stomp my feet just because we disagree and I've got a headache that could kill a moose."

"Kill a moose?"

"Don't hassle me, Ryan. I've had a hard night."

"Sorry." But he was smiling now. "Now about talking to Oliver—"

"You don't give up, do you? Look, Ryan. All I'm asking you to do is trust me. I'm not a complete idiot. Yes, I misjudged Dennis. But I saw his love for Oliver. I saw Oliver's love for him. The guy's a jerk. But not a murderer."

She watched his jaw clench and unclench. Finally he said, "Maybe he's not behind these so-called accidents."

"There." She smiled at him. "That wasn't so painful, was it?"

He didn't smile. "But he may be manipulating Oliver. And I need to find out. And you don't know how crafty criminals can be."

If only he knew how wrong he was. She looked down at the

bedcovers again. Her lies were going to catch up to her someday. Somehow she had to get some distance from him.

"Now what did I say wrong?"

She shook it off. "Nothing."

"Just trust me, honey...."

"Dang it, Ryan! Don't you 'honey' me. I need to make the decisions about Oliver's care. I will talk to Oliver and try to get more information about Dennis. But I can't have you upsetting him. I can't have you cornering him, and pulling that friendly-cop act, and getting him to betray his father. I've seen it before. Can't you just trust my judgment on this?"

He looked down at her and she could see that he couldn't—he couldn't just believe she was right about something.

How could she trust him with the truth when he wouldn't trust her? "I think you probably should go."

"Yeah," he said. He turned to go, then stopped at the door. "I'm glad you and Oliver are okay."

"Thanks."

She rolled over in the bed to face the wall.

SHE HAD JUST WOKEN UP FROM A NAP WHEN ROBIN BRENHAM swept in wearing a cherry red silk suit with matching nail polish. She plopped her oversized bag on the foot of the hospital bed.

"Fab handbag, Robin."

Robin held it up. "Stella McCartney leopard print. Isn't it something? Fab pjs you're wearing, by the way."

"La Perla. From my former life. Don't remind me."

"That's all right. I've got just what you need. Doc said it was okay."

She plopped herself down next to the handbag and pulled it open. She held up a leopard-print flask: "French press coffee. Great beans I got last time I was in the City. And—" she pulled out a white paper bag. "Chocolate croissants from Mama Thu's. This'll make it all better."

"You are a life saver."

"Yes. One of my many talents." She handed her a leopard print mug that matched the purse.

Camilla sniffed and sighed with pleasure. "Ooh. Real coffee." She took a sip.

"Good?"

"Heavenly."

Robin leaned back against the foot of the bed, apparently ready for a long talk. "So, tell me all about it. I heard at Santos' Market that Captain Ryan was at your house when this happened...?"

"You heard it at Santos' Market?"

"Gossip central. Sandy, Ms. Zelda's gardener informed the stock boy, and the clerk checking me out told me."

"Great. So I'm topic number one in town again. After last night's blow-up with Mabel Rutherford."

Robin waved a manicured hand. "That woman's always making news. You should hear some of the things she's said about me." She tore off a bit of croissant and chewed thoughtfully. "So how much has the grapevine exaggerated?"

"About Ryan? He wasn't at the house. He was just passing by."

"Uh huh. I heard you kissed him."

"That was a couple of hours ago right here. How could they know that at Santos'?"

"The nurse is the school principal's sister, and she told her cousin, who was picking up an order at the market."

"I've got to get out of town."

Robin laughed, but Camilla didn't think it was funny.

"Don't worry about it, Camilla."

"People are saying awful things about me."

"No they're not. They're saying you're bringing Ryan out of

his shell, and they say you're cute—that's from Manuel at the garage—and that you seem sweet. Nothing bad."

"Except that I'm an embezzler."

"No one believes that. They trust Ryan's judgment more than the old battle-axe's. So, how was the kiss?"

"With Ryan or Mrs. Rutherford?"

She laughed. "So you do have a sense of humor."

"When I'm not being crotchety."

"That's okay. I didn't mean to tease you about it. I'm just really glad to see Ryan showing an interest in something. Everybody's worried about him."

"Why are they worried?

"Why?" Robin picked at her croissant. "Well," she paused and cocked her head while she thought about it. "He's quitting."

"I heard that," she said casually.

"He's been acting like a recluse ever since Angie left. He's a great cop—don't get me wrong—but it's like he's a secret agent or something."

Camilla laughed, and it felt good. "A secret agent? He doesn't really blend into the woodwork, that guy."

"I don't mean like that. I mean it's like you can see him every day and not really have a clue what's going on inside him. And now, out of the blue, he's leaving us."

"Well, you know what happened—with Sara, don't you?" Camilla paused, not sure how to say it.

"About her death?" Robin nodded. "Of course. But that's the thing. He's never said one word to anybody about what happened. He just acts like everything's okay, goes about his business, and then, bam! He up and quits."

"After his divorce it must have been tough to stay on."

"Yeah. Angie owned that little Stockdale he's living in, and when he asked me to list it for sale, I figured he was just trying to move on. I've got an apartment I told him he could rent once it sells, and he just shrugged. He never said he was going to leave. Like I said, he just totally Does.Not.Talk.About.It."

"Poor guy." Camilla picked at the red napkin holding her croissant. "I think he's still really grieving about it." She didn't feel right telling about how he'd broken down when he'd told her about Sara. The more she saw him around other people—and the more she heard about him from Robin—the more she wondered why he'd opened up to her about it.

Robin arched an eyebrow. "You've been in town two days. How do you know all about it?"

Camilla took a bite of croissant and pondered how to answer without contributing to the gossip, but Robin just nodded as if she'd answered.

"He's told you," she stated.

Camilla nodded.

"So it sounds like you guys are close...?" Robin let it hang there.

Camilla felt herself blush, and just shrugged. She had no idea what they were. Except in a dangerous position. That she was sure about.

"Good," Robin said. "Like I said, you're gonna bring him out of his shell. He seems like a really great guy, but just so, so...."

"Overbearing? Pushy? Difficult?"

"I was going to say quiet, but all those words work too."

"An oak tree," Camilla muttered.

"That's a good way of putting it."

"Anyway, so I guess the for sale sign on the Honeymoon Cottage will be coming down?" She grinned.

Camilla shook her head. "I'm not staying."

"You're not? Oh." Robin seemed disappointed. "So are you thinking of leaving together?"

"Of course not!"

"Well then why are you leaving?"

How could she stay in a town where every thing she did was

broadcast all over town the minute she did it? But Robin actually seemed hurt, and she felt herself babbling. "I just need to find a new place to start over. Somewhere I can make a fresh start, where nobody knows what happened at my last job."

"This is a good place for fresh starts," Robin said eagerly. "You haven't had a chance to get to know the place yet. I made a fresh start here after my divorce."

"Divorce?"

Robin shook her head. "No changing the subject. My personal drama can wait for another time. Why can't you stay here?"

"Mabel Rutherford has told everyone in town I'm a criminal."

"So? Nobody believes anything she says. Okay, some do. But you can't live your life worrying about the Mabel Rutherfords of the world."

She'd spent her whole life worrying about others' opinions. How could she stop? "Anyway, I need to sell the house to pay off my debts."

"It's too bad you can't keep the Honeymoon Cottage," Robin mused. "I think you and Oliver would do well there. They need some more kids on Cliff Drive."

"Can't afford it," Camilla said. Who cared if that news would be all over town by evening? "I owe a truckload of money and the sale will bail me out—no pun intended."

Robin laughed. "That's all right. But you don't have to leave town. I've got a cute rental above Santos' Market. The one I was trying to palm off on Ryan."

Camilla shook her head. "Santos' Market? Gossip Central? I don't think so."

"Well then you'll get the gossip before everybody else." She grinned. "Okay, so the apartment occasionally gets aromatic when Santos' has a special on tamales, but other than that, it's darling. Pine floors, big windows...."

Camilla shook her head again. "Nope."

"No?" Clearly Robin had gone into real estate agent mode

and was in full sales-pitch. "It's got an ocean view. Well, sort-of an ocean view. Really a glimpse of blue between the rooftops. Okay, more of a view of the seagulls roosting on the roof. But it is cute—that's no lie. And it's just big enough for you and Oliver."

"I can't. I need to get a job. I need a big city with a lot of companies for that." A place to get lost in a sea of anonymity.

"What do you do?"

"I was an accountant in the payroll department of Cordova Computing. Before I got fired."

"Cordova Computing?" She whistled. "Wow. That's a heck of a reference." She paused. "So, you have an accounting license and all that stuff?"

Camilla nodded. "Yeah. All that stuff. But I don't have a job, Robin."

"That's a bummer. Well, I guess you can't use them as a reference after what happened. But you didn't do anything wrong, right? Is there anyone you used to work with who could vouch for you? Say you were honest and trustworthy and brilliant and all that?"

"Actually Felix Cordova told me he'd write me a reference once it's all straightened out."

Robin lit up. "Really? The astronaut genius guy himself will vouch for you?"

She nodded. "Yeah. He had to let me go until the payroll problem gets resolved, but he told me I could come back when my name is cleared."

"He did? So you do have a job! That's great."

"No. I can't go back there."

"Why not?"

"Everyone there knows what happened."

"That you were the victim of a crime, but your boss—one of the smartest scientists in the world—believes in you enough to give you a second chance?"

"Well, when you put it that way it doesn't sound as bad as my way."

"Which is?"

"That everyone would think of me as a criminal and no one would ever trust me."

"Well, that's a stupid way to think of it."

Camilla stared at her.

"Well, it is. Man, if I could get a reference from Felix Cordova I wouldn't ignore it."

"I guess."

"No guessing. Gee, girl, you know what you need?"

"What?"

"More chocolate." She handed her the pastry bag.

CHAPTER NINE

THE LOOK ON RYAN'S FACE WHEN HE ENTERED THE SUBSTATION must've showed what he was thinking, because Joe jumped to his feet.

"What's up, Sir?" Joe and he rarely bothered with "sir" and "deputy" when they were alone, but Joe obviously realized he wasn't in the mood for small talk.

"Sit down, Serrano."

Joe sat back down at his desk. "Yes, Sir." He watched Ryan warily. "Is something wrong?"

Ryan felt like a lion whose pride had been attacked. He prowled back and forth across the office, shaking with anger. He had to pull himself together. This was getting him nowhere.

"Yeah," he finally said, stopping in the middle of the floor. "Something's wrong."

Ryan grabbed a rolling whiteboard from the corner, yanking it so hard it banged into the opposite wall.

"This is going to stop, now."

"What's going to stop?" Joe asked.

Ryan could feel the adrenalin surging through him. He was on the trail of a mystery and he wasn't going to stop until he solved it. And what if he didn't solve it before he was scheduled to leave town? That wasn't an option. He would solve it. Then he could move on with a clear conscience, knowing he'd done his job right.

Joe was still staring at him.

"What?" Ryan barked at him, still seething.

"You have that look."

He could have said, "what look?" but he didn't bother. Bloodhound Knight, they used to call him back when he was in the homicide department. When he got like this he felt like he was in the zone, every clue laid out before him, every step clear.

Like this was the job he was meant to do, he thought. But this was the last time he'd ever be a cop. He wondered if he would ever get away from the sense of responsibility for others. None of that mattered now. All that mattered was protecting Camilla.

He turned to Joe. "You want me to show you how to run a big case?"

Joe lit up. He'd only asked Ryan about the big cases a dozen times since he joined the department last fall, but there hadn't been anything big to work on in Pajaro Bay. Until now.

"Absolutely, Sir. I'd love to."

"Okay." He tossed his notebook on Joe's desk. "We've got one. Read me the info off the top page."

"Can't I even get a cup of java first?"

One glare from Ryan and Joe sat up straight in his chair, at attention. "Ready, Captain."

Ryan wrote across the top of the board: Dennis H_____. "We're hunting a fugitive. He's wanted for payroll embezzlement."

"Oh." Joe smiled. "Yeah, she is cute."

"He's also going to be wanted for attempted murder, as soon as I can prove it. She's in the clinic, recovering from an accidental gas leak at her cottage. So's her little boy."

"Oh." The smile was gone. "Are they okay?"

"For now. And we're going to keep them okay. Pay attention. This guy's clever— nobody's put the pieces together."

"Until now."

"Until now. Here we go."

Sacramento, Fresno, then Salinas, then San Jose. The marker squeaked as he wrote the places across the top of the board. "This is what we're starting with. Oliver said he'd lived all these places. I'm going to presume he was telling the truth when he said that's the order they traveled in."

"When did he live in L.A.?"

Ryan stopped, pen poised over the board. "He didn't mention L.A."

"He said my tamales smelled like Olvera Street last night. That's not something he'd know if he'd never been to El Pueblo. Trust me on this one."

"Okay. We'll put L.A. off to the side since we don't know where it fits into the pattern. There may be others, too. We don't know how many places Dennis dragged the kid over the years."

They both looked at the board.

"Now what?" Joe asked.

"Look at the next page of notes. We know he was in Sacramento at a particular time."

Joe turned the page.

"Read me the info."

Joe read and Ryan wrote: Joyce Ashford-Henning. Deceased March 9th. Two years ago. Ryan added the contact info for Paul Graham at Sacramento Homicide below.

"So, we've got some info on Sacramento. He was there with his wife and kid two years ago. His wife died in a car accident. He was using the name Henning. Now, turn the page."

They repeated the process under San Jose: Camilla Stewart, arrested March 23rd. This year. Then he listed the crimes: Cordova Computing Payroll, $1.2 million. Savings and checking accounts of Camilla Stewart. Camilla. She was so innocent. Even now she had no idea how much danger she was in. He wanted to rush back to her bedside at the hospital. Seeing her and Oliver last night, choking, helpless, it had shaken him. He had seen a lot of crime victims over the years, but this was different. He needed to protect them. Not only that, he needed her. Needed to see her smile. Needed to feel the touch of her small hand.

He took a deep breath. Let it out slowly. He was getting involved, and that was dangerous to her. He had to keep his distance. He had to be on guard at all times, or he couldn't keep her safe. How could he be close to her to protect her, but be unmoved by her, be untouched by her presence? He had to find a way.

But first, he had to figure out what Dennis's next move would be. This was how to protect her and Oliver now.

Joe was still watching him warily.

"These are our parameters," he told Joe.

"For what?"

"Look at the board."

On the left was Sacramento, with Oliver's mother's death two years ago. On the right, Camilla's arrest and Dennis's disappearance, last month.

"They left Sacramento some time after Oliver's mother died. He was calling himself Dennis Henning then. That might be his real name —or just another lie. But we know he was there two years ago."

"I get it," Joe said. "He was last in San Jose a few weeks ago. That's when Dennis, then using the name Hutchins, disappeared. Everything else has to fit between those two dates." Joe sat back in the chair. "So how do we figure it out?"

"This is where we start digging."

"Where do we start? CODIS?"

Ryan shook his head.

"Why not?"

"We would first need to find a sample of Dennis's DNA. Then

we'd have to submit it and see if there are any other crimes where DNA was collected that matches ours."

"I see. Because there wasn't any violent crime they might not have any crime scene to collect DNA from."

Ryan let the part about violence pass, and just nodded.

"What about his son? We could get his DNA and do a partial-match search."

Ryan paused. "Tempting, but I'm not sure we can get an okay for that. Relative matching is usually used for missing persons, or if the relative is also a criminal already in the database."

"Well, Dennis is missing, isn't he?"

Ryan pictured himself trying to make that argument to Camilla. Her blistering response when he asked to swab her little boy's cheek so they could nab his father would not be pretty. "Let's let that go for the moment. We may not have to approach Camilla yet."

"You'd think she'd want to catch the creep."

"It's not that. She's not on Dennis's side. I'm sure. She's just not exactly on my side, either."

"Not speaking to you, huh?"

"For someone who got ripped off by Dennis Hutchins, she's pretty adamant that he wouldn't hurt her or the boy."

"Denial."

He didn't want to tell Joe about his feelings for Camilla—feelings he couldn't even explain to himself. "For now, let's go back to the basics. We need to figure out his M.O."

"That's easy. He robs payrolls from large companies."

Ryan nodded. "I've got to call the fire inspector and get an official report on the accident at Camilla's. Do a quick database search and see how many similar crimes have been committed in those cities in the last couple of years."

The inspector was out, so Ryan left a message. When he got off the phone, Joe was shaking his head at the computer.

"Nada. I've tried every variation I can think of, but there's really nothing like the Cordova Computing payroll in those cities during that time."

Ryan sat down in his chair, then got right back up. "We're looking for the wrong thing." He went over to the board again. "We're not seeing it. It's here somewhere."

"You're the expert, Ryan. I trust your gut quicker than most men's hard evidence."

"Let's work this through. He's been moving around a lot. Taking his kid with him. Not being a high-profile enough criminal to get a real heavy duty manhunt after him. You steal too many payrolls from major corporations and you'll be caught. It's not a low-profile offense. So let's assume he hasn't been doing that. Let's go at this a different way. We're assuming he's stealing payrolls from large companies because he stole from Cordova Computing. But what if his main crime isn't the robbing of the payroll, but the robbing of Camilla, and the payroll was just a bonus? He not only took the payroll, he cleaned out all her accounts when he skipped town. He charmed her. She thought they were getting married. Then she found he'd skipped with all her money. What does that sound like?"

"A confidence man." Then Joe whistled softly. "A gigolo."

A gigolo. The word hit Ryan in the gut, hard. They had been engaged. She had trusted the man. He had touched her, been with her.

"Um, Ryan?"

Joe was looking down at Ryan's hands. Ryan saw that he'd clenched the marker so tightly that the ink had left a smear of red all over his palms.

He wiped his hands on a paper towel and came back. He hoped the blood-red on his hands was not a sign.

"Where were we?"

"Dennis is a gigolo."

Ryan clenched his jaw. "Right."

"He charms women and rips them off?"

Ryan nodded. Camilla was so innocent, she'd never encountered a man like Dennis before. It wasn't her fault. "Okay," he said, trying to keep this businesslike and not get wound up with thoughts of ripping Dennis to pieces. "Let's narrow it down by city."

He looked at the board. "Let's start with Salinas."

"Why Salinas?"

"You ask a lot of questions."

"I'm trying to learn."

"Right. Sorry." Ryan tried to stop leaping from one conclusion to the next without thinking. He was here to teach Joe so he could do this job safely and effectively. So he'd learn how to do this without Ryan around. He had to slow down. "We start with Salinas because it has the smallest population of these cities."

"Of course."

"So it's our best shot at finding a particular crime. What are we looking for?" He waited, trying not to be impatient, while Joe mulled it over.

"Has he left his kid with other women?"

"No. Camilla seems pretty sure this is the first time he's done that."

"So we're looking for other women who've been ripped off, maybe after he promised to marry them or something like that."

"Right. He claims he loves them and then cleans out their bank account, that kind of thing. So what's the code, Joe?"

"487. Grand Theft," Joe said immediately.

"Right. We are looking for similar cases in Salinas."

"That could be a large number."

Ryan's mind was leaping ahead, but he tried to remember that being a teacher was important. "How do we narrow it down to a manageable number, Joe?"

"His description?"

"Good." He wrote on the board: WM 5'10", late 30s, clean cut, Br/Br. "Camilla never had a picture of him. That's a typical con artist trait, by the way. Somehow they never get into a picture. What else?"

Joe looked at the board. "The time frame."

"Exactly. It had to take place between Joyce Henning's death and Camilla's arrest. Not only that, we have to allow for him to spend some time in each of these places. He was in at least one other city before he went to Salinas. He arrived in San Jose at least three months ago."

All that info went on the board. It was beginning to look like a sea of red notes.

Ryan set down the marker. "I'm going to go get you that coffee. While I'm gone, call Salinas PD. Ask for Rojas in Records. See if you can get a hit on anything matching the M.O. we've got so far. Give her time. It might take a while."

By the time Ryan got back from Santos' Market with two cups of coffee and a couple of sopaipillas, Joe was ready with the info.

"Rojas says hi. She said some really nice things about you."

Ryan brushed that off with a wave of his hand. Joe looked really excited about something, though, so Ryan prompted, "and?"

"You're not going to believe this. Renee Rojas is a former beach volleyball player."

Ryan knew Joe was really into beach volleyball, so he just raised an eyebrow.

"No, it's relevant," Joe said. "She remembered the case. Melissa Everette claimed a man cleaned out her bank account. This was about a year ago. The guy matches the description. And get this— the guy's name was Dennis Hedrick."

"Wow. I guess he really likes those H's." Ryan put down the coffee and wrote on the board: Hedrick went under Salinas. "Okay, we've got Henning in Sacramento, Hutchins in San Jose, and Hedrick in Salinas. Want to bet whoever he ripped off in Fresno and L.A. knew him as Dennis H, too?" This was going to be easy. "Now, I want you to get me Melissa Everette's phone number. I want to talk to that woman today."

Ryan went to his desk and started to dial. "I'm calling the county office to run all this by the sheriff. We are definitely on to something. Once I talk to Ms. Everette, we'll be close to catching that SOB."

"Wait a minute, Ryan."

Ryan stopped with the phone in hand. "What?"

"Don't call the sheriff yet. I told you deputy Rojas played volleyball. There's more."

Ryan put the phone down. "Such as?"

"You can't call Melissa Everette."

"Why not?"

"You don't recognize the name?"

"No. Why would I?"

"Remember the last Olympics? Melissa Everette was the beach volleyball coach for one of the teams. She was way hot."

"Yeah, Joe, I know you have a thing for the sport."

Joe grinned. "Amazing athletes. And they wear really nice outfits."

"Uh huh. So what? You want to talk to her yourself because you're a fan?"

"I can't talk to her—neither can you. She's dead."

Ryan sat down in his desk chair. The creak of the springs sounded like the hinges on Camilla's front door. He felt a chill wash over him. "Please don't tell me her gas tank exploded."

"I don't think so. I don't remember the details, but it was some sort of freak accident."

"A freak accident," Ryan repeated dumbly. He stared out the window at Calle Principal. "A freak accident," he repeated.

"I'll look it up."

It didn't take long. Soon Joe was reading him the report: Melissa Everette, 27-year-old Olympic medalist, fell while hiking in the Pinnacles. The volleyball coach had gone hiking early Tuesday morning and was found late that afternoon. She had apparently slipped off a path and fallen 100 feet to her death.

"Right," Ryan said. "A trained athlete fell off a hiking path on a clear day in the middle of the summer? And nobody questioned it?"

"Why would they?" Joe asked. He kept skimming the report, hitting the highlights: She had told friends she was going hiking. She did it all the time. Had a cell phone, safety equipment, etc. When she didn't come back a friend called for a search and they found her. No signs of foul play.

"Of course not. This guy is incredible."

"You think it's Dennis whatever-his-name-is? How could he get her out there alone?"

"I don't know. But he did. First his wife dies in a freak car accident, then one of his victims dies in a freak accident."

"How do you know it's not just an accident?"

Ryan rubbed the back of his neck. He suddenly realized how tired he was. "Because it gets better."

"Better?"

"Or worse. Oliver's mother died when her gas tank exploded in a freak one-car accident."

Joe frowned. "A freak accident?"

"And I met Camilla because her car stalled on Calle Principal. Turns out she had a puncture in her gas tank that could have blown her and the boy to kingdom come."

"Oh." Joe was beginning to look as sick as he felt himself.

"Two days later, she and Oliver are in the clinic because the wall heater in the cottage malfunctioned and they were almost killed by natural gas poisoning."

Ryan stood up and went to the whiteboard, gazing at the ocean of red ink in front of him. "Camilla accused me of being paranoid."

Joe came and stood next to him. They both stared at the lists of random info from all over the state.

"Ryan, I have an awful feeling that you're not paranoid at all."

"Now what?"

Camilla answered the knock on the cottage door only to find Ryan standing there.

"I'm glad to see you got home safely."

"Yes, Captain Ryan. We actually managed to make it the four blocks from downtown Pajaro Bay to our cottage all by ourselves." Actually, Robin had insisted on driving them, but she was not in the mood for more of his overprotectiveness.

He held up one hand. "Peace. I didn't come to argue. I came because I have orders from my boss to talk to you."

"From your boss? What are you talking about?" She stepped aside and he came in.

She might have slammed the cottage door just a bit when she closed it, because she saw him wince. "Long night, Ryan? Maybe you shouldn't spend your nights spying on people.""

"Please, Camilla."

She tried to tone down the anger she felt at the sight of him. She wasn't really angry at him. She was angry at the way he made her feel. All helpless and squishy inside. She wanted him to kiss her again, but she wanted him to leave. She was just a big old mess of contradictions. But it wasn't his fault. She needed to keep up her defenses, but that didn't mean she had to be rude.

"Sorry," she conceded. "I've just had the wits scared out of me, I'm tired, and Oliver's feeling headachy and cranky. It hasn't been a good day for anyone."

He nodded. "I'm sorry. I don't mean to add to your bad day. But we really need to talk."

"That sounds serious," she said with an attempt at a smile, but he didn't smile back. She led him into the kitchen and they sat at the table. "Want some coffee?"

"Yeah," he said. He watched her as she put the blue kettle on the stove to heat. He seemed to be looking at her funny.

143

"What? The stove's okay. After the fire inspector left, Zelda Potter pulled some strings and had the gas company inspector in here and checked everything for safety."

"Count on Ms. Zelda to get the job done."

"I don't know how she found out."

"Nothing stays secret in this town for long."

"I guess. Anyway, they didn't find anything wrong except that upstairs heater. The safety valve on it was missing, so the whole unit's now disconnected. It can't happen again."

"I'm glad. I'm really glad you're safe."

He seemed to really mean that. Of course he did. He'd probably consider her his helpless charge until she left town.

She poured two cups of coffee and after he declined cream and sugar, sat down across the table from him. "Who's your boss?"

"Uh." That seemed to catch him off guard. "My boss is the county sheriff. He's stationed over in the county seat, and I report directly to him. I had to call him to tell him what's going on."

"So what is going on?"

He looked down at the cup in his hands, and she was struck again by how strong his hands looked. He seemed to be such a strange mixture of strength and softness—strong physically, but almost little-boy lost at times.

He looked her in the eye and she realized this was not one of those times. "I'm here to inform you of the preliminary results of our investigation into Dennis's activities."

"Keep your voice down!" she said sharply. She got up and went to the back door, which stood half-open to the yard. She glanced out to make sure Oliver was still sitting out on the grass, playing with his model truck, then shut the top half and came back and sat down. "I don't want to upset Oliver. You clearly have something to say, so spit it out."

He opened up a small notebook and began reciting facts: Dennis had probably committed similar con games all over the state in the last few years. He had never been caught, or even identified, being known by various aliases.

"I'm not surprised. I didn't figure this was the first time he'd ripped someone off."

Ryan continued coldly, matter-of-factly, reciting a list of locations and dates. He handed her printouts from a couple of newspapers. Then he sat, watching with those cold eyes, while she read.

The first story was of a woman's funeral—"Oh my God," she gasped. "Poor little Oliver." His mother had been beautiful, with the soft, trusting eyes so like Oliver's. Her hair was dark like his, and a lock of it fell down over her forehead in the picture, looking so much like little Oliver's lock of unruly hair that Camilla felt the tears well up in her own eyes at the similarity. "My poor boy." His mother had died in a car accident two years ago. "Hey. It says Oliver and Dennis's last name is Henning."

"Turn the page."

The next page seemed totally random. Another funeral notice. She almost asked him to explain, but just started reading. Some woman in Salinas had died in an accident while hiking. She had been around Camilla's age. "I don't get it. It's really sad that this woman Melissa Everette died so young in some random accident, but what's it got to do with—?"

"—She'd filed a report a month before her death claiming she'd had her bank accounts cleaned out by a guy she was dating. With her death the case was closed, since there was no complaining witness and not enough evidence to file charges."

"And you jump to the conclusion—"

"This happened during the time Oliver says he lived with his dad in Salinas."

"But that's not enough—"

"He matches the description of Oliver's father. And his name was Dennis Hedrick."

She sat back in the chair. "It can't be."

He just watched her, waited for it to sink in.

She felt herself reeling. She'd been so focused on the way Ryan made her feel, on her own sense of helplessness and her desire not to depend on him, that she hadn't really taken him seriously as a cop. But he'd done the investigative work and found out the truth. No matter how absurd this seemed, no matter how much it contradicted what her gut had told her about the relationship between Oliver and his father, Dennis really was dangerous. He really was a killer. He really was threatening the life of his own son.

She finally whispered, "you were right."

"About Dennis? I'm afraid I might be."

She nodded. "I can't believe this could be true—"

He started to protest, but she stopped him. "—but I'm not an idiot. I'm not going to sit here and deny it when it's staring me in the face."

His body language changed then. He relaxed his shoulders then, and took a sip of his coffee.

"Yeah," she said. "We're on the same page now." She lifted her coffee cup to her lips, and realized her hand was shaking.

He put his hand over her other hand, which she noticed she was clenching. "It's going to be okay, Camilla. I'm not going to let anything happen to you."

She stood up and went over to the kitchen window, stared out for a bit. She couldn't think straight. How could this be? She just couldn't believe Dennis wanted his own son dead. Her, maybe. But Oliver? "How can I protect him?"

Ryan came over and stood behind her. He put his hands on her shoulders and she found herself leaning back, resting against his chest. He didn't do anything but stand there, solid and alive and supporting her.

After a minute she turned around to face him and he took a step back and put his hands in his pockets. "What do I do, Ryan?"

"You keep doing what you're doing, and allow us to help you."

"Us?"

"The sheriff's office. We'll keep close, we'll make sure you and Oliver are safe."

She nodded. "Should we leave the cottage? Go hide somewhere?"

He sighed. "I talked to the sheriff. At this point we think you're better off just staying put and keeping to your normal routine. But you won't be alone."

She shook her head. No. She had to escape. She felt the adrenalin rush through her. "No. I want to run." She looked around, trying to quickly think of what to pack, what to leave behind, where to go.

"Camilla!" Ryan took her by the shoulders again. His strength calmed her, and she took several deep breaths.

He let go. "Good. Feel calmer?"

She nodded.

"Running isn't a good idea. You might find yourself alone somewhere he could get to you. Somewhere without protection. Remember, he doesn't attack openly. It's not like he's going to come at you in the street. As long as we stay close by, you'll be safe. He needs to stage these so-called accidents carefully. He must need time and secrecy to set things up. We won't give him that time or that secrecy. We're going to be here 24/7."

"For how long?"

"For as long as it takes to make sure you and Oliver are safe."

CHAPTER TEN

THEY HEADED OUT TO DINNER TOGETHER JUST AS THE SUN WAS starting to go down. When they came out of the cottage gate, Oliver gasped.

Camilla's heart leaped into her throat, but then she saw it wasn't fear, it was car lust.

Oliver ran over to Ryan's car. "It's a Mustang!"

It sure was. It was a "1966 Tahoe Turquoise Mustang convertible with Pony interior," Ryan informed Oliver. "Hector just finished it today." The boys were in car heaven.

Camilla couldn't believe it. It seemed very un-Ryanlike, somehow. It was a teenage boy's dream car, from the glossy blue paint to the shining chrome trim, to the cream and blue seats. "Do we dare sit in it?" she asked.

He laughed. "Sure. It's not fragile. Well, not very." He opened the passenger door for them. After checking that Oliver's shoes were relatively clean Camilla let him scramble into the back seat. "Seat belt on," she reminded him.

"It's got a pony on the seat!"

Oliver and Ryan talked about cars the whole way to town—all

four minutes, which was definitely not long enough for Oliver. "Can't we drive around more?"

She shook her head. The sun was beginning to set and it was after 6 p.m. "Time for dinner. Aren't you hungry?"

They pulled to the curb on the main drag and got out. Oliver was captivated as Ryan raised the convertible top "in case the fog comes in."

Oliver looked warily up at the sky. "It won't dare rain, will it?" He made it sound like a serious crime.

Ryan assured him that a heavy mist was the worst that could happen, and Oliver watched anxiously while the motor whirred and the top settled into place.

"Where to now?"

Ryan pointed down an alley. It didn't look promising, but she was beginning to trust that he knew what he was doing.

She held Oliver's hand while they walked, and at the end of the alley they saw a wooden sign: Feuille d'automne. "I take it this is not Mel's Fish Shack?"

"No. We're entering the land of free-range herbs."

Inside she was astonished. What appeared from the alley to be a little hole-in-the-wall opened out at the back to a view not unlike the one behind her cottage. The restaurant's back wall was all glass, and outside, metal tables and chairs ringed a cliffside patio overlooking the glistening sunset over the bay.

"Outside or in?" a young Asian woman asked with a smile.

Camilla hesitated.

"It's Sam Spade tonight," the woman said.

"Then probably outside," Ryan said.

They settled out on the patio at a table for three. Oliver kicked his feet and looked sullen when he opened the menu printed all in French, but then an older lady in a gorgeous long silk dress appeared—the same woman Camilla had seen at the fundraising dinner in tie-dye and braids—and she soon had Oliver in a jolly mood. "So, sir, it appears we have run out of raw oysters with bitter vegetables and slime. Perhaps you would settle for a plate of fish and chips?"

She turned to Ryan and Camilla. "Oliver is in the same class with my granddaughter, Ly. She's in the kitchen having her supper. Perhaps he will come in for the show later?"

Ryan nodded. "I bet he'll enjoy that. But first we'll eat."

And grill him for clues about his father. Camilla had agreed with Ryan that they needed to get more information from Oliver, but she wasn't sure how they were going to pull it off.

After she and Ryan ordered (steamed fish with spicy sauce and cellophane noodles, and a bowl of the famous chowder), they settled back in their chairs.

"So, Oliver," Ryan began. "How are you liking your new school?"

Oliver smiled. "It's pretty good. No tests yet."

"Is it better than your school in San Jose?"

Oliver stiffened.

"It's okay, Oliver," Camilla said quickly. "I knew you when we lived there, so it's not telling anything to talk about it."

He frowned. "It's okay," he mumbled.

She and Ryan looked at each other. Man, this kid could shut down in an instant.

She leaned over to Oliver. "You don't have to worry. You know we are here to take care of you and keep you safe. We don't want to hurt you in any way. You can trust us."

He nodded. "I know. But it's a bad idea to talk too much."

"Why?" Ryan said, focusing in with that laser look he got when he was onto something.

Oliver shrugged. "Don't go running off at the mouth, Daddy always says."

Camilla felt the anger rise in her. She really could do violence to that man. He was setting his own kid up for a lifetime of problems, and apparently he didn't care. Obviously he didn't care. He wanted his own son dead.

Camilla wrapped her arms around Oliver. "It's okay," she whispered. "Don't worry about anything. You are safe here."

He leaned into her arms and sighed. She rubbed his hair for a moment, but then he pulled away. "Can't I go hang out with Ly?"

Mama Thu came up in time to hear that. "He's welcome to eat in the kitchen with her if you'd like."

Camilla sat back in her chair. "Is that okay?"

She was asking Ryan if Oliver would be safe out of their sight, but Mama Thu said, "Of course. I'll give him his fish and chips there. Ly will be thrilled."

Ryan nodded agreement.

She set their bowls of chowder in front of them, along with a pot of fragrant tea. "Come on inside, Oliver, and we'll get you your supper." He ran ahead of her into the restaurant, obviously glad to get away from their questions. "And now you two can have a relaxing sunset meal," she said happily, and followed him inside.

"Great," she said. "She wants to fix us up. That blew our chance to talk to him."

"We weren't going to get anything out him, anyway." He poured the tea into tiny cups for them both. "I don't want to pressure him, either," he said. "I know you are concerned about him—and I think you're right to be. But we've got to find a way to win his trust." He turned that astute gaze on her. "And I think you're doing it. You seem to really understand him, in a way I don't."

She shrugged. How could she explain that she knew exactly what it was like to be in his shoes—afraid to tell the truth about his past, afraid that he might slip up and give something away that would hurt his family. She looked out at the bay. "But now we've wasted this chance to talk to him."

"Is a romantic sunset meal such a terrible idea?" he said softly.

It seemed no matter how much she knew being around Ryan was a bad idea, it kept happening. Why did she want to spend time with this man, even when he drove her crazy? There was something the same about them. Both of them needed something. But it would never work.

She could never tell him about her father. In her own way she had as many secrets as Oliver. She couldn't explain her own dad to a cop, of all people. The humiliation, the constant fear of exposure. And then worse, her own criminal past. He would never understand.

She never talked about it to anyone. In college she was terrified someone would find out, and kept everyone at arms' length, never really opening up to anyone. Ryan couldn't possibly understand. But maybe as long as they kept their relationship superficial, things would be fine. After all, she had been reliving that kiss in the clinic all day.

He was still waiting for an answer from her. "No," she said. "Having a nice evening together isn't a terrible idea." Maybe the key was to ignore the future and just live for the moment.

She relaxed then, talking about the view, and the food, and for a little while just enjoying the present instead of worrying about all the problems hanging over them.

She found herself sharing a secret smile with Ryan when Mama Thu brought them another pot of tea and informed them that it was flavored with special herbs she'd grown herself.

When they had eaten the delicately spiced food and been brought cups of steaming Vietnamese coffee, Ryan moved his chair over closer to hers and put his arm around her. She rested her head against his shoulder as they both watched the water turn golden, and then orange, and then deep crimson as the sun went down. She leaned into him, relishing that same ocean-and-man scent she had noticed at the hospital. She felt so safe with him. If only this moment was real, and not just an illusion built on lies—him using her to solve his case, her keeping secrets from him. If only this was built on something real....

"We should go," she muttered when the sun finally

disappeared and the view below them had turned to points of glittering lights from the wharf to the amusement park.

He helped her up and they went inside.

The light and noise inside felt jarring after the quiet outside. A large group was gathered in the corner and laughing. She heard a high, squeaky voice say "Oh, Sam!" and everyone laughed. Oliver sat with a little girl and they whispered and giggled through the whole thing.

She looked at Ryan in confusion.

"Sam Spade," he said. "The local jazz station plays old radio shows on weeknights at seven. This is detective show night."

"Radio?" He started to explain, but she held up her hand. "Don't tell me. It's a Pajaro Bay thing."

"Yeah. What can I say? It's just something people are into here. It's a quirky town."

She nodded, watching all the people just hanging out together, having a good time. People who clearly belonged here and felt at home here. She wondered if she'd ever find a place like that for her and Oliver.

RYAN LET THEM OUT OF THE CAR IN FRONT OF THE COTTAGE. "Go put on your pajamas and I'll be there in a minute," Camilla told Oliver.

She leaned in the open passenger-side window and looked at him. "Are you planning on staying out here all night?"

He hoped she wasn't going to start another argument. He gave her his most calm, talking-Mabel-Rutherford-out-of-filing-yet-another-complaint voice: "The county office has authorized me doing this, Camilla. I won't disturb you at all, I promise. But it's not wise to leave you unguarded."

She raised an eyebrow. "I know. I got the message when you showed me the funeral notices."

"Okay," he said. "So you're not going to fight me on this?"

She shook her head. "I'm not stupid, Ryan."

"Never said you were."

"But you seem to think I'm helpless and unable to make any decisions."

Now it was his turn to be exasperated. That wasn't what he thought at all. "Just because you need protection, that doesn't mean I think you're stupid."

"Fine. But you need to talk to me about these decisions, not make them without discussing them with me."

"Okay. Got it."

She leaned forward into the car, and her beautiful green eyes bored into him. "And you are never, ever to question Oliver about his father without me there." She took a big breath. "Ever."

"Okay," he said. "Got it."

"I don't want him upset. I understand what you're trying to do, but we have to work together to get information from him without traumatizing him. You may think grilling him is the highest priority, but I think taking care of him is."

"Okay," he said. "Got it."

"You sound like a parrot. Are you making fun of me?"

"I'm trying to be agreeable and non-confrontational."

She laughed out loud at that. "Geez, Ryan. I'm not Mrs. Rutherford."

He smiled. She looked so adorable leaning in the window that he was tempted to reach over and kiss her, but didn't. "You have no idea how glad I am of that."

Something of what he was thinking must have burned in his eyes, because she glanced away quickly, then started to blush.

"So I'll be out here keeping an eye on the cottage," he said to break the tension.

"I—I don't want you to do that."

He frowned. "I thought we agreed—?"

"That wasn't what I meant." She paused, the blush grew on her face, then she looked him in the eye. "Are you going to stay in your car all night?"

He nodded. "I'm on duty now. We're going to make sure no other accidents happen."

She paused. "What I mean is, do you have to sit in the car?" She took a deep breath. "I mean, it's awfully cold and cramped to spend the night out here. Maybe, I mean, could you guard us from inside the cottage?"

He must have looked surprised, because she said a flustered: "I didn't mean, you know, anything personal by that, you know...." She stammered to a stop and stood there, looking helpless.

Her blush was now bright red. It was so cute he wanted to say something more. He was so tempted to say they could share her sleeping bag, but he was here on official business and that would be unprofessional, so he just said, "I won't be sleeping. My job is to keep an eye on things. I'll be glad to come inside, Ma'am."

She laughed. "All right, Captain. Come on in and I'll make you a cup of my famously lousy instant coffee. We don't want you to fall asleep on the job."

HE SAT IN THE KITCHEN NURSING HIS CUP OF TERRIBLE COFFEE, listening to the soft murmur of Camilla and Oliver's voices in the living room as they settled down to sleep. He felt the sense of life in the little cottage, the warmth she had already brought to this abandoned little house, and to his life.

You're leaving, you're leaving, he kept silently repeating to himself. This is your last job. Don't get attached. But he worried that it was already too late for that.

CHAPTER ELEVEN

The next morning Camilla had trouble taking her eyes off Ryan. He was still in his uniform, but with sleepy eyes and rumpled hair, he seemed almost little boyish—a little boy in a man's body.

The three of them sat around the kitchen table eating their cereal. Ryan and she had agreed, in a whispered conversation before Oliver woke up, that she would be safe enough during the day while Oliver was in school. They had another deputy on loan from the county who would watch the school, while Deputy Serrano watched the cottage. That way Ryan could get a few hours sleep, and then he'd be back that afternoon.

She crunched her cereal thoughtfully, wondering how Dennis would try to get to them—if he'd try to get to them. It was still hard to believe this was really happening.

"My, this is cozy." Ms. Zelda swept in the kitchen door.

Ryan immediately stood up. "Ma'am."

Ms. Zelda turned back to the door and Camilla saw there were two people behind her: a skinny young guy in a black top hat and an androgynous-looking person with short blond hair and big, sad eyes.

"Sandy," Ms. Zelda said. "See that the chimney sweep makes a thorough inspection. We can't have the Honeymoon Cottage going up in smoke."

Sandy nodded and directed the top-hatted man toward the living room.

"Um," Camilla said, but got no further than that.

"Sandy is my man-of-all-work, Camilla. He'll see that the job is done properly." She turned to Ryan. "It's time for Oliver to go to school."

"Yes, Ms. Zelda," he said. "Come on, kid."

Oliver wiped his mouth with his napkin, jumped to his feet and ran off for his backpack.

Ryan helped Ms. Zelda into a chair while Camilla watched.

She was dressed head-to-toe in gray today, from a felt fedora with a gray feather, to tiny suede boots on her feet. In her arms she held what Camilla at first took to be an elaborate fur muff, but then realized it was a Persian cat when it reared its head up to look disdainfully at her.

"Ophelia," Ms. Zelda said. "She's a monster, but she needs her outings."

"Yes, Ma'am," Camilla said, at a loss.

"You may go now, Ryan," Ms. Zelda said with a dismissive nod.

He nodded to her, glanced at Camilla with a little half-smile and went to get Oliver. Camilla heard the front door creak and then they were gone, and she was alone with this overwhelming woman.

"I see you have already begun work on the cottage."

Ms. Zelda set Ophelia on the floor, and Camilla saw the cat wore a silver harness and matching leash. It sat and glared at Camilla.

"I'm sorry, Ms. Zelda. I mean—"

She waved a hand at her. "No apologies are necessary, Camilla. I am glad to see you are working on the place. The broken windows were a terrible thing. Weather damage could decimate this darling home if it's not nipped in the bud."

Camilla let out her breath. "Oh, good. I didn't want to do anything against the rules, but I had to start some of the basic repairs right away." She stood up. "Would you like a cup of coffee? It's terrible, but it's hot."

"Sounds lovely. We'll have time to talk over your plans while Sandy supervises the chimney sweep." It wasn't a request.

Camilla made Ms. Zelda a cup of coffee and offered her a cookie, which the lady accepted with a regal nod.

She sat back down across from Ms. Zelda and waited, feeling like she was trying to impress the queen with instant coffee and packaged cookies, and failing miserably.

"Now. Why is there a for sale sign on your cottage, Camilla?"

That wasn't a question she'd been expecting. "Um, because I'm selling it."

Ms. Zelda raised an eyebrow, and Camilla quickly stammered, "I'm not trying to be impertinent. That's why it's for sale. Because I'm broke."

"Didn't Dennis pay for the house in cash?"

"Dennis? How do you know—"

Ms. Zelda waved a hand. "Shall I call Felix?"

"Felix?" Of course she would know him. "Have you talked to Mr. Cordova about me?"

She shook her head. "I haven't spoken to young Felix in several months."

Young Felix. The man had a daughter Camilla's age.

"But you do know he's a neighbor."

She shook her head.

"He owns a beach house a couple of miles down the coast. Quite an ostentatious place, not to my taste, but he wanted a home for all his electronic toys. Interactive video walls and all that sort of thing. We certainly wouldn't have let him do that with a Stockdale, so he built himself a 10,000-square-foot pseudo-Adobe monstrosity." She shook her head. "Glad you aren't trying to do anything like that."

"Yeah, well, I don't exactly have the resources to do anything wild, even if I wanted to."

"But the point is you don't want to. You appreciate what the Stockdale mystique is about."

"Do I?"

She smiled. "Yes. Even if you called this a drunken leprechaun cottage, you appreciate the history of the place now."

She wasn't even going to ask how Ms. Zelda knew she'd called this a drunken leprechaun house. "What makes you think I appreciate this place? I'm trying to sell it."

Ms. Zelda frowned. "I will have to talk to Felix. He isn't pressuring you to repay the money Dennis stole, is he? That's most inappropriate."

Ms. Zelda—" she paused, trying to choose from among the dozen questions that came to mind. "Do you know Dennis Hutchins?"

"Of course. Although he called himself Dennis Henning when I met him."

"When did you meet him?"

"When he bought the cottage, of course. Which is why I know you cannot sell it."

"Of course I can sell it. It's in my name." Was Ms. Zelda going to stand in the way of what she needed to do? She crossed her arms and glared. "I have the right to sell the property... ma'am."

"Now don't get ruffled, young lady. Of course you have a legal right to sell it, that's not what I mean. I mean you cannot. It wouldn't be right, not for little Oliver, and not for you."

Camilla felt panic rising in her. She had to sell. She had to leave town. She felt the familiar panic—get away from the criticism, get away from the people who would judge her—and she had to take a couple of deep breaths to talk herself down from it.

Ms. Zelda just watched her.

Finally, Camilla said, "I don't understand, Ms. Zelda. Are you going to make it difficult for me to sell?"

She put up one hand. "My dear, you are so impatient. Drink your coffee and have another cookie and I'm sure we will reach an amicable agreement. I am not here to make your life difficult. You are too quick to assume that you have enemies all around you." She reached down and scratched the cat behind the ears, and it glared back at her. "Ophelia here is the only one who is truly hostile. Everyone else is on your side."

"She looks like a nice cat," Camilla said dubiously, while the cat glared back at her.

"No, she's not," Zelda said matter-of-factly. "She's an awful beast. But we're used to each other. She was abandoned in a barn as a kitten and got her little mind pretty twisted by the time she was found and brought to the shelter."

Somehow Camilla wouldn't have pictured Ms. Zelda adopting a shelter cat, and she told her so.

Zelda laughed. "Why not, my dear? I'm nothing but an old mutt myself. Miss Abigail Potter from a run-down truck farm in the Central Valley." Then that sharp look focused in on her. "You are what you make of yourself, Camilla. It's up to you to define yourself. Don't let others do it for you."

"I guess." Camilla leaned down to pet the cat, but it reached out and took a swipe at her. "Ouch!" She pulled away, and the cat hissed at her like it was the one who'd been attacked.

The cat glared at her with an expression exactly like her mother had always worn. "I've seen that look before," Camilla muttered, rubbing the scratch on her hand.

"Where?"

Camilla almost told the truth, but then shook her head. "It doesn't matter."

Ms. Zelda shook her head. "Mabel Rutherford has her own problems that have nothing to do with you."

Camilla didn't correct her.

"But you have a lot of people rooting for you. Give us a chance to help."

Camilla straightened up in her chair. "Ma'am, I need to get your permission to do these improvements. Is that going to be a problem?"

Ms. Zelda took another bite of her cookie. "These are very good. Does Santos' Market carry them? I will have Sandy buy us some."

"They're just store-brand cookies."

"Things don't have to be expensive to be good. Like this little place." She nodded toward the living room. "You've noticed the fireplace."

"Of course," Camilla said, giving up on directing the conversation and letting Ms. Zelda go her own way, which seemed inevitable anyway.

"This is the very first Stockdale. Jefferson Stockdale's honeymoon cottage. He came to Pajaro Bay as a young man, and met Ramona Robles. Her family owned the Robles Pottery in town. They made dinnerware, Mexican-style tiles, that sort of thing."

Camilla nodded, trying not to be impatient. "The stuff on the fireplace."

"That came later. After they met. It was as if they freed each other. He had been building conventional houses on contract."

"He knew how to build regular houses?"

"Of course, my dear. Haven't you noticed that despite all the odd angles, the joints are perfect? He was a woodworker and a trained architect."

Camilla looked up toward the kitchen ceiling. No, she hadn't really noticed. She'd been so busy dealing with the problems that she hadn't really looked at how the ceiling beams had perfect dovetail joints. She leaned back in her chair and smiled. "I haven't been paying attention."

"Of course not. You've been too busy."

"But I noticed the fireplace tiles."

"Yes. Ramona had been working in her family's pottery, following the standard, mass-produced designs from which her family made a living. After Jefferson and Ramona met, he started making these cottages, first this one, then more and more as people fell in love with them. And she—well, you can see what she did. She started developing new arts and crafts designs and producing them in her family's kilns. There are Robles tiles in many of the California craftsman homes throughout the state, as well as in every Stockdale."

"They were meant for each other."

"Yes. But their son died in the war, and there were no heirs. So when Ramona finally passed years ago, the place sat empty. It hadn't been repaired in years, and it just fell to pieces. We in the historical society purchased it from the estate, but we hadn't gotten around to working on it, when Dennis came along."

Camilla perked up. "So you actually met Dennis?"

"Oh, yes. He was a fast talker, but I could see underneath the polish he really wanted the house."

He really wanted this house? That had never made sense to Camilla. When the real estate agent told her she'd sold Dennis the house and he'd insisted on putting it in Camilla's name, she at first didn't believe it. Now she knew it was true, but still... "Why? Did he say why he bought it?"

"For his son, of course."

"His son?"

Ms. Zelda nodded, and took another sip of coffee. "This coffee really isn't that bad."

Dennis wanted the house for Oliver? That didn't fit with what she and Ryan had realized about Dennis's motives. She had believed Dennis was a doting father, but Ryan had corrected that misperception. She knew there must be more to the story, so she waited for Ms. Zelda to continue the story.

"I see you don't believe me," she finally said after another bite of cookie and another sip of the awful coffee. "Well, that's all right, my dear." She patted Camilla's hand. "But this place is what you and Oliver need."

"No, Ms. Zelda. What we need is the money we'll get from selling it. Then we can make a new start somewhere else."

"You must stay here. Dennis was adamant about that. He wants his son raised here."

The nerve of that man. He'd stolen from her, and then thought he could dictate what she did with her life? Was he completely crazy? But then she realized he might very well be crazy. After all, if he was everything Ryan claimed he was, he must be nuts. Still, he couldn't stop her from selling the house.

"He really was quite insistent on that point," Ms. Zelda said, obviously reading the anger on Camilla's face.

"Well, we can't always get what we want," she muttered into her coffee cup.

"You want what's best for the boy." It was a statement, not a question.

"Of course I do. But I am not going to indulge Dennis's whims. He left Oliver in my care, and I have to decide what's best. Dennis is a criminal. He doesn't know what's best for his child."

She froze, stared down at her coffee. "Criminals don't make the best parents," she muttered.

"I'm sure they don't. But they can love their children, even if they fail in other areas. It's human nature to be able to hold several mutually exclusive opinions at the same time, my dear. That's Fitzgerald, I think, though I'm probably misquoting him."

"Whatever. Selfishness is not love."

"No, it's not. But Dennis's purchase of this place was not a selfish act."

"How do you know?"

"Because I'm very old, young lady." Camilla glanced up and

caught the twinkle in Ms. Zelda's eyes. "I am not easily fooled by quick-talking scam artists."

"You saw through him?"

"Of course. He's what we used to call a gigolo. A fool who takes advantage of other fools."

"Ouch."

"Sorry, my dear. But I believe in being honest. You were a fool to trust him. You know that yourself—in fact I do wonder why someone as bright as you fell for such an obvious man...."

That sentence lay there for a minute while Camilla said nothing, thinking furiously about it herself. Why had Dennis fooled her? You would think she had seen enough dishonesty in her life to spot it. But there was something deeper there, something inside her she hadn't faced. She had been thinking about it ever since Dennis disappeared, but she kept turning her mind away from it instead of really facing it. Some time she would have to face it. But not now.

"No matter," Ms. Zelda continued. "You were a fool to trust Dennis. But you are not a fool to love Oliver. And Dennis was not a fool to trust you with his son."

Camilla shook her head. "There's more to the story than that."

She tried to think of how to explain about the so-called accidents, but Ms. Zelda waved her hand in the air, dismissing it. "I'm sure there are other parts to the story that I do not know. But I know what Dennis said, and what showed in what he didn't say."

"What do you mean?"

"He told me he was buying the cottage for his son, and for the woman who would be his son's guardian."

"Did he say that, or did you read that between the lines?"

She smiled. "He said that. The term 'woman who would be his son's guardian' stood out to me, as you might imagine. So he never intended you to be his wife."

Camilla shrugged. "It's not like I really loved him."

"You just loved his son."

She nodded. "Yes. And you're saying that's what Dennis wanted?"

"That's what he said."

"He's a born liar."

"True enough. But as I said, I don't believe what I'm told, I believe what I know is true."

"I'd like to be that way."

"You already are. You just have to learn to listen to your own judgment, and not be swayed by others."

"I felt it in my bones that Dennis loved Oliver, but then when Ryan told me he didn't—"

"—Ryan is a good young man, but why do you doubt what you feel in your own bones?"

That struck home. She wondered. Why had she assumed Ryan was right? You couldn't trust cops to tell the truth; they always had their own agendas. Why did she believe Ryan instead of herself? "Good question. Very good question."

Zelda nodded. "So. I will talk to Felix so you don't have to sell the cottage."

"No, Ms. Zelda. I don't want you to do that."

She raised an eyebrow. "You're sure? Yes, I see by your expression you are."

"I pay my debts. I'm not a deadbeat. But I will respect the architectural integrity of the cottage when I make the improvements. I promise."

"I'm sure you will." She gathered Ophelia into her arms and stood up. Camilla watched as the cat went perfectly limp and buried its head in the crook of Ms. Zelda's arm. The cat was a monster—and a gentle lap cat. Two contradictory things, depending on who she was dealing with.

"Finished, Sandy?"

The little man came back into the kitchen, nodded silently.

"You've seen the chimney sweep out?"

Another nod.

"Very well. I am sorry we will not be neighbors for long, Camilla. I have enjoyed our conversation, and I would have liked to get to know you better. I think you show a lot of promise."

That felt good coming from Ms. Zelda. She had the nerve to call her a fool when she deserved it, and it made the compliment mean something. Honesty. Something she might want to think about.

"Thank you, Ma'am. But we haven't talked about what I'm changing in the house. Or about the historical society."

Ms. Zelda waved the hand that wasn't holding the cat. "I don't think we'll have any problem approving your plans."

She and her tiny entourage swept out, and Camilla closed the door after them.

AFTER ZELDA LEFT, CAMILLA TOOK A BROOM UPSTAIRS TO THE TINY attic room and began sweeping furiously, kicking up dust everywhere. It's human nature to hold several mutually exclusive opinions at the same time, my dear. It may be human nature, but it was still wrong.

How could she be an intelligent, adult woman, and be fooled by an obvious con man? Even more, how had she been fooled by the type of man she'd spent her whole life dealing with?

She got angrier and angrier while she swept, until she finally sat down on the hardwood floor and had a good cry. The truth was there, right in front of her. But she'd been avoiding it for all these weeks.

That stupid cat looked just like her mother. It had been neglected until it became a bitter and angry little animal. She'd never thought of that side of it, being so focused on getting scratched that she never paid attention to what made an animal mad enough to attack.

But she was paying attention now. Her dad was Dennis. It hit her like a lead pipe to the chest. All this time she'd been so angry at her mother, blaming her for the coldness, the cruelty, the abandonment. But her dad had been the real problem.

She'd always made her mother the bad guy. But her mother hadn't started out a bitter, hateful old woman. Her mother had once been in love. She'd seen the old photos, years ago. She remembered how shocked she had been when she'd realized the beautiful, happy young woman clinging to dad's arm in the wedding photos had been her own mother. It was like her mother had been a completely different person then.

Of course she was a different person. She was a woman in love with a rising young executive who'd promised her the moon and stars.

All her mother's dreams of a good life and social standing were wiped out when she found herself married and pregnant with the child of a con man. Her father wasn't an up-and-coming executive, but an out of work handyman who went from one get-rich-quick scheme to the next, lying and manipulating all the way. He used people, ripped them off, and smiled all the while he was doing it. Like it was a game.

But her dad had loved her. Worshipped her, really. His little apprentice. His little darling daughter. She had basked in that love, soaked up that adoration, at the same time trying to fight off the anger and bitterness—and hate—that her mother constantly spewed at her. Mutually exclusive beliefs. Love and hate.

Her dad was Dennis. She couldn't get over the thought. That was why Dennis had been able to get under her skin so quickly, why she'd fallen for every lie, believed every stupid trick he'd used. Because she'd been taking her dad's side all her life, determined not to be judgmental like her mother.

But dad was the one to blame. He wasn't a lighthearted con man who made mistakes but meant well. He was the one who lied, who disappointed them, who kept letting them down.

Her mom couldn't take being married to someone like him. She'd stuck it out until Camilla turned 18. Then she'd taken off, disappeared. Camilla went to college, and dad ended up in prison. And mother had gone who-knows where, somewhere she could escape the mess she'd made of her life. They'd each found an escape.

But her mother's crime wasn't in abandoning her father, as she'd always thought, but in abandoning her child. She'd always stood up for dad, but not for herself. Somehow it was easy to take dad's side. Because he was a lovable con man. And because he loved her unconditionally.

But dad wasn't the victim here. Just like Dennis wasn't. It was Oliver who was paying the price for his father's immaturity and selfishness. Just like she'd paid for her parents' mistakes. Somehow it was so much easier to see the pattern in Oliver's life. It brought her own life into sharp focus. Forced her to face what she'd spent a lifetime denying. To think that the parent who loved her had been a creep, and the parent who hated her had been the victim, had been too hard to face before. But now, seeing Oliver, apparently loved by his father, a monster who had killed his child's mother... The truth was so stark and brutal, she had to deal with it.

No, her dad wasn't a murderer. But her mom had been married to someone as dishonest and scheming and selfish—and charming—as Dennis Henning.

Her whole life had been based on a lie. No wonder she was so screwed up.

Her mother's bitterness had colored her childhood. "You're just like your father." "You're going to end up a criminal just like him." The endless litany of criticism had never really been about Camilla at all. Camilla had been the tie to her father. The thing her mother couldn't escape. The evidence of her mother's mistake. So she had paid, oh how she had paid. She was her father's daughter. And her mother would never forgive her for that. It had been a relief when she'd gotten old enough to run—first to throw herself into schoolwork and then later into college, her last ties with her mother severed by mutual agreement.

"Don't call me when you get arrested."

Those were her mother's final words to her when she left for college.

Not, "gee, honey, I'm so proud of you for getting a scholarship." Not, "I can hardly wait for you to come home on winter break." But an assumption that soon enough, she'd end up like her father.

That was the horror of her arrest last month. It was the words of her mother's scorn come to life. Her own worst fear—that her mother's opinion of her was true—being proven right.

None of this had ever been about her. None of it. Her mother's life, and her father's worship. She hadn't deserved either.

Being around Oliver, Camilla finally got it. It had taken her 24 years, but she was finally going to get over her childhood. Because she had to. For Oliver's sake, and her own. It was the only way to keep history from repeating itself.

Oliver looked just like his father. What if she had fallen for Dennis—really fallen for him. What if she'd built her life around that man, and then, like her mother, been so disappointed that every reminder of him sent her into a rage: "You blush just like your father, Camilla. It's that red hair and freckles, just like him. Ugly."

No, even then, she couldn't picture herself being cruel to little Oliver the way her mother had been to her. She couldn't.

But, in a way, she'd been as cruel to herself as her mother had. Why had she believed all the lies about herself? She knew it wasn't true about Oliver. She hadn't been any older than him when her mother had been running her down. It was hard to picture herself as small as Oliver. But she forced herself to, really trying, for the first time, to see what her mother had seen.

She got a glimpse of something awful, something that her own heart couldn't fathom—taking all that deep disappointment and bitterness and directing it at a child. But she could see how it had happened. Not excuse it, maybe never even forgive it. But for the first time, she could see it for what it was. It had never been about her at all. It had been a sad, lost woman's disappointment turned on the nearest target.

She wiped away her tears and stood up. She was done crying.

Sure, her mother had been wrong. It was always wrong to blame a child for its parents' mistakes. But her mother was dealing with a disappointment far worse than anything she'd had to. She had been infatuated with Dennis, but she hadn't married him (thank God). She hadn't had a child with him, hadn't bound her life to him. She had luckily found out what he was before any real harm had been done to her. She'd lost money, and her reputation, and her home and job. But not her heart. No wonder she remembered her mother as a bitter, cynical woman who constantly worried about what the neighbors thought of her and blamed the world for her problems.

Her mother had been a victim too. A victim and an abuser. Two mutually exclusive things at the same time.

Camilla picked up the broom again. She had a lot of work to do here.

There was enough victimhood to go around. She wasn't going to perpetuate it any more.

Oliver would not be a victim. She was going to protect him from his father, and she was going to teach him to protect himself—to believe in himself from the start, so he wouldn't make the mistakes she had made. She was going to take him away from the past, far away where none of this could ever hurt him again.

His life was going to be different. She was going to make sure of that.

She got back to work.

RYAN SHOWED UP AT THREE IN THE AFTERNOON, JUST LIKE HE'D
promised, and had picked up Oliver on the way.

Camilla watched the two of them from her window in the
attic room. They were laughing together outside the cottage, and
then Oliver took Ryan by the hand and pulled him across the
back lawn to look over the cliff edge.

She saw Oliver was pointing down to the amusement park
and talking in a very animated way. She didn't have to wonder
what he was talking about. Ryan ruffled his hair and laughed
with him, and her heart caught in her throat. It all felt so right.

Then Oliver ran across the lawn and picked up a pine cone
and they began tossing it back and forth like a football, little
Oliver feinting and running around Ryan while Ryan pretended
to be tricked by the play.

Then Ryan scooped him up and carried him toward the
kitchen door and they were out of sight.

She felt the stirring of some sense of comfort she had never
experienced before. Her boys were home. She hurried downstairs
to meet them.

"I have a present for you," Ryan said when she met them in the
living room.

She didn't tell him she felt like she'd already received a present
at the sight of them. She gave Oliver a big hug.

"What's the present?"

He went out the front door and then came back, carrying
two boxes.

She looked at the labels. "Air mattresses?"

Oliver helped Ryan unpack the boxes and he jumped up and
down on the foot pump to help blow them up.

Then they both sprawled across the mattresses. "It's heaven,"
Ryan said. "You should try it."

The sight of him lying on his back on the floor made her

think completely inappropriate thoughts, and she suddenly blushed.

He looked up and caught her eye, and then he slowly grinned. "Come on." He held out his hand to her.

She stood still, blushing and trying not to plop down on top of him. The thoughts she was having were dangerous.

"You should get some real mattresses, but these'll do until you get proper ones."

She shook her head. "It's too hard to move mattresses."

He sat up, the smile gone. He crossed his arms across that muscled chest. "Right. Gotta pack light."

"That's right," Oliver said. "Don't want to get tied down." He sprawled on his mattress and wiggled his arms and legs like he was making a snow angel. "But we can pack these when we go, huh Camilla?"

"Yeah," she said, ignoring Ryan's frown. Why did Ryan even care that they were planning to move away? For that matter, why did she care? He wasn't the man for her, and she had to stop letting her hormones distract her from the truth. She had no business flirting with a cop. She had no interest in getting involved with a guy she was just going to leave behind. "The mattresses are really nice, Ryan. Thank you. We'll take them with us when we leave."

CHAPTER TWELVE

WHEN RYAN'S CELL PHONE RANG DURING DINNER, HE QUICKLY checked it, then relaxed. It wasn't the dispatcher. He excused himself and stepped out the back door to talk in private.

"So why did you call?" Leah sounded more annoyed than ever.

Ryan held his cell phone up closer to his ear. "I'm glad to hear from you. I've left you three messages."

"I was out yesterday evening with girlfriends. You don't have to check up on me, Ryan. I'm a grown-up."

Of course he had to check up on her, but she didn't understand. "I'm glad you're okay."

"Of course I'm okay, Ryan. You need to relax."

But he couldn't relax. He had to know the people he cared about were okay. "So do I know the girlfriends?"

He could hear Leah's exasperated sigh clear from Sacramento. "Oh, Ryan. I'm twenty-four."

"What does that have to do with anything?" His concern about the people he loved had nothing to do with their age. Why didn't she get that?

"But what about this woman you're seeing?" Leah asked. "She has a little boy, right? And you guys have started dating?"

He felt a jolt in his gut. "How did you find out about that?"

"Joe Serrano, of course. You're not the only one who can be a detective. So, tell me about her."

"There's nothing to tell. She's got some trouble and I'm helping her out."

"Is that all?" She sounded disappointed. "I was kind-of hoping she might be changing your mind about staying...."

"No," he said firmly. "We haven't even—I mean—"

Her laugh came through loud and clear. "It's okay, big brother. I know about the birds and bees—don't you remember? You're the one who gave me the talk before my first date. Then you scared my date so badly he wouldn't even hold hands with me."

"I didn't threaten him. I simply explained that every action has a consequence. If he made you cry, I would make him cry."

"As I recall, your words were something like 'if she doesn't tell me you were a perfect gentleman on this date, I will hang you from the goal posts by your jockey shorts.'"

"He got the message."

"Yeah. It's amazing I ever dated anyone, Ryan."

"Is it wrong for a big brother to be protective?"

Another sigh into the phone. "Oh, Ryan, you're hopeless. Maybe this woman can get through to you. No one else ever has."

CAMILLA WAS HARD AT WORK ON HER MAKESHIFT WORKTABLE ON the lawn when the cell phone started ringing again.

If that was Ryan calling one more time to check on her she was going to scream. It was hard to believe she had only known that man for one week. He seemed to think he had to check on her every second of the day. They had agreed that Dennis wasn't going to attack her in broad daylight. That wasn't his style. And Joe was sipping coffee in the kitchen right now. So why couldn't Ryan trust her not to get into any trouble for five minutes?

Maybe because he could tell how incompetent she was. Camilla pushed that thought back. Ryan didn't know her, not really. He couldn't actually see through her public façade to her real self below, even if it felt that way sometimes.

Camilla laid the broken window on the pair of sawhorses, and set the screwdriver on top of it. She looked out at the bay, a peaceful glisten far below her perfect working spot out on the backyard lawn, and started counting to ten. The phone kept ringing.

She heard a boat toot its whistle and watched the gulls circle the wharf. "Eight, Nine, Ten," she muttered, then reached into the back pocket of her jeans for the phone. "What?!"

"Yikes. Sorry." It was Robin's voice. And here she'd gotten herself all revved up to yell at Ryan for nothing.

"Sorry, Robin. I'm in the middle of something. Didn't mean to yell."

"Oh. Okay." Robin said, then paused.

Camilla ran a hand across her forehead to wipe off the sweat. "I didn't mean to bite your head off. I'm just stressed. Are you okay?"

"Yeah, well...."

Something was really bothering her. Usually Robin was so bubbly.

Camilla held the phone more tightly. "Is something wrong? Are you all right?"

"I kind of have a problem."

"Do you need help?"

"Yeah." Robin sighed. "I really need your help."

"Are you hurt?"

"No! Nothing like that. It's a personal problem. And... well, I didn't know if I should ask you for help. I mean, we've only known each other a short time, but.... Well, listen, are you really busy? Could you maybe come by my office for a cup of coffee?"

Camilla felt some warm stirring inside her. A friend. She had always pushed people away too quickly, afraid they would learn the truth about her. Here, at least until she left town, was the first stirrings of an actual friendship.

Camilla looked at the disassembled window. What could it hurt? "Nope," she said. "I'm not busy at all. And I would love a cup of coffee."

Robin gave her directions—down Alvarado Alley past Santos' Market—then they hung up.

She drove down and parked in front of Santos' Market, then walked down the street until she came to a little cobblestone alleyway—no more than a walking path between some little cottages, really. She was standing there, wondering if this was Alvarado Alley, and why the heck these people didn't put up signs on their streets, when she glanced back down Calle Principal toward Santos' and saw Mabel Rutherford coming her way.

She ducked into the alley, hoping Mrs. Rutherford hadn't seen her. She felt like a fool for allowing that woman to control her, but she just wasn't in the mood to face her.

She walked farther down the cobblestone way, passing several tiny storefronts. The first one was a little wine shop with artificial grapes hanging from a wooden sign. Next came a place with seashells and funny-looking mermaid sculptures in its window, then finally a nice-smelling place with african violets in glazed pastel pots and cut flowers in galvanized buckets grouped near its open door. Then the alley dead-ended in front of a storefront with a closed green door.

"Hi."

She turned around and found Robin grinning at her. "I saw you go past." She pointed back up the alley. "I'm the second door on the left. I need to get a better sign."

Camilla nodded, not wanting to admit she'd been too rattled to notice.

"Hey, are you looking at this?" Robin came up to stand beside her in front of the green door.

Camilla noticed a FOR RENT sign in the crooked oval window next to the door.

"I've got a key. Come on in." Robin opened the door and ushered her inside.

The place was even tinier than her cottage, just a single room about four paces across, with a high, raftered ceiling rising to a point. The floors were oak, the walls were freshly painted cream, and it was cute in that Stockdale cottage way, with divided-light windows in the back facing onto a little garden full of roses. "Great garden, isn't it? It belongs to the florist next door. You'd have a great view."

"I would have a great view? What are you talking about?"

Robin ignored her and went into her real estate pitch: "It's cozy—"

"—Just big enough to bump your knee every time you turn around."

"It's got a lot of charm—"

"—Charm is just another word for creaking floors and crooked doors, Robin."

"The last renter loved it—"

"—So much they moved out and it's for rent again."

"Not true. I know her. The acupuncturist who rented here loved the place and hated to leave."

"Why did she? Not enough people wanted to get poked with needles?"

"No, smarty. She got so much business she moved into a big place over on Vincente Alley."

"Well, I can see why. This place isn't big enough to store all her bandaids."

"They don't need bandaids with acupuncture, silly." Robin grinned at her. "You're just playing hard to get. But I know better. It's perfect for you. You do most of your work on a computer, don't you? You could make a little space like this work."

"I don't have a computer. The police seized it as evidence.

179

Why on earth would I want to rent this place? It doesn't have a kitchen, or, well, anything."

"Not to live in, Camilla. For your accounting business."

"My what?"

"Oh come on. Haven't you ever thought of running your own business?

"No." She had thought of it, actually, but never even dared to let it get beyond the daydream stage. Who was she to start her own business? Why would anyone trust her with their accounts? It was way too much for her to dream of.

"Why not?" Robin asked, undeterred. "It wouldn't take much money to get started, and you have an accounting license, don't you?"

"Yeah, I haven't lost my accounting license. Yet. But—"

"Don't you like Pajaro Bay?"

"It's not that." She went over to the back windows and looked out at the flowers.

"Then what? You have a cute house, a nice kid, a really great guy."

"The house is for sale, the kid's not mine, and the guy is leaving town even before I do. And he's a pain in the butt. I don't even like him."

"Well you sure don't look at me like you look at Ryan. Thank goodness for that. I'd have to let you down easy."

Camilla smiled. "Well, Ryan's not exactly easy himself."

"All the better. You can spend the next fifty years figuring him out."

"No."

"He'll stay here and keep us safe, and you'll keep us from going bankrupt. It's perfect."

"You're not listening, Robin."

"One of my best qualities."

Camilla shook her head. "That's debatable."

"Well...." Robin opened one of the back windows, and the

scent of spearmint wafted in on the warm breeze. "See how nice it is? You'd have flowers outside your window all summer, and in the winter, you can light a fire in the little stove." She pointed at a cream-colored wood-burning stove in the corner.

"No central heat is what you really mean," she said.

"It's just big enough for a desk and chairs, and you would be just down the alley from me. Free gourmet coffee anytime."

"Good thing," Camilla said. "Since there isn't enough room in this place for a coffee pot."

Robin laughed. "So you'll do it?"

Camilla shook her head. "Are you crazy? I'm not opening an accounting office in Pajaro Bay. Whatever gave you that idea?"

"We need a local accounting office. Really desperately need one. There's no place within forty miles to get your books done."

"That's not my problem, Robin."

"But you know how to do Quickbooks and taxes and payrolls and all that jazz."

"Well, sure," she said, dismissing the idea of owning her own business, in a darling office, in a charming little village, with the local cop as her personal cabana boy. It was ridiculous. A life like that only happened to other people, not her. "I mean, I have a degree in all that jazz, but—"

"Fabulous. I'll be your first customer. Starting now."

"And my last. I can't do that."

"Why not?"

"Can you imagine what Mabel Rutherford would say if she found out I was handling people's money?" She shuddered at the thought. It would be a constant battle to hold her head up, and soon enough, people would find out she wasn't to be trusted, and then where would she be?

"Who cares about Mabel Rutherford? You'll start with a few clients—like me—and then it'll grow as word spreads about how wonderful you are."

Boy, did Robin have her pegged wrong. "What makes you think I'm so wonderful?"

She smiled. "You have a degree in all that jazz, remember? And Felix Cordova recommends you. That's good enough for me."

"Well it's not good enough for me. I still have to sell the cottage—then what am I supposed to do? Sleep in the garden? And why are you pushing this, anyway? What's it to you what I do for a living?"

Robin looked crestfallen. "Don't you realize what today is?"

She shook her head, then it finally struck her. This wasn't about her at all. She started laughing. "Oh, you poor little thing. April 15th. Tax day. Of course."

"And I need help."

"That's your emergency?"

Robin looked sheepish. "You wouldn't think it was funny if you saw my desk." Then she perked up. "Please come see my desk. Pretty please? I'll buy you pastries and give. And if you can figure out how to make that stupid electronic filing thing stop arguing with me I'll pay you the same amount I was going to pay the tax office over at the county seat."

Robin looked so helpless at that moment that Camilla couldn't stop giggling. "All right. I'll do it. But on one condition."

"What's that?"

"You don't try to rent me any more places in town. I really have to leave once the cottage is sold."

Robin wrinkled her nose. "Can I cross my fingers behind my back before agreeing?"

Camilla stood there tapping her foot. "The filing deadline is in"—she glanced at her watch—"about seven hours."

"I'll do it!"

CHAPTER THIRTEEN

It was the next weekend before Camilla, Ryan and Oliver headed out for their day at the beach. The sun was out and the Mustang's convertible top was down as they drove down toward the beachfront.

"Are we really going to the amusement park this time?" Oliver asked.

"Yes. I promise. Last weekend was just too busy." Camilla didn't want to tell him that this would be the last weekend all three of them would be together in Pajaro Bay. She had almost finished fixing up the cottage for sale. She had gotten the whole second floor repainted, with Ryan and Oliver's help, and once they got the living room done, she'd start on the exterior. It was really coming together.

But they were coming apart. There had been no more so-called accidents, but Ryan was still hanging around the cottage. It had started to feel natural. And now it was going to end. Ryan's two-week notice was almost up. He was going to take off on some cross-country adventure without a backward glance.

And she and Oliver would soon be heading off to whatever

city seemed the best place to start over. She had been studiously avoiding deciding what city that was going to be. As if avoiding it would make it go away.

"Here we are," Ryan said. The Mustang came to a stop in an overcrowded parking lot in front of the most run-down beach shack she'd seen in Pajaro Bay.

"This is the famous Mel's?"

"Yup." They got out and headed up the worn wooden steps to the restaurant.

"They weren't kidding calling it Mel's Fish Shack, were they?"

He laughed, and opened the squeaky screen door for them.

Inside the place was dark and deafeningly loud—with the Beach Boys tunes that blasted from the speakers doing their best to compete with the sound of fifty voices talking at once.

"Let's sit outside," Ryan shouted in her ear.

She nodded. They made their way through the crowd to the ocean-front deck at the back of the restaurant.

When they stepped out into the sunshine again, she took a deep breath and shook her head to clear the din from her ears. "Wow."

He laughed. "Yeah. This isn't Mama Thu's."

She smiled back at him, remembering the quiet deck, the sun setting over the bay, and his arm resting lightly around her shoulder. Was it only a week ago?

Now they were keeping their distance, almost afraid to pursue something that couldn't possibly go anywhere.

They found a small table at the edge of the deck. It was stacked with plates and cups from the last diners who'd just left. "Grab it!" Ryan said.

She and Oliver sat down and in a moment Ryan returned with a plastic tub. They cleared the table, and then wiped it down with some napkins.

"This is fun!" Oliver said.

"Then why is it so hard to get you to clear your plate at home, young man?" she said, but grinned at him.

When the table was clean they all sat there, and Oliver kept pointing at things—a surfboard with a shark bite out of it hanging from the shack's outside wall, a tank full of lazy goldfish just inside the restaurant door, netting decorated with green glass floats that covered the deck's railing.

"Here are your menus," said the green-haired teenaged waitress who finally juggled her way through the crowd to their table. "Hey, Captain Ryan. It's good to see you." She gave him a big grin. "It's been a long time."

He nodded grimly and looked down at the laminated menu.

Camilla put a hand over his, knowing he was still uncomfortable when people pointed out his reclusiveness, and he looked up and smiled at the girl. "Yeah, Nan. Nice to see you, too. And you've got an after-school job. Good for you. Keep those grades up, kid, and you'll be ready for the academy in no time."

The girl smiled happily and disappeared back into the crowd with a promise to come back with three bottomless sodas. "She's planning on becoming a forensic psychologist—at least she was last time I talked to her," Ryan explained.

"You know everyone in town, don't you?" Camilla said.

He nodded. "Just part of my job—my almost ex-job."

"Part of who you are," she said.

"You sound like my little sister," he said grumpily, and buried his face in his menu. It was like he was fighting his true nature. He seemed to truly care about everyone around him, but he seemed at the same time to want to avoid connecting with people. Why? Because he was afraid to get hurt? That was her reason, but how could it be his?

Soon Nan was back with the promised sodas, and they were ordering from among the extensive choices—all variations on deep-fried seafood.

"We'll start with three cups of chowder," Ryan said.

"That's right," Camilla agreed. "We're still doing comparison testing."

That finally brought a smile back to his face.

"Onion rings?" the waitress asked.

They all nodded.

"Calamari?"

"What's that?" Oliver asked.

"deep-fried squid," Camilla explained.

"Ooh, gross!" he said happily.

"That's a yes," Ryan interpreted for the waitress.

Once again, as she had been repeatedly over the last week, Camilla found herself struck with how good Ryan was with Oliver. She felt bad she had accused him of wanting to grill Oliver, when actually he was always very gentle with him, protective. That was the term she kept coming back to with him. Protector. That's what drove him. And yet she resented that part of him. She could never live with such a smothering man. She added that to the list of logical reasons why they didn't talk about where he was going after this weekend.

He cocked his head to one side to listen to something Oliver was telling him. She noticed how one strand of hair kept falling in front of his ear when he did that, and wanted to reach out and tuck it behind his ear.

She did.

He froze when her hand brushed across his cheek.

"Your hair was out of place," she said quietly.

"Thank you."

She looked out at the water.

"So you plan to leave as soon as you sell the cottage," he said suddenly.

She nodded.

"We're leaving?" Oliver said.

"Of course, Oliver," she told him. "You know I said so."

"That was when we first came. Now it's different."

"But nothing's changed," she said.

Oliver looked from Ryan to Camilla, and she wondered if he had read too much into Ryan hanging around. Did he think this was permanent?

She started to put her arms around him but he wiggled away. "Can I go look at the fish tank?" he asked suddenly.

Camilla nodded.

"You had to be honest with him," Ryan said gruffly.

She nodded. "I know. But he's already lost his mom and dad. It's hard to keep uprooting him." Hard for her, too.

"But I'm responsible for you until you leave," he said.

That was always it with him. He was responsible. He had to protect them.

He frowned. "Even if I haven't done a great job so far."

"I don't know about that. We're still alive, aren't we."

He didn't look satisfied with that.

"You do a good job of protecting people, Ryan."

"Not good enough." He sounded so bitter.

"But Sara's death wasn't your fault, either."

"Of course it was my fault." He looked out at the water, and she watched his profile. His jaw clenched and unclenched repeatedly. "I misjudged how the perp would react."

"That doesn't make it your fault. You're not psychic, Ryan. You're a human being."

He dismissed that with a shake of his head. "I misjudged the danger." He shook his head again, vehemently. "You're going to tell me like everyone else that it wasn't my fault. That she might have died even if I hadn't walked with her to the store. But she was my responsibility. If I'd handled it right in the first place, Sara would be alive."

"That doesn't make sense, Ryan. You can't blame yourself for what someone else did."

"Let's change the subject."

"Okay." How could he think he was responsible for something no one could have predicted?

When the plates piled high with calamari and onion rings arrived, Ryan waved to Oliver and he came back to the table to eat.

The chowder was extra-thick, creamy, and just as artery-clogging as Ryan had promised. Camilla took a big bite of an onion ring. "Ooh, my breath is going to smell awful after this."

Ryan leaned toward her. "Let's see." His lips brushed across hers, and she was startled by his public display.

"Ryan!"

"Hey!" Oliver said.

"It's okay, kid. Trust me. I'm a professional."

Oliver shrugged and bent over his chowder. They all ate in silence for a while, and Camilla wondered how attached Oliver was getting to Ryan. She could handle it (yeah, right), but he was just a child, a child who had lost so much already.

When he finished eating, he asked to be excused again. "Don't eat so slow. We have to go on the rides." He went over to the deck rail to look out at the bay, probably watching the Ferris wheel go around.

"He must be pretty confused about what's happening," Ryan said, reading her mind.

"I think it's confusing for all of us," she said.

"Yeah. Listen, Camilla. I don't know what you're planning to do once you sell the cottage."

"Yeah?" she said, watching his face.

"Well," he said hesitantly. "I know you plan to leave town."

"I have to. I have to make a new start. Somewhere fresh."

"Somewhere fresh." He said it quietly. "Somewhere with no past to tie you down."

"Yeah?"

"Well, I'm going to be heading out, too. And there's room in the car for both of you to come along."

She shook her head.

She was being pulled in all these directions. First Robin planting the idea of opening her own business here, and now Ryan saying she could run away with him. But what did she want? What was best for her and Oliver?

"It's too soon to decide, of course," he said. "But, I'm just sayin'..."

"Let's keep it open," she said, not wanting him to say any more, though her heart had started thumping in her chest at the tentative promise in his voice. "Let's see what happens when the cottage is sold."

He nodded. "Yeah. My place hasn't sold, either. So I'll be in town for a couple more weeks, too."

She looked down at her hands, realized they had started to shake. He was saying what she had been thinking—hoping—even dreaming. "Maybe."

He leaned in closer. "We'll leave it open. See where we go from here."

His lips met hers, and this time she opened her mouth to the kiss, felt the taste of him again. After keeping a distance from him for days, it felt so good to sense his warmth against her lips, the scent of him, the taste of him. An alarm buzzed in her ears, and they broke apart.

"Gee, Ryan, you make bells ring when you kiss me."

But he didn't smile. "Knight," he said into the phone. He listened, then said, "On my way, let Serrano know and alert coast guard we might need them."

He stood up, threw some bills on the table. "Gotta go."

"Wait—"

"Missing kids at the amusement park. Gotta go." He took off at a run.

Camilla rounded up Oliver and they headed out.

"Are we going to the rides now?" he said anxiously. "You're not backing out again, are you?"

"I'm not backing out," she said absently. "We'll go to the amusement park."

They headed that way, but all the time she was looking for a tall man in a khaki uniform.

"THERE HE IS!" OLIVER POINTED OUT TO THE SAND, WHERE RYAN'S uniform could be spotted in the center of a group of onlookers.

They headed that way. As they got closer she could see him more clearly. He stood out, not only because of his height and the uniform, but because of his expression, his stance, everything about him. This was a different Ryan than she'd seen around the cottage all week. This was the guy you wanted in a crisis. His eyes looked like lasers, scanning the crowd, taking in every detail, focused, intense. She remembered the annoyance she'd felt at his overprotectiveness toward her and Oliver, and now saw its flip side, the sense of personal responsibility he carried for everyone in his charge. She realized she needed to cut him some slack. This was who he was, and she should try not to chafe so much under the weight of his smothering. At least for the short time they had left together.

His eyes passed over her, noting she was there, but not acknowledging her on the edge of the crowd.

At the center of the group, where he stood, a woman was babbling in Spanish, hysterical. He listened to her calmly, all the while those eyes watching, assessing everything going on around them. She could see the tension in his body, feel even from ten feet away how responsible he felt for some missing kids he'd never even met. If her child were missing, this is the guy she'd want looking for him. She pulled Oliver a little closer. She felt a sense of pride in watching him, though he wasn't her man. He and she were—what, exactly? They couldn't ever be a couple, not really, not with the barriers between them.

Him being a cop, her being a criminal's daughter. Him being so honest, and her carrying secrets deep inside her that he couldn't ever understand. Still, she felt that foolish pride in "her man," and watched him as he did the work he was obviously born to do.

"What candy?" he said suddenly, interrupting the mother in mid-sentence. That laser gaze focused sharply back on the crying woman. He repeated the question in Spanish.

She said something else to him, and he smiled at her gently. Spoke to her reassuringly in Spanish, patted her arm.

He strode off through the crowd as if they didn't exist, and they parted to let him through.

The crowd followed him, but his long strides quickly outdistanced them.

Camilla, still keeping Oliver close, stood at the rail separating the wooden boardwalk from the beach itself, and watched him from a distance.

He went straight up to a concessions booth, spoke to the attendant, nodded, then took off at a run down the main boardwalk, through all the rides. She lost sight of him when he ducked in between two of the amusement park rides a hundred feet away.

He was gone a few minutes, and it seemed the crowd watching held their breath.

Then he came into view with two little kids, no more than five years old, each clutching a huge wand of cotton candy.

She watched as he lifted them up onto his shoulders and came striding back. As they got closer she could see their little faces were completely smeared with sugar, and he was joking with them, making them smile.

Just then Joe Serrano pulled up next to her in a lifeguard Jeep. "Where's Ryan?"

She pointed.

The mother of the children came running when she saw the

kids, and he let them down when they met, stepping back as she smothered them with hugs and kisses.

The crowd still watching burst into applause.

Ryan saw Joe's Jeep alongside Camilla and Oliver, and came over.

"False alarm?" Joe asked.

Ryan shook his head. "She told them they couldn't have any cotton candy because it would rot their teeth, and then they disappeared."

"So you realized they were hiding from her?" Camilla said.

He nodded. "They're perfectly fine. Just very sticky."

"Gracias a dios," Joe said.

"That's what their mom said," Ryan said. "Will you call in the all-clear?"

"Sure, Captain. And congrats."

Ryan shrugged it off and turned to Camilla and Oliver. "I'm going to have to go in and write up the report. Sorry. It's my job."

"And you're good at your job."

He shook his head. "Not always. I got lucky."

"No. You're good. You figure things out more quickly than most people do." She stood in front of him there on the sand, gazing up at him. She couldn't get past that silly pride in him, and found it odd how offhand he was about what he'd just accomplished. She had never been this close to a cop before, and she'd never really thought about the endless stream of daily successes and failures they must go through, with people's welfare—their very lives—in the hands of very mortal and flawed men and women just doing their best. "I'm proud of you," she said tentatively.

He seemed startled. "Proud?" Again he seemed to shrug it off, like being praised made him uncomfortable. "It's nothing."

She wondered if he really believed that, and if that was why he was quitting. What he'd just done had saved that family hours of grief—at the least—and he brushed it off as nothing.

"What's wrong?" he asked. Her face must have gone from jubilant to dismayed in an instant.

"Are you sure you want to quit this job?"

He stepped back. "Yes," he said shortly. "Of course."

So she just nodded up at him. "Just asking. So Oliver and I are gonna go on all the rides while you write up your report."

"It's about time!" Oliver said. "First the roller coaster!"

"Whoa, young man," she said. "After that big lunch I think we'll start with something tamer and work our way up to the thrill rides after we've had a chance to digest everything."

Ryan gave her a thin smile. "Have fun." He walked away and was soon lost in the crowd.

She let Oliver lead her over to the rides.

JOE MET HIM AT THE STATION WHEN HE WAS STILL FINISHING UP HIS report.

Ryan looked up from the computer screen. "How's the Dennis research going?"

Joe threw his hat on the hat rack and went to his desk.

He returned with a stack of papers. "Quite a few possibles came in yesterday. I've been trying to eliminate 'em as quickly as possible—some have been apprehended, some don't match the description. But there's at least one bad one."

Ryan put in the last period on his report on the missing kids and turned away from the computer. "Bad one?"

"Yeah." Joe shuffled the papers while Ryan went over to the whiteboard and took out a pen.

"First one is in L.A. The timeline doesn't fit, but parents of a college coed reported she'd been ripped off by a con man who promised to marry her. The description's perfect, the guy's name was Dennis Harrison, but the crime was reported long before the pattern starts."

Ryan wrote it on the board under L.A. with a big question mark. "I'd hate to think there are two different Dennis H's running around California pulling this garbage. That's going to be hard to track." He took the copy of the complaint Joe handed him, read it quickly. "No wonder her dad was mad. He's an attorney, and saw right through the guy. I want to talk to the girl."

"I couldn't find any listing of the girl. Her name's Dora Favre."

Ryan wrote it on the board.

"But I've got a call in to the family. We'll see if there's any chance it's a match."

"Sounds like you've made some progress."

"Yeah. But the next one is the bad one."

"A death?"

"Yup. Accidental, of course."

Ryan looked at the board and shook his head. He had to solve this. "This isn't going to happen again. It stops here." This was his last weekend on the job. And Camilla kept talking about leaving town. He couldn't let her and Oliver leave until they solved this.

He turned back to Joe, who was looking at him quizzically. "Just thinking," he told him. "So what's the dead girl's story?"

"Not a girl."

Joe handed him a printout.

Ryan took it and examined it: "You have got to be kidding me. She drowned in a bathtub and nobody questioned it?" This was getting frustrating.

"They did an autopsy. She dropped a hairdryer into the tub while taking a bath and it shorted out."

"Right. This guy is screwing with the system now." He wanted to break something. This guy thought he could get away with anything. He was making a game out of killing innocent women.

"Who was she?" Joe gave him the report: she'd been a nurse, single woman, 43 years old, honored for her work with terminally ill children. "Not the kind of woman to make a stupid mistake like that." He read the rest of the report, read between the lines: a caring woman who deserved happiness after an early failed marriage. Ripped off and murdered—she deserved justice. He had to get it for her.

"There's a picture for the board—and this is a find," added Joe. "We got a picture of the perp."

Ryan grabbed it from him. "Why didn't you say so? That's huge."

A grainy engagement photo had been printed in the Fresno paper. "Worthless," he said after a minute staring at it.

"It might help some?" Joe said.

Ryan shook his head. The nurse, Shirley Worth, gazed happily out of the photo. She had a fine-boned face, with a bit of gray hair showing. Next to her stood Dennis "Hastings." His head was turned sideways to face the woman, making him look like the adoring fiancé he was pretending to be, and not coincidentally making identifying him from the picture nearly impossible. "Look how he posed in the picture."

"So?"

"You don't see his face clearly. He's essentially facing away from the camera. We can't get much more than height and coloring from this—and we already have that from Camilla. He's being careful. The woman probably insisted on the picture, and this was his way of making sure he wasn't identified from it."

"You think he's that smart?"

"Oh yeah. He's that smart. Look at the different women he's fooled. His wife was a teacher. Then there was an Olympic team coach. Then a nurse. Then an accountant. These aren't stupid women. They aren't gullible. They're living successful lives on their own. But he's getting under their skin somehow. He's putting them at ease. He's offering them love, and they don't notice it's a con until he's ripped them off."

"But why the murders?"

Ryan shrugged. "Maybe he's just afraid of being caught. He doesn't want anyone pressing charges against him. He's figured out the perfect way to keep them from testifying. And he's clever. He's making sure no signs point to him. Every one of these deaths was investigated, and every one was ruled an accident." He looked at the board again. "All in different jurisdictions...."

"Why?"

"Why different jurisdictions? So no one puts it together. If he stayed in one city—even one as large as L.A., the pattern would raise red flags. But if he's moving from place to place, and never commits the same crimes twice in the same jurisdiction—"

"—no one realizes he's doing it."

"Exactly. Until us. We're going to nail him. This SOB is good. Really good. I find it hard to believe there are only five victims. He must have been doing this for years—maybe long before Oliver was born, before he married his wife."

"But all those murders, wouldn't the pattern be found out before now?"

"Sometimes criminals get away with it for years before they're finally caught." He pushed thoughts of Sara's killer—a three-time loser wasted on meth—out of his mind. No time to think of that failure. He had to protect Camilla. "Maybe—" Ryan thought about it, and Joe watched him silently until he continued, "—maybe he wasn't always killing. We've got to widen the search. Find out where he was before this. I want you to get more background on Joyce Ashford. Find out where they married. We've got to go back farther on this guy."

Joe worked on the computer for a while. Ryan kept going over the papers, knowing he was missing something. He had to figure this out. He was running out of time. The perp was going to make another try for Camilla and Oliver. He just knew it.

"No marriage record in the state of California for a Joyce Ashford."

Ryan pulled out the file on Oliver's mother. "The obituary says she was born in Milwaukee, Wisconsin. See if you can find out if they married there."

"Bingo!" Joe said shortly after that. He read off the marriage info—Dennis Henning and Joyce Ashford. Milwaukee, Wisconsin. "I know what's next," Joe said. "Search for matching crimes in Wisconsin."

Ryan paced the floor while Joe worked.

"Con artist named Dennis Henning had been arrested in a number of petty cons, but they stopped about nine years ago." He double-checked. "That's around the time he got married."

"And the time he moved to California. So we've got a lead on him." He asked the next question, dreading the answer. "How many of those victims are dead, can you figure it out?"

"Here's the weird thing," Joe said.

Ryan looked up.

Joe looked excited. "He didn't kill 'em."

"None of them?"

"None of the victims back East. None of them are dead, far as I can tell. I'm going to have to do more research, but at least the last three I've checked appear to be alive. And they testified against him and he went to jail several times, plea-bargained out, served short sentences. The usual pattern for a petty crook. Nothing happened to the victims."

"He didn't want to go to jail after he was married?" Ryan muttered. "But then why would he kill his wife and go after his son?"

"Maybe he went nuts," Joe offered.

"But there's no pattern to this."

"Maybe it's just random," Joe said.

"Nothing's random. There's always a pattern. Even insane people have patterns—quirks, habits, obsessions, trademarks. In fact, the more insane, the more consistent the m.o. tends to be. It's part of the obsessiveness of the criminal."

"But what's the pattern here? Why would Dennis Henning be a petty con man for years, then get married and have a kid, and start killing his victims—starting with his wife and the mother of his son?"

Ryan looked at the white board with its sea of red marker scribbles.

"I don't know. I really don't know."

CHAPTER FOURTEEN

C AMILLA'S M ONDAY MORNING STARTED WITH A MESSAGE ON HER cell from Robin. She stopped by the real estate office after dropping Oliver at school.

"Hey, Camilla. Thanks for coming."

"Hey, Robin." Camilla plopped down into the chair in Robin's office. "What's up?"

Robin handed her a mug of steaming coffee (two sugars, a dash of cinnamon), and Camilla sipped it. "I could get used to this." She had gotten used to it. They had been meeting for coffee practically every day.

"Yeah, well...." Robin sat back down at her desk and began shuffling papers around.

"What's the matter? Don't tell me your check to the IRS bounced." She laughed.

Robin shook her head. "I got an offer on the Honeymoon Cottage."

"What?" She set down her coffee mug. "That's great." She didn't feel like it was great, though. She was really torn. One part of her was really going to miss Pajaro Bay. Miss the guy who felt like he belonged with the house. With her.

"Wow," she said. It was really sinking in. She was going to be free of this—free of Dennis's hold on her; free of debt; free of the drag of her reputation following her around town. She could really go away and start over now.

"Yeah, well," Robin said. "I need to get in touch with your real estate agent. Go over the details." She sounded really unhappy about it.

"It's good news, Robin. Thank you for finding a buyer."

"Well, you know, they've only seen the exterior, and they peeked in the windows while you were gone on Saturday afternoon. I'd be glad to put them off for a while if you want me to—like maybe until sometime next year." She laughed, but it wasn't a happy sound.

Camilla shook her head. "No, I'm ready to sell. I'm ready to move on."

"I was really hoping it would work out differently."

"I know." She looked at Robin. "Part of me was, too. But it's got to be this way. I want to sell the place—I have to sell the place. It's not an option. It's what I need to do to get on with my life."

"And what about Ryan?"

She felt tears behind her eyelids and blinked them back. "Ryan?" she said cheerfully. "He's cute and all, but it wasn't going to happen between us."

"It wasn't?"

She shook her head. "Nah." Those stupid tears pushed forward, trying to get out. She turned away from Robin for a minute and sipped her coffee until she got herself under control. "He's not looking for anything, and neither am I. Just one of those things."

Robin looked at her for a good long while, then just said, "all right, Camilla. If that's the way you want it. What's your agent's number?"

She pulled out the flyer she'd kept stuffed in her purse and rattled off the number.

"I'm sorry, Camilla."

"Why?"

"I feel like I'm doing something wrong getting an offer on your place. Maybe I can put it off for a while."

"No. In this market who knows how long it'll be 'til another offer comes along. Go ahead."

"I'm going to miss you."

"We just met a couple of weeks ago."

She looked hurt. "I don't make friends that easily, Camilla. I thought you were one of those people I'd really become close friends with." She added, trying to make it light, "Maybe even tell you the gruesome details about my divorce. I guess not."

She realized she'd really hurt Robin. But Robin couldn't really be her friend—not if she knew everything about her. So she just put her hand out to her across the desk. "I'm sorry, Robin. I thought that about you, too. We could have been buds. But I've got to go away. It's what has to happen to get my life together."

Robin pulled her hand away. "I know. I'm glad I could find you a buyer. See ya around, soul mate."

Camilla left her coffee mug on the desk and walked out, smiling half-heartedly at Robin when she closed the door.

She felt rotten. She'd closed off a friendship before it could even get started. She'd done that before. That was why she had no one to turn to when everything fell apart. But what could she do? She had to leave.

"OOH, I JUST HATE THAT WOMAN," CAMILLA SAID SOFTLY AS SHE hung up the phone that evening. Oliver was asleep on his air mattress in the living room, and she and Ryan were sitting at the kitchen table, enjoying a cup of cocoa before she went to bed.

"What woman?"

"That Thea Paris. My real estate agent. She agreed to meet

Robin and me here tomorrow morning but she's being a real creep about it. She's always such a snot."

Ryan laughed. "A creep and a snot. You sound like a little kid."

She made a face at him. "I don't care. She makes me feel like a little kid with her perfect hair and perfect wardrobe and her so-superior attitude. When I told her about the sale, she acted like she was all offended, just because she didn't come up with the buyer herself."

"Maybe she's mad because she has to split the commission with Robin."

"No. I think she just hates me." She brushed her unruly curls self-consciously. "Do you think I should get my hair straightened?"

"What are you talking about?"

"I don't know. Thea has the best hair. Perfectly straight black hair to her waist. Would you think I'd look better like that?"

He laughed. "You? With straight black hair?"

"Not black. But straight instead of curly. And maybe makeup to cover my freckles...." She looked at him, feeling as awkward as judgmental people always made her feel. "I'm not exactly elegant-looking."

He laughed again. "Thank God for that. You're pretty perfect just the way you are, Camilla."

The way he looked at her when he said it made a thrill go down her spine, and she felt herself start to blush.

He frowned. "I—I don't suppose...?"

She looked down at her hands, clasped around her mug of cocoa. "Suppose what?"

"You've thought about what I said?"

She kept her eyes on her hands. The knuckles were white from gripping the cup. Ryan was saying exactly what she wanted him to say, but it was wrong.

"It wouldn't last," she said softly, still looking at the cup.

"Why?"

"Because—you don't know anything about me."

"That's why we could spend more time together. To find out if it would last. That's what dating's for."

Not for her it wasn't. Dating was an ordeal of her pretending to be Camilla Stewart, bright, college-educated accountant for a high-tech firm; good, law-abiding person with no skeletons in her closet, or relatives in San Quentin. Dating was a strain. And she couldn't take care of Oliver, or get on with her own life, under that strain.

So she shook her head at the mug of cocoa.

The kitchen chair creaked as Ryan leaned back in it. "I see."

"There's still a 30-day escrow until I get the money."

He waved a hand. "So you're saying I have thirty days to change your mind."

That wasn't what she was saying at all, but the thought of leaving him was suddenly too much for her to take.

She stood up and took her mug over to the sink to dump it.

He was behind her, resting those big hands on her shoulders. "So there's a chance?"

No, she thought. Not a chance in Hades she was going to open her heart to him when he'd reject her once he realized what a façade she'd created to cover her true self. No. No chance at all.

She turned to face him and kissed him, hard. Her mouth opened and his matched hers, letting her stand on tiptoes to explore the surprising softness of him while her hands reached up to brush the rough stubble on his face.

They came up for air, and he whispered into her curls, "I'll take that as a yes."

His mouth found hers again, hungry, claiming her, and she let go, let all the doubts go, not wanting to lose this moment, ignoring what would come after she came back down to earth. When the kiss ended she rested her head against his chest, felt his heart pounding as hard as her own was.

"Can you stay in town until the escrow closes?" she whispered.

"Of course I will.

"And then where will we go?"

"Wherever the road takes us."

She felt her breath catch in her throat. She wasn't running alone any more. She could run with him. They could do this together.

She glanced out toward the living room, where Oliver slept. She walked over to the kitchen doorway and watched the boy sleep. She stood there for a long time, listening to his steady breathing.

It was right to run away. Wasn't it? To run away from their work, their family, their friends. Run away from everything they didn't want to face.

Somewhere in the back of her mind she felt the big doubt looming. This would end badly. It had to. Anything built on a lie would collapse eventually.

But that was for tomorrow, or the next day, or a year from now. For now, she could pretend that this man, this man so far out of her league, was hers. And she was his.

She turned back to the kitchen, where Ryan stood, the yearning in his eyes making all other doubts disappear from her mind.

She took him by the hand. "We'll go with you, Ryan. We'll go as far as the road takes us."

RYAN CAME INTO THE KITCHEN WHISTLING THE NEXT MORNING. "I feel like whistling myself," she said to him, and he grinned in response.

He gave her a quick peck on the cheek and she blushed and

pulled away, since Oliver was sitting at the kitchen table watching them.

She poured Oliver's cereal with hands that shook. She was exhausted, running on pure adrenalin. They'd stayed up all night making plans, dreaming of this wild, unfettered future together.

This was really happening. Everything she'd hoped for was coming true—and more.

She had come to town planning to sell the cottage, pay off Mr. Cordova for Dennis's theft, and move on somewhere new with a clean slate.

She had never dreamed she'd find a man to share this new adventure with her.

He sat down at the table next to Oliver and ruffled the boy's hair. "How's it going this morning, kid?"

Oliver shrugged. "Okay, I guess."

She frowned. She wondered if Oliver had overheard any of her conversation with Ryan last night. She didn't want to upset his world any more than it already was, but this was a good thing. For him and for her. For all of them.

She sat down opposite her two boys and picked up the milk. She poured some over the boy's cereal. "Oliver?"

He looked up with such a wounded expression she wondered if he knew what she was going to say.

"I told you last night that someone decided to buy the cottage, right?"

He nodded. Slumped his shoulders and took a spoonful of cereal.

"So, that means we can move to a new town now, just like I've been telling you."

He nodded to his cereal bowl.

"But—" How could she tell him this? "We're going to move on with Ryan."

Oliver looked up with wide eyes.

"What do you think about that, buddy?" said Ryan. "We'll head cross-country in the '66 Mustang, and see where the wind takes us."

"Good idea. We've been here too long," Oliver said quietly.

"It's only a couple of weeks, kiddo."

"Yeah, but Camilla's restless. I know how it is. Gotta keep on the move, daddy says."

Ryan's eyes narrowed in on the mumbling boy. "He does?"

"Yup," Oliver said. "Don't put down roots. Don't let anybody get too close. Don't ever let anybody catch up to you."

Camilla set the milk down on the table. She'd heard those words before. Throughout her own childhood. "We have to make a fresh start where no one knows us," she said quietly.

"Yup. You sound just like daddy." Then he looked up at Camilla, and the expression on his face broke her heart. He was smiling, but his eyes had a resigned look in them, a look far-too old for his eight years. "It's time to go. We were getting to like it here too much."

She leaned toward him. "What do you mean, like it too much?"

He smiled brightly with the sad eyes boring into her. "Like daddy always says, it's dangerous to get too comfortable. Got to keep on the move. Don't let the past catch up to you." He looked down at his cereal again. "Time to move."

He got up from the table, and she stood up to give him a hug. He pulled away from her before she could get her arms around him.

"It's okay, Camilla. We gotta keep runnin'. They can't catch ya if they can't find ya. I'm gonna pack. I'll be ready in ten minutes." He ran out of the room.

"You don't have to do that now," she called after him. "We aren't moving until the escrow closes—we haven't even signed the papers yet."

Ryan said something to her about how Oliver would come around if they gave him time, but she only half-heard him. She was thinking hard. Everything Oliver said was exactly what she knew to be true. They couldn't stay. If they did, the past would catch up to her. If they did, people would find out she wasn't who she claimed to be. Ryan would reject her, and she just couldn't take that rejection.

But that was all a lie. It was the lie of the con man. The lie of her father. The lie she'd lived with all her life, and was now teaching to Oliver. When you're scared, run away. When things get tough, run away. When you have to face criticism, or judgment, or blame, run away.

She had spent her entire life running away, and now she was running again.

No more. She had to end it now. Not in thirty days when the escrow closed. Now. Before she got in any deeper. Before she fell for the fairy tale. Before she believed things would work.

She looked up at Ryan. He was staring at her, seeing something of what she was thinking transparent on her face. But his look was uncomprehending, lost. How had she ever thought he was cold? The look of longing, of fear on his face was so like Oliver's it broke her heart.

"We have to talk, Ryan."

He froze, coffee mug in hand. "Babe, that is not the thing to say to a guy after a night like last night." He gave it a brave smile, but it quickly faded when she didn't laugh.

She looked away from him, trying to think. Oliver was right. She sank down into the chair.

"Hey, hon." He reached across the table to take her hand but she jerked away.

"What's wrong?"

"We can't go with you." The words came out so quietly she wasn't sure he'd heard them until he reacted.

"What do you mean?" Those heartbreaking blue eyes were making this impossible so she looked away from him again. He tried to make a joke of it: "We have a thirty-day escrow, babe. I've still got twenty-nine days to go—and nights."

"No."

"I don't understand—last night...."

She couldn't speak.

"Camilla, please—"

She shook her head. She couldn't say anything.

She looked away, toward the living room where Oliver bent over his backpack. His shoulders were hunched and his expression was shuttered, closed in, retreating to some place inside where he didn't have to think or feel or deal with another loss.

It was that expression that made her sure she was right. She couldn't run, not for Oliver's sake, and not for hers.

She closed her eyes, forced back the tears.

When she opened her eyes again, Ryan was standing there, the most lost and wounded she'd ever seen him. She wanted to love him. To believe he was her one true partner like in some fairy tale.

But it was a lie. Their love was a lie. And she could not lie to herself any more.

"You're dumping me?" He looked stricken, but anger was starting to seep in behind the hurt, and his voice rose. "Why? What did I do?"

"Nothing."

"I don't get it. We said so much last night—Is that it? Is it too fast for you?"

"No. It's not that. It's the whole plan. Don't you see? I can't run. Didn't you hear what Oliver said?"

"He's just a kid. He'll understand."

"He has to learn not to run away. I won't have him hurt again."

"You're the one hurting him, Camilla, not me."

My name isn't even Camilla, she wanted to say, but there was no point. He knew nothing about her. She'd let him believe something that wasn't true, let him fall for the illusion she'd created for him, and now it was over.

He was furious now, and the words came pouring out of him, fast and angry. "You're not making any sense! You tell me you love me and then dump me? Was it a game?" He pushed a chair across the linoleum floor with a screech that hurt her ears.

She put her head in her hands. "I'm not explaining it well."

"No, you're explaining it perfectly. You have been playing with me, pretending to care."

"No, Ryan. That's not it. I wasn't pretending that. That wasn't a lie."

That laser-sharp mind of his caught the implication. "Then what was the lie?"

She shook her head. "You don't know anything about me, about my life. You don't understand."

"How can I understand if you won't talk to me."

"There's nothing to talk about, Ryan. You don't know me at all."

"I guess I don't."

He headed for the front door.

The creak of the old wooden door closing wasn't cute, or melodramatic. It was a rusty pair of iron hinges shutting Ryan out of her life.

She found she was standing in the kitchen of the Honeymoon Cottage clutching a box of cereal, with Oliver staring at her in shock, and her soul mate walking out of her life forever.

WHEN RYAN BLEW INTO WORK, JOE HAD THE COAST GUARD RADIO station turned up loud and he was bent over the radio, listening.

"Why aren't you at the Honeymoon Cottage?"

"Switched schedule. There's a new guy on duty today, so I had him take the morning shift." Joe turned back to the radio.

"What's happening?" He put his hat on the rack and came over to listen.

"Rescue out by the lighthouse," Joe explained. "All Coast Guard personnel involved."

Ryan glanced out the window at the street. The fog was in, but that was normal. There hadn't been any bad weather for days. "I thought the seas have been calm," he said. "Is it a fisherman?"

Joe shook his head. "Kids partying at the lighthouse island, it sounds like. Someone got swept off the rocks."

"Again?"

"Yeah. That place sits out there abandoned and those kids think it's party central. They forget the lighthouse was put there a hundred years ago because the waters out there in the middle of the bay are dangerous."

Joe turned the radio down a notch. "Sounds like they have it under control. The kid just got picked out of the water." He turned to Ryan. "He's waterlogged but alive—gracias a Dios." He stared. "What happened to you?"

"Nothing." Ryan went over and plopped into his desk chair. Nothing but his heart getting stomped on by a two-faced woman. No. He just couldn't believe all his instincts about her were wrong. She was a good person. But for some reason, she didn't want him.

"Are you all right, Ryan?"

Joe was still staring.

"Fine. I've got to finish these last reports so I can go." His desk was covered with papers. "What's all this?"

"More reports. One from Salinas—the detective who took the statement from Melissa Everette faxed us his notes. One from L.A.—background on the girl whose parents reported the fraud. She was killed in a boat explosion."

Ryan hit his fist on his desk. Another death.

He looked up at Joe. "Sorry."

"I didn't find anything useful in the reports. But then again,

I'm not Bloodhound Knight." Joe came across the room to stand over him. "Are you sure you're okay?"

Ryan looked up at him. "I'm fine." At Joe's skeptical expression he explained, "Camilla dumped me."

Joe looked stricken. "Oh, no. I really thought—"

"I don't see why it matters so much to you," he snapped. "I knew we were both leaving town when I met her."

"Oh," Joe said. "It just seemed you both needed a new start, and maybe if you and she got together you'd...." Joe let it peter out.

"What? If we got together we'd live happily ever after, with her sticking around and me being the cheerful cop on the local beat, and everything would be perfect. Well, it's not going to happen!"

Joe looked at him, shocked. No wonder. He'd never said anything like that to anyone in this town. He'd never opened up to anyone.

Except Camilla. Except the one person who told him from the start she was leaving. Who told him there was no future for them. Why hadn't he listened to her?

"I'm sorry, Ryan."

Ryan shrugged. "Sorry about yelling. I'm sure we've been the main topic at Santos' checkout line, but it's not going to happen." He shuffled the papers around on his desk, stacking them up into piles by city.

"So, how does that affect—"

"The case?"

"Yes. Are you still going to—"

"—Work on it? Of course." He ran a hand through his hair.

"But isn't this your last day?"

Was it? He'd called his boss over the weekend, told him he'd be willing to stick around for another thirty days. But now what? "We have to resolve this, one way or another. My personal feelings don't have anything to do with that. There's still a possible killer loose, possibly in our town, and we're going to catch him."

He looked at the now-neat stacks on his desk. Everything neat, and tidy, and professional. The way he'd wanted to leave the job. And he had to go and mess it up. He'd blown it. Now the woman he lov—he stopped himself. Camilla and Oliver were leaving. Soon. And if he didn't catch Dennis before they left, they'd be in danger for the rest of their lives.

With another shake of his head he brought himself around to the problem in front of him. No more emotions. Emotions messed with his head, made him lose objectivity. Had he been wrong about this case all along? What had he missed?

He cleared his throat. "All right, Joe. Give me the rundown on what's we've got here."

Joe went over it, pointing out the places where they were still waiting on information, going over his notes on autopsy reports and fraud investigations in the cities they'd found. Joe was learning quickly. He had gone from the greenest rookie to a good cop practically overnight. But Ryan still knew Joe didn't have the real-life experience to handle everything that might come his way. But he couldn't take care of him forever. Joe would learn after he was gone. He had to.

Joe was still talking, now about a couple of other cities with possibles.

"How possible?" Ryan asked.

Joe went through the reports. Scams, women ripped off. But none of it struck Ryan as being right for Dennis. "We'll keep them in a separate file for now. Maybe they'll tie in later." Later. He had to figure this thing out soon. "There has to be something here I'm missing. Something different. So far everything is too perfect."

"Well, the boat accident in L.A. is different."

Ryan perked up. "In what way?"

Joe grabbed the page. "The investigators didn't fully accept the accident idea. They thought—but couldn't prove—that someone might have tampered with the boat."

"Aha. That is different."

"Yeah. It's the first time someone didn't immediately buy the accident theory."

He handed Ryan the paper. "But they found nothing conclusive.

Ryan read the report. "The boat was far out in the water. No witnesses. And the body was never recovered, so they couldn't do an autopsy—there might have been signs of foul play this time, so he had to explain her disappearance with a staged accident. This guy is really bright."

"Bright?"

"Yeah. Just because he's an amoral psycho doesn't mean he's not smart. That's the problem. Criminals are usually stupid, with poor self-control. They get into a bar fight while on parole because somebody looks at 'em sideways. They're criminals because they don't have the common sense to do anything better."

"But not this guy."

Ryan shook his head. "This guy is smart, and comes up with clever ways to get what he wants. Without leaving any traces behind."

"They did find a partial fingerprint on the boat engine. Let's see—" Joe pulled out another page. "Right pinky. Smudged. Not exactly helpful."

"Yeah, but now when we catch Dennis we might have proof of murder."

Joe shrugged. "But we're not any closer to finding where Dennis is hiding. And I don't see how we're going to find him."

"Yeah. It won't do us any good if we don't catch the SOB." Ryan looked it all over. Maybe he was tired. Maybe he was depressed. But he just couldn't see a pattern in the info. Nothing jumped out at him.

He rubbed his hand over his eyes. There had to be a pattern there, but he wasn't seeing it.

"I really thought you two were a good match," Joe mumbled.

Joe was back at his desk, writing a report on the computer. Ryan watched him. "Why did you think that? I mean, she's cute and all, but I don't know...."

"She stands up to you. She tells you off when you need it. She brings you out of your shell. And she's a good mother to that boy. Oliver told Marisol that Camilla was a good second mom. Those were his words for her. A good second mom, since his first one had to go away. Sounds like a good woman to me."

He shrugged. "She is a good woman. A good person. She just decided she didn't want to be with me."

"Is that what she said? She doesn't want to be with you?"

"Not exactly. We just couldn't agree on things."

"Like what exactly? You left the cap off the toothpaste, or what?"

"No." He swiveled his chair away from Joe and glared out the window at Calle Principal. "She says she's staying in town after we already agreed to leave together."

Ryan saw Robin Brenham walking down the street outside. She got into her blue hybrid import. She must be heading out to Camilla's to sign the papers. The Honeymoon Cottage was sold. So why did she think she had to stay?

He turned away. This wasn't getting him anywhere.

"It doesn't sound like she dumped you. It sounds like you're disagreeing on geography."

"There's more to it than that." But what? She had started to say something, but then he'd said something wrong, as usual, and she just got exasperated with him. Why? Because he wanted to keep her safe? She always got mad at him when he said he would protect her. But wasn't that what a man was supposed to do?

"Flowers," said Joe. "That and an abject apology always works wonders. Trust an old married man."

The phone rang. Saved by the bell. "Get it, Serrano."

Joe shrugged and picked up the phone.

"Pajaro Bay sheriff's office. Deputy Serrano speaking." Joe's shoulders slumped and he put his head down. He sighed loudly in a long-suffering way that gave away the caller's identity.

"Yes, I see that, sir. I see. Another seven chickens."

Ryan stifled a snicker.

"I will be happy to take the report over the phone for you, sir."

Joe listened some more. "Perhaps we could discuss this later, sir? No, I understand you're a taxpayer, sir. I certainly do take this seriously."

Ryan smiled evilly. "Go take the report, deputy."

"Yes, sir," Joe said to the man on the phone. "Why of course I'll be glad to come see the evidence. Yes, sir. I do think it's a terrible crime. I am not taking it lightly at all, sir. I'll be out as soon as possible, sir. No, I'm sure you won't disturb anything until I get there. No, sir, I don't think it'll be necessary to block off the barn with crime scene tape. Thank you, sir." He hung up.

"Have a good time, deputy," Ryan said.

"Thank you, sir." Joe grabbed his hat and notebook and headed out the door.

At least now Ryan would have some time to think in peace. Why was Camilla so mad at him? She seemed to kind, so loving, but then he'd say or do something that just set her off.

He wasn't getting anywhere with this. He threw himself into his work, trying not to think about her any more.

He started working through all the papers on his desk, city by city. He carefully read through each report before filing it, still hoping to find some clue that would lead him to Dennis.

He worked for a half hour on the papers, finding nothing, with no sounds except the occasional codes coming in over the Coast Guard radio's frequency. They were still out by the lighthouse, trying to catch all the kids who were apparently trying to hide from them on the island.

He shook his head, and flipped to the next report in his stack.

About the boat explosion. Joe was right. There was nothing much there, especially since the body wasn't recovered for autopsy. But at least for once there was some suspicion that it wasn't an accident. He set that page down, read the next.

Nothing but general background on the girl killed in the boat explosion. Well-off family in L.A. Only child. Father was a lawyer and mother was a real estate agent. Bright girl, but suspended from high school twice, dropped out of college. Really clever, her teachers said. Came up with ingenious ways to get away with things. After school she bounced around, having minor contacts with the law here and there—passenger in a drunk driving incident with some kids, skirmish while partying at a club. Bailed out every time by her parents. Never held accountable. Spoiled. Her picture showed a good-looking young woman with glossy black hair, perfect makeup and a snooty look on her face.

Ryan froze.

He was having one of those Bloodhound Knight moments. The clues shook together like puzzle pieces. He stared at the picture of Dora Favre: no body recovered. Mother was a real estate agent. Waist-length black hair and an arrogant expression. Got away with everything she ever tried.

The answer had been right in front of him all along. Waist-length black hair. "I always feel like she's looking down her nose at me." Mother is a real estate agent. Clever but amoral.

No body recovered. Because Dora Favre was at Camilla's house right now.

He tried Camilla's cell phone. It went straight to voicemail. He left a message.

Called Robin Brenham's number. Straight to voicemail. Left another message.

He called the dispatcher and gave her the code for crime in progress, backup needed.

The Coast Guard was still out at the lighthouse. Joe was

somewhere halfway up Pajaro mountain. He knew backup from the county took seventeen minutes to get here by chopper over the mountain from inland.

He had the dispatcher call in everyone ASAP and then he was out the door to the car.

The closest backup was seventeen minutes away. And he knew seventeen minutes from now would be too late.

CHAPTER FIFTEEN

THE FOG SHROUDED THE DAY, MAKING EVERYTHING IN THE LITTLE cottage feel hushed, isolated from the whole world. Camilla stood at the kitchen sink, doing the breakfast dishes, trying not to think about the path she'd just embarked on.

She had locked herself in the bathroom for a while to have a good cry, and now she was cleaning up the mess of the morning dishes—the mess she'd made of her life.

"Oliver," she called. "Get your stuff ready for school, hon."

She looked out the kitchen window at the back yard. She couldn't see anything more than a few feet away. It had an odd look, the fog almost glowing, with the sunshine just beyond the fog bank making it seem solid, like a gray screen lit from behind by a pure light. Muted, soft, alone.

Ryan was gone. She had sent him away. Dumped him. Now she had to face whatever came next on her own. She wiped her hands on the dishcloth and set it down on the counter. Squared her shoulders. She was doing the right thing. Ryan had never been the right man for her. She'd known that from the start. She could never tell him the truth. Could she see herself living a lie for the rest of her life? Never being able to be honest with the man with whom she shared her life? No.

Sending him away had been the right thing to do. That didn't make it easy to live with.

"Oliver?"

No answer. She went into the living room. His sleeping bag was still on the floor, his pajamas discarded on top. Backpack gone.

"Come on, honey. No messing around today. I've got a lot to do."

She looked in the tiny bathroom. Went upstairs to the second floor, even up to the little room on the third floor, where just last night she and Ryan had escaped to talk about their future—

Enough of that. Where was Oliver?

"Oh, no." Had he been upset by their argument? She knew how fond he was of Ryan. After thinking they were staying together, running away together, now she was dumping Ryan and not running. Had she added another loss to his young life?

"Oliver!" She shouted it, but was met with nothing but silence in the house. At least as silent as the old cottage ever got. She stood in the middle of the living room and strained to listen: the creaking of old timbers, the tree branches rustling against the shingles, the whisper of the waves far below the cliff out back. But no sound of a little boy's footsteps.

"Oliver, please. Where are you?"

She was getting frightened now. Something was off in the cottage. It was like the little house was menacing all of a sudden, and she began to wonder if Dennis was lurking somewhere around. And if he was, could he have cornered his own son for some awful scheme?

Again she ran through the house, searching frantically in every tiny spot Oliver could have crawled into.

Then she rushed back downstairs, looking in, behind, around anything big enough to hide a small boy.

She threw the dutch doors open and ran outside to the back yard. She saw a flash of yellow on the lawn.

It was Oliver's backpack, lying haphazardly in the grass, abandoned. She was really scared. She ran to the cliff, looked down over the dizzying edge. Nothing. Fog blocked her view of the cliff face, and of, God forbid, the ground far below.

"Oliver!" she shouted.

She looked around the yard, then saw that the shed door was standing open.

She went in. Even though the fog had been thick her eyes still took time to adjust to the dark little building.

"Oliver?" she whispered, somehow feeling like she shouldn't shout in here.

Where could he be? She absently noted the hum of the freezer still running, the jumble of 100-year-old junk. Something was different in here. Things had been moved around.

But she didn't have time to register what was different, because she saw a shadow on the floor, out of place amid all the cast-off treasures.

She bent over. It wasn't Oliver.

"Robin?" She lay too still, a gash in her forehead oozing dark. Camilla shook her shoulder, whispered her name. "Robin?" No response. Camilla felt for her wrist. She could feel the pulse, she could see her chest rise and fall. She was alive, but how badly hurt? And how did she get hurt?

Oliver wouldn't have hurt her. This made no sense. Dennis must be around somewhere.

She stood, fumbling in her coat pocket for her cell phone to call 911—and then realized the phone was in her purse back in the house.

"Hold on, Robin. I'm going for help."

Only the hum of the freezer answered her.

She turned to go, then froze. The freezer. That's what was different in here. The stack of windows had been moved away from the freezer, and the scratched white door stared blankly back at her.

No! She'd heard of children hiding in freezers, suffocating, unable to get out.

She pulled the door open.

And screamed.

Her first thought was that Dennis looked so peaceful.

Dennis Hutchins' dead body lay curled up in the freezer, almost as if he were sleeping. Sleeping on a pile of money. All around him were plastic bags full of cash. It was poetic somehow to see him that way, with the money he cared about so much cradling him in death.

Poor little Oliver. He was truly orphaned now. "My poor little boy." That was all she could fit into her mind. Poor child, so alone.

Except for her. What had happened here? Robin hurt, Dennis dead. Had Oliver stumbled across all of this? If he had, who knows how traumatized the poor child would be. She had to find him. She had to call 911. She had to get help. Now.

She started to close the freezer door on the awful sight, but her own name caught her attention. She paused, the door open and the cold blast from the freezer hitting her in the face. There was an envelope, hand addressed, with her name and old address in San Jose. She carefully picked it up from its resting place among the bags of money, and slammed the door shut. She had to get help.

"You ruined everything."

The voice was female, from behind her. Camilla shoved the envelope into her pocket and turned around.

In the doorway of the shed, with that shimmering foglight behind the figures, Camilla could only see one taller, and one shorter person, side by side, with the gray swirling around them.

"Thea?" Relief surged through her. "You found him. Thank

you, Thea. I was so worried about him. We have to call Ryan. Something terrible has happened, and Robin is hurt, and—"

Then she saw the shape in Thea's hand. A knife? At Oliver's side?

Thea? This day was becoming surreal. First the discovery in the freezer, now her real estate agent holding a knife on her little boy.

"Why do you have a knife?" she asked stupidly, too shocked to put it all together.

Thea smirked at her in that superior way she always did. "Why he wanted an idiot like you...."

"Dora killed daddy," Oliver said, standing in the shadow. "My daddy's dead."

"I know, sweetheart." She took a step forward to put her arms around him but Thea raised the knife.

"What's going on? I don't understand."

"You are the dumbest of them all, Camilla. Put your hands up and come out of there."

She obeyed, her hands raised like in some old gangster movie. "Dumbest of them all? You were behind all the killings?"

Thea smirked at her. "Even now you can't understand what's happening to you." She grabbed Oliver by one arm and dragged him back a few steps as Camilla came closer. "That's far enough."

This was unbelievable. "You punctured the gas tank."

"I wish you smoked," Thea said.

"Huh?"

"Smoked. Cigarettes. The fumes would have blown you up out on Highway One and you never would have gotten to this Godforsaken town. You really have been a pain, Camilla Stewart."

Camilla shook her head, keeping one eye on Oliver and watching the shining blade hover close to his neck. "Why did you want that to happen, Thea?"

"Dennis was mine," she said simply. "You tried to steal him, but I stopped you."

"I don't want him—didn't want him," she corrected, flashing back to the image of that body in the freezer and feeling her stomach turn over.

Thea had done it. "You killed him."

For the first time, Thea looked upset. "He was mine, and you ruined everything." Unbelievably, a tear ran down her perfectly made-up cheek, bringing a streak of mascara with it.

"You were his girlfriend?"

She sneered, the sad look gone. "You thought you could take him, but you failed."

Oliver was frozen in the woman's grasp. She had to get him away from this crazy woman.

"You can have Dennis," she said. "Just let us go."

"Have him?!" Thea twisted Oliver around in front of her and put the knife against his throat. The boy cried out in pain. "He's dead, Camilla. And it's this little brat's fault. I can't ever have him. Our love was perfect. He told me I was the only one he'd ever felt this way about."

Camilla bit her lip to keep from saying that was exactly what Dennis had told her, too. She had to keep her talking. "But he was married, Thea."

"To that horrible woman. She didn't love him the way I do."

"She was a school teacher."

"Kids, kids, kids!" She dragged Oliver across the grass toward the cliff face. "Who needs kids? They just cause trouble."

Camilla followed, staying a few steps behind. She had to keep her talking. "How do they cause trouble, Thea?"

"He thought he could buy me off. Me! His one true love."

There was another one of those phrases that had crossed Dennis's lips so easily. And this woman had really bought the act, hook, line and sinker.

"Please, Dora," Oliver whimpered.

"Dora?"

"She was one of the ladies daddy saw after mommy died."

She saw the glint in Thea's eyes. "You knew him before Joyce Henning died." It was a statement. She knew now that everything Ryan had said was true—a serial killer was stalking her and Oliver. A crazy murderer had killed Oliver's mother and who-knew how many other women. But the killer wasn't Dennis.

"You killed them all." She said it with certainty now.

Dora dismissed the other women with a wave of the hand holding the knife. "They stood between us. He would have come back to me, if it weren't for all those b—"

"—Don't cuss in front of Oliver," she said automatically before realizing how stupid that was.

She watched Dora edge closer to the cliff, with Oliver held in a death grip in front of her.

"Why did you kill Dennis?" It was a dangerous question, but she needed to distract her, buy a little more time.

Again that look flashed across Dora's tear-streaked face: sadness, loss, then back to anger. "He thought he could buy me off. Me!"

"What do you mean?" she asked, edging a step closer and trying to keep her face neutral.

"He was afraid for his son." She spat it out contemptuously. "He said he'd give me a million dollars to go away and leave him and his son alone. But he loved me. He told me he did."

"Of course he did," she said soothingly, but saw the flash of anger in Dora's eyes.

"Me! Not you. Not this brat." She leaned back against the stone wall now, maneuvering Oliver closer to the edge.

If only she could think of a way to get to Ryan. But she had sent him away. If only his famous intuition would kick in, make him realize what was wrong. If only.

"Where's the deputy guarding the cottage, Dora?"

"Gone." There was a world of horror in that single word.

The look in the killer's eyes told her there was no point

hoping for a miracle. No one was guarding them. No one would come rescue them. She had to get out of this on her own.

She held her hands out to Dora. "Let Oliver go. He's not the problem. I am. I stole Dennis from you. Take your revenge on me."

Dora didn't bother to answer, just twisted around to face the cliff. Camilla followed, hands still raised.

"He loved his son more than me. More than me! No one ever turns me down."

"Don't do this. You can still get away. Take all the money." She swallowed hard. "Take Oliver."

"Camilla?" The look of betrayal on Oliver's face cut her like the blade at his throat would, but she didn't have time to explain it to him.

"He's your only connection to Dennis now. He's what's left of Dennis. Keep him alive, take him with you, and you will still have Dennis with you."

Dora paused, then motioned with the knife. "Come closer, Camilla, or I'll stab the brat."

She came closer, hands still raised.

Dora moved away from the cliff, the knife at Oliver's throat. "Climb over the wall, Camilla Stewart. You're going to have an accident."

Camilla obeyed. She stood on the narrow edge between the waist-high stone wall and the drop-off. The fog looked like a fluffy gray pillow below her, but she knew that was an illusion. She'd fall through the cloud like lead through empty air.

"As long as Oliver is still alive, you'll still have Dennis," she said, trying to reach that clever, crazed mind and convince her.

If Oliver went with Thea, Ryan could still save him. No one could hide from her overprotective oak tree. He'd find Oliver if it was the last thing he did.

But if Oliver went over the cliff after her, there was nothing Ryan could do to save him.

"I'm the one you want, Thea. Not Oliver. With me gone, you're home free. You can escape."

Dora shook her head. "You're both going to die."

RYAN WAS OUT OF THE TRUCK ALMOST BEFORE IT STOPPED IN THE gravel in front of the honeymoon cottage. He had his service revolver in hand, but down at his side so he didn't accidentally shoot the wrong person.

There were a bunch of cars parked. The deputy's, Robin's, Camilla's rust bucket, and another.

The deputy's car was empty. Where was the guy? Not a good sign. He hadn't called in before going wherever he'd gone.

A car he didn't recognize was parked behind Camilla's convertible. He checked it out. A rental.

He called dispatch, reporting the missing deputy and giving them the rental's license number. He whispered into the mike, then turned the volume down so it wouldn't squawk and give away his location.

He wanted to run through the gate and burst in and save them, but he knew that was stupid.

He forced himself to slow down. Maybe nothing would happen. There was no reason for Dora to know she'd been found out. He had to take it slow. They were probably drinking Camilla's horrible coffee in the kitchen. He just had to keep his cool.

Not make a mistake.

He opened the redwood gate and went through. The cottage looked still. He stood and listened for a minute. Nothing but the sound of waves on the beach far below, and the flapping of a shutter or something.

He crept up to the front of the cottage, and peeked in the

lopsided window. Nothing looked out of place behind the wavy glass.

He tried the door handle. Unlocked.

He slowly opened it, dreading the creak of the hinges.

They didn't make a sound. Had she oiled them?

He stepped through the door, checking the corners and scanning the room automatically.

No one was there. The sleeping bags were on the floor on top of the blow-up mattresses. Oliver's pajamas were in a heap on top. That was how it looked when he'd left. Nothing looked off.

But if nothing was wrong, Camilla should be here. They should be sitting in the kitchen—the kitchen where he and she had just fought an hour ago. They should be going over paperwork for the house sale.

The sound of a shutter or something banging was louder. He crept into the kitchen, cleared it—no one inside—and went to the back door.

He peeked out the small window next to the door. The fog was really thick here, so close to the ocean. Everything looked shadowy. But he could see no one in the back yard.

The door to the shed was standing open, flapping back and forth in the wind. That was the source of the sound. But why would they be out there?

Slowly, he opened the kitchen door.

Finally, he heard voices—not from the shed, but from farther away.

The cliff.

Two voices. Camilla's and another female. He listened for a moment. Not Robin. A voice he had never heard before. Angry, but in a cold, controlled way. Bad sign. Dora Favre was too much in control. She was capable of anything.

He crept out the door. Started to make his way toward the cliff, thanking the fog for keeping his movements invisible to the two at the edge of the yard.

Three. He could see three figures now. One was alone, on the wrong side of the shadowy stone wall at the cliff's edge. The other two were a few feet away, right at this side of the wall. A taller figure and a shorter one.

Too close. Oliver and Dora, presumably. Which made the person right near the cliff edge Camilla.

He crept closer, listened to the voices, trying to predict the next movement before it happened.

"Take him with you, Thea. He's all you have of Dennis," Camilla said. Good girl. Trying to stall for time.

"I'll jump, I promise." Bad. She'd better not. He'd recovered the bodies of idiot tourists who'd tried climbing the cliff face on a dare before. He had to stop her before she went over.

"Now, Camilla Stewart. Jump or I stab him."

He crept closer. Stabbed. Not shot. Good. He needed to distinguish her arm with the knife from the shadows or a shot from this angle might not save the boy.

As the breeze swept the fog into currents and eddies he realized he suddenly had a clear line of sight to the cliff. He ducked behind the nearest bush and peered out. Camilla was facing his way, and Dora, with Oliver clutched tightly to her side, was facing toward the cliff.

He raised the gun. Which hand held the knife? He saw that the knife was down by her side, close to the boy, but not at his jugular or anywhere a sudden jerk from her would cut the boy.

Then Camilla saw him, and her expression, as it always did, gave her thoughts away. Dora twirled, saw the officer bearing down on her with gun raised, and pulled Oliver over the edge of the wall with her and jumped.

He ran forward, but he couldn't possibly reach the cliff in time.

But Camilla did. She leaped sideways, catching Oliver's wrist as Dora leaped. The boy cried out and Ryan heard a snap as his wrist broke, but Camilla held on through the boy's screams.

When he got there, Camilla was gripping Oliver's broken wrist with both hands, and slipping in the soft dirt at the cliff's edge.

He grabbed onto the boy's midsection with one hand and tried to put down his gun with the other so it wouldn't misfire when he dropped it. But he felt himself pulled over the wall by the small boy's weight.

He looked over the edge and saw that Dora had Oliver by the ankles and she dangled freely, the fog and its 100 feet of empty space beneath her flailing feet.

Oliver continued to scream and Camilla was slipping, but Ryan ignored them and leaned farther over the wall.

"Don't drop him!" he shouted at Camilla, and trusted her to hold on.

He let go of Oliver and leaned over the poor child's body, pressing the boy down against the ground with his heavy weight. He grabbed Dora's hands, jerking her grasp away from Oliver.

She pulled at him, her beautiful face a mask of pure, insane hatred. "I always win!" she screamed. "Always!"

"Not this time." He pulled as hard as he could, forcing her back from her death. He felt Oliver disappear from beneath him and then he was alone in his battle with the flailing woman, gravity and her crazed desire to take one last victim giving her the power to pull him farther over the edge.

He refused, using all his strength to pull her back up, inch by inch, until she was at the top of the cliff and he had her pinned on the sweet grass inside the stone wall.

He lay there a moment, gasping for air, hearing her sobs mingled with Camilla's soft murmuring in the background:

"I've got you, Oliver. I promise I'll never let you go."

CHAPTER SIXTEEN

"Robin's sleeping," Dr. Lil told her in a whisper as they stood next to Oliver's bed in the clinic. "She has a concussion, and her cut on the head required five stitches, but she'll recover."

"And Oliver?" Camilla looked down at the sleepy boy, just barely keeping his eyes open.

"He's going to be okay. His wrist is broken, but he'll heal quickly—from that." Dr. Lil gave her a quick glance that told volumes. Her little boy had a lot of healing to do to get over what he'd been through. They all did.

She leaned over him and kissed him on the forehead.

"Daddy's dead," he whispered.

"I know, sweetheart. Sleep now. He's in heaven watching over you, keeping you safe forever and ever."

"With Mommy."

Camilla let the tears fall. "Yes. Your parents protected you. Now I will keep you safe forever. I will be here when you wake up. Let yourself go to sleep now, honey."

She brushed the hair from his forehead gently, and he closed his eyes, and she watched his chest rise and fall.

"He's pretty heavily sedated now. He's in shock. But he's

resilient. Val DiPietro can put you in touch with a good counselor to help him work through the grief."

She nodded. "We'll all need time."

Dr. Lil patted her on the back. "You have time now. And you have the whole town behind you, to help you through."

She nodded. "I'll be asking for all the help I can get." They were staying here, no matter what the consequences. She owed Oliver that.

"Good girl. You'll make it, kid." Dr. Lil gave her another quick pat and then left the room. "Captain," she said as she went out.

Camilla heard Dr. Lil whisper some words of condolence about the dead deputy. The guy had been found stabbed, with his pants unzipped, only a few yards away from his car. So Dora had taken one more victim with her before she was caught. She had a long list of victims to pay for. But she would never hurt anyone again now.

Ryan came up behind her. She looked up from the sleeping child.

"I'm so sorry, Camilla. I blew it."

Camilla went over to the window on the other side of the room, where a pair of softly padded chairs waited. She sat down and gestured him to the other seat.

He sat.

"What do you mean, you blew it? You saved at least three lives today, and caught a serial killer."

"The county deputy's dead. Robin's badly hurt, and so is Oliver, and you almost died."

She felt the anger rise in her.

"Ryan!" She said it softly so she wouldn't wake up Oliver, but with pure exasperation. "You're an idiot, you know."

"I know," he said, forlornly. "I should have seen the pattern sooner."

"No. You're not an idiot because you saved us from a horrible death and caught Dora Favre today. You're an idiot because you think that's not enough. You aren't responsible for what she did. You stopped her before she did even more damage." She shoved her hands in the pockets of her sweatshirt and felt something. She pulled it out. The letter addressed to her. The one she'd found with Dennis's body.

She shuddered.

"What's that?"

She held up the envelope. "I found it when I discovered... the body. It's a letter addressed to me." She examined the envelope. "It's in Dennis's handwriting."

"That's evidence," he said.

"I guess it is. But I didn't know that when I picked it up." She looked at the back, where the envelope had been hastily torn open. "Can I look at the letter inside before turning it over to you? It's addressed to me."

He nodded.

She pulled it out.

Dear Camilla,

If you get this letter you're going to be really mad at me. I, Dennis Henning, stole the payroll from Cordova Computing. Take this letter to the police and they will know you are innocent, so that's okay.

"Okay! What were you thinking, Dennis?"

"What does it say?"

"I'll finish it and then you can read it, okay?"

He nodded, and she continued reading.

I'm sure you're really pissed. If you let it out, you wouldn't blush so much. That's the cure, you know. Being true to yourself instead of pretending things don't bother you.

If you get this letter you have Oliver, and I'm not coming back. Here's the thing: I got into a jam. It's my own fault, I made the wrong woman angry. I'm going to try to get rid of her before she does any more damage. But it might not work. I'm not a violent guy, Camilla. I'll try, but I might not succeed. I can't go to the cops for obvious reasons, so I've got to try to man up and solve this on my own.

But you're my insurance policy. If I don't come back and you get this letter, that means Oliver is all alone. I need someone who can take care of him, and I picked you because you're the perfect person.

"Poor little boy," she whispered. "Dennis knew what was coming."

His mother had insurance when she died, so there was a big chunk of change set aside for him, all legal money, not laundered or nothing. I used it to buy a little place in a town you've never heard of. The house is in your name, and the keys are in this envelope. It's The Honeymoon Cottage in Pajaro Bay, California. It'll give Oliver what he needs: safety and love. It'll give you what you need, too—no more running. You play those old tapes over and over in your head. They tell you you're going to screw up. They tell you you're just like your father. You tell yourself all those lies you learned from your parents. You think you're destined to be just like them. Until you stop telling yourself those things, you'll never be free. Stop blushing, Camilla. Tell yourself the truth. Tell the world the truth about yourself. And tell my son the truth he needs to hear. He needs to know he's not destined to be like me. You can do this—better than I ever could, because you understand Oliver better than I do. You're just like him. Don't let him repeat our mistakes. Give him the chance to be different.

I'm mailing this letter today, then going to solve my problem. If I get back in time, you'll never see this, and you'll never know about any of this. If I don't get back in time to intercept this letter, you'll find it in your mailbox.

Tell Oliver I love him. Take care of him. Don't let him grow up to be like me.

"I won't," she whispered, fingering the scrawled *Dennis* at the bottom of the letter.

She handed the letter to Ryan and he read it through silently.

"Wow," he said when he finished. "So Dora found the letter when she killed Dennis. She must have confronted him before he had a chance to mail the letter. Then she used the key to the cottage to lure you there, planning to kill you and Oliver in another 'accident'. What a scheme."

"Yeah."

"So you were right. He loved Oliver more than his own life."

"And you were right. Someone really was trying to kill us."

"So now what?"

"Now what? I'm doing what it says. Staying here and giving Oliver the life he needs." He hadn't understood her when she tried to tell him before, but maybe he could now.

"I have to stop running away. I have to make a stand somewhere, and it might as well be here. Do you get what I'm saying?"

"No." He said it flatly. "You're doing this because Dennis told you to?"

"No. Of course not. This is what I was trying to tell you at the cottage. As long as I'm afraid I can't teach Oliver to be brave. I would always be hiding behind a lie."

"What lie?" He lasered in on that. "What lie, Camilla?"

"I've been ashamed. Ashamed of who I am, where I came from. Ashamed of what I've done."

"What have you done?"

"I lied to you about everything."

She noticed Ryan had stood up. He had his hands clenched at his sides and she could see his knuckles were white.

She looked up at him. "What's wrong?"

"What's wrong?! You tell me our whole relationship is based on a lie, and that's why you can't leave with me, and then you ask what's wrong?"

"Keep your voice down!" She glanced over at Oliver, but he was fast asleep.

"I asked you to stay a few hours ago and you said no. But a con man uses you, causes all this trouble, and when he snaps his fingers you jump."

"You have it all wrong, Ryan."

"Yeah. Apparently I do."

"Sit down, Ryan. I have things to tell you."

"I don't think so," he said, so coldly that she jumped.

She looked up at him, but he wasn't going to listen to her. How could he? "You don't understand," she said helplessly.

"No. I don't. You're staying here because Dennis wants you to, but what I want means nothing."

"I'm not staying for Dennis. I'm staying for—"

"—for Oliver. But I don't see why."

"Because I have to make a stand somewhere."

"A stand for what?"

"For myself. For my life. I am not going to run."

"Because a con man tells you to?"

"Keep your voice down. Dennis could read me like a book. Remember—those were your words. He's right. I run every time someone looks at me sideways. I'm trying to run away from other people's judgment of me. But that's not going to work. Because I'm never going to stop judging myself."

"That's a bunch of mumbo-jumbo he came up with to manipulate you."

"No it isn't. Don't you see, Ryan? The problem isn't Mabel Rutherford, or Dennis, or Thea, or my mother—or even that grumpy old cat of Miss Potter's."

He looked at her uncomprehendingly.

"The voice putting me down is inside me. Until I stop running from it, I'll never be free. I could go clear across the country—the world—and it'll still be there. I've got to stop running from it. I have to stay here."

"You won't even discuss it with me." He couldn't get beyond that.

"No," she admitted. "This is something I have to do. And if you would stop running away yourself, you'd see I'm right. Stay in Pajaro Bay with me, Ryan." How could she explain? This was about being deserving of him. It was about being honest, and holding her head up, and then, only then, being able to build a relationship with the man she loved. "Please stay here, and face everything we need to face with me."

"Don't try to project all Dennis's psychological garbage onto me, Camilla. I know what I'm doing."

Of course he couldn't understand. Because she was just hitting him with all this. She's never really talked with him about his decision. And he knew nothing about her. He had never really known her at all. She'd never given him the chance.

He stalked to the door.

"Ryan?" she said to his back.

He stopped at the open doorway, but didn't look back.

"Please stay. Let me explain."

The door closing behind him was the ending of one part of her life. It was time to begin the next.

"I CAN'T BELIEVE IT'S MINE," SHE SAID AT NINE A.M. ON A SATURDAY morning three weeks later. She looked at the green door of the little office in Alvarado Alley.

Robin handed her the keys. "It is. For a very reasonable lease rate with option to buy."

Camilla unlocked the door and stepped into the little building. "It's really tiny." She was feeling overwhelmed with doubts. Was she crazy to do this? She had been so sure that staying in town was the right thing to do, but now, faced with a new business, and no customers, it seemed ridiculous.

Robin came in after her and took three steps forward, stopping in the center of the room. "What do you mean it's small? It's big enough to hold a dance party." She twirled around in a circle, then put a hand to her forehead, where the healing scar still showed bright red. "Ooh. Maybe I shouldn't have done that."

Camilla put a hand to Robin's shoulder. "I'd offer you a chair, but I don't have one."

Robin smiled. "I'm fine." She walked around the room, examining everything. "I love this little wood stove. Think how nice it'll be in the winter. And think of the flowers outside all summer." She opened a window to the garden in back. "It'll work. You can fit a desk and a computer and that's all you need, isn't it?"

"Since I didn't sell the cottage I don't have money for the computer. I'm still cash-poor until Dennis's case works through the courts and the money he stole from me is returned. If it ever is. I'm pretty low on the list of victims needing reimbursement."

"Well, you have enough to live on for now, right?"

She nodded. "Now that I sold the car to Hector at the garage. I think he overpaid because he was stoned, but I couldn't afford to wait for him to come to his senses."

"Oh, honey. You'd be waiting a lifetime for that...."

She shrugged. "I'll pick up another car as soon as I can scrape the money together. He'll make the profit from me when he sells me one of his fixer-uppers."

Robin laughed. "He'll probably turn your old convertible into a luscious little gem and then sell it back to you for a fortune. I wouldn't worry about him. He's nuts, but he's good at what he does."

She smiled.

"So what do you need to get started in business? We'll make a list."

They sat in the middle of the floor, and Robin took a notepad out from her purse.

Camilla started ticking things off on her fingers. "I really should get a used computer. I actually learned to do books by hand in college, believe it or not. I can do double-entry accounting with nothing but a pencil and a pad of paper. But a computer would make reports look more professional."

"You can use mine in exchange for a discount on the fees you charge me."

Camilla nodded. "And a chair. I should sit somewhere."

Robin wrote it down. "Yeah. Sitting's good."

"And I guess I better find a chair for clients—if I get any."

"We'll go over the hill to the city tomorrow and you can pick up a couple of cheap chairs. You'll be back by then, right?"

She nodded. "I promise I'll be back late this evening."

"You're not going to tell me where you're going?"

Camilla shook her head. "I appreciate you loaning me your car. But I'll tell you about my trip when I get back. I promise. I'm coming clean on everything now. Just something I have to take care of right away."

Robin nodded. "Tell it when you're ready. I'll be here." She looked around. "So, what kind of chairs?"

"Chairs?" Then Camilla stopped thinking about what she was planning for the afternoon and brought her mind back to the present. "Yeah. Let's see. A desk chair for me and a couple of regular chairs for clients. We'll get the desk chair tomorrow, but Mabel Rutherford's got a pair of nice straight-back chairs that'll work for clients. Much cheaper than new."

Robin stared at her. "You're kidding."

"Nope. I have to face her sometime. I'm not leaving town, so I have to get used to dealing with her."

"Wow. I guess you are clearing up all your unfinished business. You are a better man than I, Gunga Din."

"Kipling. I hated that English class in college."

Robin laughed. "I was an English major. And my ex-husband was an English professor, so I got my fill of the classics."

Camilla grinned. "Aha! Another clue."

"Yup. Stick around, girl, and you'll learn all the gory details eventually."

"I have time. I'm not going anywhere." She looked around the room. "Do you really think I'll have enough room for everything in this little place?"

"You don't need space for a coffee machine. Mine's just down the block. Two sugars and cinnamon, just the way you like it."

"It's a deal. Chairs, a computer as soon as I can get my hands on one. And some clients. Clients would be good."

"I'm your first client."

"You know you don't have to do that."

"Yes I do. I took the English classes in school. You took double-whatever math."

"So, I have one client."

"Two." Zelda Potter's hat today was strawberry red, with a huge brim that almost—but not quite—overshadowed her aura of unflappable cool. "The historical society's finances are in deplorable condition. The fault, I am sorry to say, of the organization's president."

Camilla and Robin scrambled to their feet and Camilla brushed the dust off her jeans. "I thought you were the president," she said.

"I am, my dear. You're hired. Sandy!"

Her silent assistant entered with a cardboard box stuffed to the brim with papers.

"Where should this be placed, my dear?"

"On the floor, I guess. What is it?"

"Your assignment. Make sense of this shambles, and you'll be set in this town for life."

"You don't even know how much I charge."

"We can afford it. Here's a deposit." Ms. Zelda handed her a check big enough to cover a used desk, two wooden chairs from the Junque Shoppe, and—she quickly calculated—a down payment on a computer and some software.

"Call me when you have it straightened out." She swept out with as much drama as she'd swept in.

"How on earth did she know I was opening an accounting office before I even got a sign on the door?"

Robin smiled. "I heard about it at Santos' market about an hour ago."

"So everyone in town knows by now."

Robin looked over her shoulder to the open doorway. "Yup. I think the rumor was started by the guy who's renting the apartment above the market. See you later. Let me know how it goes."

"How what goes?"

As Robin left, Ryan stood in the doorway, hat in hand.

"Hi, Camilla."

"Hi," she said. She waved him in and he came all the way into the tiny office.

"Nice place," he said.

She nodded. "I heard the people who had wanted to buy the Honeymoon Cottage bought the Cat Slide Cottage instead."

"Yeah. I rented the place over Santos' to stay in."

She waved him all the way in and she sat back down on the floor. He joined her. "I was going to stop by the substation to talk to you this morning, Ryan. I'm glad you came by."

"You were going to stop by?"

She took a deep breath. "I have been seeing you around town. I don't want us to just pass each other on the street and nod, Ryan. We have to clear the air between us. Even if we can't be together."

He nodded. He held his hat in his hands and stared at it. He obviously felt as awkward as she did, but she was done with pretending. She was tackling life head on. All of it. Even the uncomfortable parts.

She looked around the room, wondering how to say, what to say, how to clear the air. "I'm not good at being honest, Ryan. My whole life has been about covering my feelings and running away."

He looked guarded, but she quickly put a hand up. "I don't want to repeat the same argument. That won't get us anywhere."

"Then what?"

She took a deep breath. "So you rented an apartment. How long are you staying in town?"

"I haven't decided. I withdrew my resignation. I'm seeing the department's psychologist. Haven't decided," he repeated.

"So are you on duty this afternoon?"

He looked surprised. "Why?" he asked warily.

"I'm going to go visit my father."

"Your father?"

"Yeah. I've never told you anything about my family—about my life before I went to college."

He nodded slowly. "Yeah. We never did talk about our pasts much, did we?"

"We never really got to know each other. I want to correct that."

He shook his head. "Now that we're not—together—any more? What's the point?"

"The point is, I guess.... I don't know." She plunged ahead. "I trust you, Ryan. I trust your judgment. I like you. I care about you. I'm asking you to come with me to see my father. Not because I think it'll change anything between us. But because I'm trying to ask for help."

He stood up and reached out a hand to help her to her feet. His calloused palm felt so good against hers she had to resist all the feelings she still had for him. This wasn't about that.

"If you need me, I'm here for you." He said it with a sureness that made her realize she'd unconsciously pushed exactly the right button with him. Ask him to be vulnerable, and he'd clam up. Ask him for help, and every protective instinct came rushing to the fore.

"You sold your car to Hector. How were you planning on getting there?"

She didn't bother to ask how he knew that. This was Pajaro Bay. "I'm borrowing Robin's."

"I'll drive you," he said. He added softly, "I happen to have a nice old Mustang. I haven't put the mileage on it I had planned. So it's available."

She smiled. "Thanks. And thanks for coming with me."

She led him out the door and locked it behind her. She was going to need all the help she could get to make it through the next few hours.

IN MARISOL'S PINK BEDROOM FULL OF RUFFLES AND STUFFED animals, Oliver sat on the bed crying, and Camilla didn't seem to be able to do anything to stop him. "Please, honey." She held him close, and he sobbed in her arms.

He reached up to put his arms around her, then winced when his cast got in the way. She winced too.

"Watch it, kid," she said with a grin. "That hunk of plaster on your arm gives you a mean left hook."

He didn't smile back, but just put his head on her shoulder and sighed.

"You have to go?" he mumbled, not looking at her.

"I do. But it's only a short trip. I'll be back soon. I promise."

"You promise?" he said tentatively, still not looking up.

She pulled away from him just enough so she could look into his eyes. "I will always come back, Oliver. I give you my word. I have never lied to you, and I never will. I promise."

"Even if I'm bad," he whispered.

"Oh, Oliver. You're not bad."

"I made them die."

"No!" She lifted his face so he could see into her eyes. "Your parents had problems. Not you. They made mistakes. But that doesn't have anything to do with you."

243

He didn't look like he believed her.

She gave him another hug. It was going to take time. "I promise you I'll take care of you. I will always come back."

"Cross your heart?"

She crossed her heart. "See? I promise."

He sighed. "Daddy said you wouldn't ever leave me."

So Dennis had talked to him about this. Another bit of info slipped out through the cracks in Oliver's armor. She was going to bust down that armor if it took a lifetime. But the first step was to give him safety. "Your daddy was right. He knew how much I love you, and how important it was for someone who loves you to always take care of you. He gave me custody because he loved you so much he wanted you to be safe, no matter what happened to him."

"Even if he died," Oliver whispered.

"That's right," she said. The counselor had recommended talking openly about his parents' deaths with him, no matter how hard it was. "Your daddy died, but he made a promise to protect you and care for you forever. It's now my job to keep that promise for him."

"So you'll come back?"

She hugged him again. "I will always come back," she repeated. "Pajaro Bay is our home forever and ever. Now let's wipe your face so you can go play with Marisol."

CHAPTER SEVENTEEN

THE CONVERTIBLE TOP WAS UP TO PROTECT THEM FROM THE coastal drizzle, and she listened to the whistling of the wind against the car as the miles slipped past.

She didn't realize she'd been quiet for so long until Ryan spoke to her somewhere along Highway 1 north of Año Nuevo.

"He'll be safe. You can count on Joe."

She pulled her mind back from the coming conversation with her father. "And Oliver will be pigging out on enchiladas," she said to Ryan with a small smile.

"Nah. Joe only cooks that stuff for the fundraisers. They eat vegetarian mostly."

"Oh."

He glanced at her again. "You gonna tell me where we're going, or do we just keep driving until we run out of road?"

She rested her palms on the pony seats and tried to make it light. "Maybe it's a secret." How could she tell him? How could she face this? She felt that desire to run welling up inside of her, but she pushed it down. She was done with that. She had decided to stop running, and now she was on a path that changed everything. She had to come clean about who she really was, to Ryan and to herself.

He smiled. "Okay, let me guess then...."

He looked out the car window.

"He's friends with little Marisol," he said, "and Joe's wife is great with kids. And of course he's safe with a deputy watching over him."

She nodded, knowing he thought she was thinking about Oliver. And she was. But not only Oliver. "It's not that I'm worried about his safety," she said. "I know he's safe now. No one's after him. But I hope he's okay. He's been so sad."

"That's expected, isn't it?"

"The counselor said it would take a long time. But I'm not sure I'm up to it—I don't seem to be able to reassure him."

"I'm sure you can do it. You're the one he trusts. You just have to believe that time will heal—" He stopped. "That's such a cliche, isn't it? I'm sorry." He was silent for a bit, then said quietly, "when my mother died that's what people said, and I thought it was stupid. You never get over it. But the pain does fade."

"I didn't know—about your mother."

He shrugged and went back to looking out the window. "We don't know much about each other, I guess. What pulled us apart, Camilla?" he said, his eyes on the road ahead.

"The lack of honesty. The lack of openness. We haven't been telling each other the truth."

"What truth? I haven't lied to you."

"No, I haven't exactly lied either. I've just left things out. Not explained."

"Been a clam."

"Yeah."

"What about? You don't seem to have any secrets, Camilla."

She laughed at that. "My name's Beatrice, not Camilla."

"No it isn't," he said confidently. "I've seen your driver's license."

"I changed it when I turned 18."

"Then Camilla is your name."

"It's the name I chose. But not the one I was born with. We're coming up on Pigeon Point," she added.

He waited until the lighthouse at the point came into view. "So, wanna stop here?"

She shook her head.

"You know," he said, "it might be helpful to know where we're going. You still haven't told me."

"We'll stay on highway 1 through the City."

"Do we cross the Golden Gate Bridge?"

She nodded.

He smiled. He thought she was playing a game with him, not struggling to figure out what to say. "So," he said. "North coast somewhere. Mendocino?"

She shook her head.

"Eureka? It might be faster to take I-5 if we're going that far."

"No."

"Marin?" He pursed his lips. "Tiburon? Mill Valley?"

She looked away from him, out the window, feeling the knot in her stomach growing bigger with each place name he came up with.

"Sausalito?"

She squirmed in the seat.

"I'm running out of city names. I'm not an expert on the north bay."

She looked at her hands in her lap. She felt that stupid blush creeping up her neck to cover her face. Tell the truth, Camilla. Then you'll stop blushing.

"It can't be all that bad," he said with a chuckle. "No—don't tell me. You made up the visiting your father story to sweep me away on a romantic getaway. No? You gotta give me a clue, darlin'."

"San Quentin," she whispered. She kept her eyes on the passing scenery.

"Not my first choice for a romantic getaway."

She said nothing. Stared out the side at the hills they were passing.

"You know there's not much in San Quentin but the prison."

"I know," she whispered.

"You aren't kidding, then. Your dad works at San Quentin prison?"

"He works in the laundry there."

He started to say something, probably because he knew that only prisoners worked in the laundry, but then he realized what he was missing.

"What's he in for?" he asked quietly.

"Forgery."

"Forgers usually go to county jail."

"Not if they are habitual criminals."

"It was his third strike?"

"Actually." She paused. "I think it was his seventh, but I'm not sure."

"How old is he?"

"Old enough that he'll never get out."

"I'm sorry." He waited a while, then said, "Is he in mainline?"

She felt a certain relief talking to him, knowing he understood all the terms. "No," she answered. "He was in the general population and working in the laundry. As close as he gets to normal life in prison. Now he's in Ad Seg."

"For Forgery? That doesn't make sense."

She felt the blush start, but shook her head decisively and blurted it out: "He's always pulling something! He wouldn't even tell me what he'd done this time, but somehow he got himself segregated from the general population." She shook her head again. "He's impossible."

"How violent is he?"

"He's not. That's the thing. He's one of those people, if you tell him the rules, he somehow ends up on the wrong side of them. Every—" she paused. "—darned time."

She saw the ghost of a smile cross his face. "I love the way you talk," he said softly.

"What does that mean?"

"Darned. Creepy. All that. It's so cute."

That was not the reaction she had expected to her telling him her father was spending life in prison. "There's more," she said.

He kept his eyes glued to the road. "What more?"

She looked down at her hands. They were clenched together, as if she were keeping the truth in a death grip in her hands. "I put him there," she whispered.

He was silent for a bit. When she said nothing more, he said, "I assume you don't mean literally."

"Yes. I was supposed to be his alibi. But the police questioned me and I screwed up and they figured out I was lying for him."

He smiled gently. "I'm sure they knew you were lying all along."

"Of course they did. I blushed and stammered and gave it all away."

"Because you're too honest to lie."

"I'm not honest! Aren't you getting this, Ryan? All those things you say about me—that I'm smart, and honest, and good, and kind. That's just Camilla Stewart, the person I pretend to be. It's not who I really am. I'm really little Bea Stewart, liar, low-class trash daughter of a con man."

"No, you're a lot more than that."

"Don't you get what I'm telling you, Ryan? I'm telling you that I am a criminal type. I am a perp. I am one of those people you have to deal with in your job."

"Don't be ridiculous, Camilla."

She crossed her arms over her chest and looked out the window for a while. Didn't he get it?

"Tell me about your father."

So she did, spilling all of it. The ridiculous, grandiose plans he'd come up with that always ended up with people getting hurt and him getting in trouble. She told him about the awful time she was in high school and her dad made headlines because he tried to get into Vacaville.

"Vacaville? The mental facility?"

"Yeah. I was so embarrassed. He was giving interviews to the local paper from his jail cell, claiming he heard voices telling him to run a Ponzi scheme. It was all a plan of his to avoid prison by being declared criminally insane. Didn't work, of course. None of his plans ever worked, in the long run."

"So was he ever out of trouble when you were a kid?"

She thought back. "There were a lot of charges. A lot of different times. Sometimes he'd get off. Sometimes he'd be gone for weeks, or months. Then it was just me and my mother, stuck in some small town near the jail he was being held in. Then we'd move somewhere else when he got out, and he'd promise my mother he'd stay out of trouble. Then he'd get tired of working all day at a carpentry job and he'd plan some grand scheme to make a big killing."

"Like what?"

"Ponzi schemes, like I said. Investment scams. One time he pretended he was psychic and tried to get a neighbor lady to give him money to communicate beyond the grave with her dead husband. My mom was so embarrassed she got a job as a cashier so she could pay the lady back and keep her family from pressing charges."

"He's a lot like Dennis."

"Yeah. Only not as good at it as Dennis was. It's amazing somebody didn't throw him in a freezer," she added bitterly.

She bowed her head. Placed both palms at her sides, pressing them against the car seat. It was warm to the touch. But she felt cold. Chilled to the bone.

"No wonder," he said.

"No wonder what?"

"No wonder you were a perfect victim for Dennis. No wonder you let everyone else's opinion hurt you. No wonder you don't have the pride you should have in yourself."

That wasn't what she'd been expecting. "You don't hate me?"

He let out an exasperated sigh. "Camilla! That's what I'm talking about. You aren't a criminal. You didn't steal from the neighbor lady. You didn't run the Ponzi scheme. Can't you see that you were just a little kid?"

He stopped speaking like something had choked him. They each turned away to look out their side of the car. He just didn't get it. How it felt to be the daughter of a guy like her father.

Slowly as the miles swept by her frustration at him cooled, and she began to realize he did hear what she'd said, but somehow he didn't seem to think it made a difference. He really didn't understand how much this changed everything. "I shouldn't have asked you to come," she mumbled.

"Why not? I can help you get through this. I know it's tough."

"Don't patronize me. You don't understand."

"What don't I understand? Wait. Are you saying he was abusive? Is that what you mean?"

"He was no more abusive to me than Dennis was to Oliver."

"Dennis didn't hurt Oliver. You've said all along he loved his son."

"Love is more than being nice to a child! It's giving them stability, teaching them confidence, helping them become whole adults!" She hit the dashboard with her fist. "He did nothing for me!"

"I just got that repaired." he said mildly. "This is an antique. Be careful with it."

"I'm sorry."

"I'm teasing, Camilla. I had no idea. This is why Oliver—"

"Why he what?"

"I was going to say why he means so much to you, but that's

not fair. I know you love him." He glanced over at her, those blue eyes making her uncomfortable, like they had when she'd first met him and felt the cool assessment in every look he gave her. He was still stuck thinking he was going to protect her. That she was some helpless victim, not part of a terrible family with a legacy of crime and a destiny to repeat her father's patterns.

"Dennis read me like a book, Ryan. Like you said when we first met. I don't know how he knew. But he knew I was like Oliver. I identified with him. I knew what he needed. He needs what I never got."

"Where's your mother in all this? Was she also...?"

"A criminal? No. Just my dad and me."

He nodded. "I see. When was the first time you were arrested?"

The question pulled her up short. He assumed she had a long history of arrests, too. She had so identified with her dad that she blended her own life story with his. What was she thinking? She had come clean to him about her father's prison record, but she was still in denial here. She wasn't dealing with the real truth, the truth behind the bare facts. Of course Ryan didn't understand. Of course he thought she was some habitual criminal. That was how she was describing herself. She laughed out loud.

"The arrest in San Jose after Dennis ripped me off is my very first brush with the law, Ryan."

"Then I don't get—"

"Of course you don't. I keep talking about my family like I've inherited a disease from them. My Secret Shame, like some ridiculous family curse." She laughed again, realizing how dumb that was once she said it out loud—brought it out of its dark corner in her mind and pulled it into the bright daylight. "I'm no more of a criminal than you are, Ryan. But all my life, my mother told me I was destined to be like my father. She blamed my dad, me, the neighbors, the police, the whole world for her unhappiness. But the whole world didn't take her seriously. Unfortunately, I did."

"You were just a kid."

"Like Oliver is."

"Aha." He paused. "I'm sorry."

"And I'm sorry I lied to you, Ryan. It wasn't fair."

"What did you lie about?"

"Haven't you been listening? They may have been lies of omission, but I was still dishonest with you. I made you think I was someone I wasn't."

"Really? So I don't know who you are? You didn't work your way through college?"

"Of course I did."

"You have a degree in accounting."

"Yeah."

"You were hired by Cordova Computing?"

"You know that."

"Felix Cordova gave you his personal recommendation."

She nodded.

"You held my hand when I, a total stranger, spilled my guts to you about my stepdaughter's death, and you tried to make me feel better."

"That wasn't anything."

"It was to me." He looked ahead. "We're coming up on the city now."

She nodded.

"Robin's actually a bit shy," he said quietly. "You probably don't know that."

"Robin? Miss soul sister herself?"

"She had a rough time before she came to Pajaro Bay, and she's only slowly started making friends."

Camilla thought about that. "I thought I was the shy one."

"She needed your friendship as much as you need hers."

"Oh." She pondered that for a while. She never imagined

Robin was anything but the confident, sophisticated woman she appeared to be. Maybe Robin—maybe lots of people—put on a brave front to keep from showing their vulnerability. Maybe it wasn't just something she did.

"You agreed to adopt Oliver," he continued.

"You know all this, Ryan."

"And you kept on working hard to take care of him even when you found out his father had ripped you off."

"Of course. What was I going to do? Dump him by the side of the road with a dollar for bus fare?"

He looked out the windshield and she watched him for a while.

"Well?" she finally said.

"Well, what? I'm waiting, Camilla."

"Waiting for what, Ryan?"

"Waiting for you to explain how you're not honest, and kind, and good, and smart."

She sat back in the seat, stunned. She'd never really thought about it. She just knew, the day she turned 18 and left home, that she was going to pretend to be someone else. Someone who was everything she wasn't—classy and smart, successful and good. Not her father's daughter, the one cops looked at pityingly when she flubbed the alibi that was supposed to keep her dad out of prison. Not her mother's daughter, an "embarrassment," a "disappointment," and all those other insults hurled at her through the years. Someone with all the qualities she imagined other people had. Someone different from what she was destined to be.

"You aren't pretending those things, Camilla," he said gently. "That's who you really are. It's the other stuff—the con man's daughter, the other insults you give yourself—those are the lies."

AT THE PRISON RYAN WATCHED HER GO THROUGH THE PROCESS FOR visiting—the paperwork, the search, the standing in long lines to take her turn. Through it all she had the same resigned look the other visitors had. All these women, patiently waiting to see their sons, fathers, husbands. All the men back there in the prison with their screwed-up lives. All the women and children out here standing by them. Even though they didn't deserve it. Even though not one of the perps in there probably deserved a minute of these women's time.

He was sick of the wreckage criminals left in their victims' lives. All these women and children, their lives put on hold for men who couldn't get it together.

He waited with her until her turn came. She clenched her purse so tightly her knuckles turned white. He wondered if her father had any idea that his adoring daughter had changed—that she wasn't coming to bring him presents and listen to his complaints about prison life, but was here to finally tell him off for all the damage he'd done to her.

He hoped this confrontation would be cathartic for her. He wanted her to stop feeling so bad about herself. He felt like such a jerk for not seeing the signs earlier. He'd thought her embarrassment was just the common guilt he often saw in victims of crime. They thought if they'd been more alert, acted more quickly, they could have avoided being victimized. He'd talked many victims through that mistaken idea.

But Camilla's problem was different. She had been victimized since birth by a jerk who had been a lousy, irresponsible father to her. He wished he had known that earlier. Maybe he could have saved her some pain.

They finally got their turn to go in to the meeting area. He felt the tension in Camilla's body ratchet up as they went in. Her body was radiating energy, and he watched her closely, worried that the stress might be too much.

Because her father had gotten himself into segregation,

there'd be no hugs and sitting together during their visit. Good thing, since he imagined hugging the jerk was the last thing Camilla wanted to do.

She sat in front of the plexiglass barrier and waited for her father to come in and sit opposite her.

He watched her, wanting so much to help her, to fix it, but felt helpless to make it okay. A father in lockdown because he couldn't even stay out of trouble in prison. How could he fix that?

When the guy came in, Ryan was surprised. Of course, what was he expecting? The guy was old—looked much older than he must be. After all the years of prison life, he had that prison pallor, that sideways shift to the eyes as he unconsciously watched for danger sneaking up on him from all angles.

The blue denim prison garb hung off his body. He didn't look well, and Ryan wondered if he had health problems. Too bad. He deserved whatever pain he was in after the trouble he'd caused.

Ryan waited, standing a few feet behind where Camilla sat, his arms crossed and his stare boring into the jerk.

After a quick, curious glance in his direction, her father sat down opposite Camilla and picked up the phone.

She picked up the phone on her side. Ryan waited to hear what Camilla had to say to the man who'd caused her so much pain for so many years.

"Hi, sweetheart," he said to her. The loud, static-filled voice was easily heard on this side of the barrier.

Camilla's back was to Ryan, so he couldn't see her face. He wished he could, because he wanted to be ready to intervene if she got too emotional.

"Hi, pop," she said. "How you doin'?"

He shrugged. "Thanks for comin' to visit the old man."

"Do you need anything, pop?"

He shook his head. "The stamps are good. They got me in the hole 23/7, so there's not much I need."

"I got you a few candy bars from vending. The guard'll give 'em to you."

He nodded. "I'm sorry, kid."

"How did you get yourself put in the hole, pop?" Her voice sounded sharp, accusing.

"Just a misunderstanding." He shrugged, resigned. "I'm just a bad apple, kid."

"No, you're not. How can you think that?"

"I was born bad. It's just the way it is. I was in juvenile hall before I was old enough to smoke."

Jerk was trying to make her feel sorry for him, after all he'd done to her? Ryan saw how hopeless it would be for her to reach her father. She wasn't going to get through to the guy.

Like he'd never been able to get through to his own father. The anger in him made him ball up his fists. He never thought about his own father, unless Leah brought it up. Why did watching Camilla make him think about it now?

But Camilla wasn't sounding angry with her father. How could she not let it out? He wanted to see her rant and rave at the old man, let him know the damage he'd done.

But she put her palm up to the plexiglass, and he put his on the other side. "I made a mess, I know," her father said. "But you're doing okay now?"

She nodded. "I'm fine. I've started my own accounting business."

His expression changed then. If Ryan didn't know the guy was a jerk, he would've described him as a father glowing with pride.

"I knew you could do it, kid."

"Thanks, pop."

Camilla told him about Oliver, about the Honeymoon Cottage and her repairs, and he gave her advice on adding insulation, replacing worn roofing. It would have been a normal conversation between father and daughter except for the circumstances.

"I wish...," Camilla said twenty minutes later.

He smiled at her. "I almost made it the last time, kid. I would've had 'em, if it wasn't for that smart-aleck frequent flier who noticed some little things."

Ryan saw Camilla's hand on the phone looked relaxed. "Like the fact you were emptying the country club patrons' wallets?"

"Minor detail. I would've made it. Just slipped a little bit. Bet you never thought your old dad could convince people he was an airline pilot, did ya?"

"No, pop." She looked at him through the plexiglass barrier. "It was real clever."

The conversation could have been funny. But it was not funny at all.

Her old man told her all about his absurd con game, bragging as if he was real smart. She listened patiently, nodding, not correcting him when he said things that were obviously lies.

How could she be so compassionate with him? What was wrong with her that when she finally had the chance to tell him how much he hurt her she just sat there, listening to his idiotic comments and treating him—

Like she treated Oliver. Ryan rocked back on his heels, uncrossed his arms. This was who Camilla was. She had this deep well of kindness, understanding and compassion. It was what he'd noticed in her the first day he'd met her. What had stood out when he'd watched her with Oliver.

This woman was special. He would never be like her, but he had to admire what she was. She was something he would never be. Loving. Forgiving.

Their appointment time was up.

He watched as Camilla felt around for her purse and then stood up, still with the phone in hand. "I'll write you, pop."

He nodded, and Ryan saw the tears in the old man's eyes.

"I'll make another appointment to visit you in a few weeks. I have to take care of my little boy, but I'll be back soon."

He nodded again, and stood, still holding the phone, clearly not wanting to let the conversation end.

"Stay out of trouble, pop." She hung up the phone, placed her hand on the glass one last time, then turned to go.

The old man watched her until the guard came to make him go back to his cell.

IN THE PARKING LOT SHE STOOD BY THE CAR FOR A LONG TIME, AND Ryan watched her. He was so angry, not at her, but at the situation.

"Why didn't you tell him?"

She looked up, startled from her own thoughts. "Tell him what?"

"How he'd hurt you. How angry you are."

She smiled. "He knows he hurt me."

"That doesn't make it okay!"

"Ryan." She shook her head at him. "I'm not angry at him."

"He was a terrible father to you." He wanted to go back in there and wring the guy's neck.

"Didn't you hear anything he said? He's been in trouble since he was a kid. He's a 'bad apple.'"

"So? He's trying to make you sorry for him, and it's working!"

"Don't you get it? He sounds just like Oliver—like me. Like we caused the things that happened to us when we were kids."

"He's not a kid!"

"He did the best he could, Ryan. It was a terrible job, but it was the best he had in him." She got into the car, and he went around to the driver's side and got in, slamming the door behind him.

"Hey. This is an antique," she said. "Be careful with it."

He made up his mind. "I'm going in there to tell your father what he did. If you can't do it, someone needs to."

259

She put her hand on his arm, that small touch restraining him. He knew she could feel the thrumming tension in him.

"No, Ryan. Don't you see? I can't fix him. I can only fix myself. I can only live my life right. I can't go back and fix what's broken in him—what must have been broken when he was just a child. All I can do is move forward. Make sure I don't repeat his mistakes. Make sure I teach Oliver not to repeat them."

"It's just so unfair."

"And you can't fix it. I know. You want to catch a bad guy, arrest him, make him pay. Neat and clear-cut. Life doesn't always work that way."

He was seething, and he wasn't sure why. Yes he was. Because he had been vicariously hoping for a confrontation between Camilla and her father. Because her forgiveness pissed him off. It felt like she was letting the creep off too easy. He needed to pay for what he'd done to her.

Like his own father deserved to pay.

"No, Camilla. I need to take care of you in this. He can't get away with hurting you." He started to stalk back to the entrance, but she ran after him and got in front of him.

She glared up at him, her curls a halo around her round face, and he was struck again by how small and vulnerable she was, how she needed him to protect her.

But then she said, "So everything you said was a lie."

"What are you talking about?"

She put her hands on her hips and glared up at him. "You said I'm smart, but you won't listen to me. You said I'm honest, but you don't trust me. You said you respect me, but you override my decision."

"I just think"—

—"No. You don't. Get in the car and drive me back, Ryan."

They drove in silence.

Ryan was furious for about thirty miles, gripping the steering wheel to keep from turning to the insufferable woman next to him and telling her off. He'd done everything for her. He'd saved her, protected her. Didn't she see this situation was black and white? There was good, and there was bad, and it was that simple.

But not for her. She saw the gray that had given him problems all his life. Either he was right or wrong. Either he was perfect, or he was a screw-up. She saw that people could be both. And that was why he loved her.

But he didn't respect her. That was the problem. He said he did, but somewhere deep inside he didn't respect anyone. Or maybe it wasn't really respect. He didn't trust anyone.

Or was it that he didn't trust himself? He stared out the windshield. What was wrong with him?

He thought back at all the times people had said those same words to him: Why don't you trust me? Why don't you respect me? Why don't you listen to me? What he thought was protecting was really smothering.

Was really fear.

Fear was behind it all. Every time someone he cared about walked out the door he feared they wouldn't come back. He felt an urgent need to go with them, to keep the world outside from touching them, harming them.

He thought back to what Angie had said after Sara had died.

She had said she couldn't live with him smothering her. She hadn't called him names, blaming him for the death of her daughter. After Sara's death, Ryan wouldn't let Angie out of his sight, and that's what had driven them apart. He hadn't given her the space to grieve, to go through what she needed to go through. He hadn't let her know he was feeling the same pain, too. He'd just been strong, and controlling, and distant. Would they have stayed together if he'd opened up to her? Who knew. But he'd never given her a chance.

He smothered people he loved. He didn't actually listen to them. He didn't actually talk to them.

He glanced over at Camilla, saw her watching him with those beautiful, wise, kind eyes. He was going to lose this incredible woman if he didn't do something.

They were coming up on the Pigeon Point Lighthouse road again. He turned in and parked.

"My mother left the house one day when I was ten," he said, staring out at the fog rolling in off the ocean. "She was hit by a car and I never saw her again. After that my father went to work and came home, and drank. It was just me and Leah. She was only a baby when my mom died, so I took care of her. It was my job." He rephrased it. "I thought it was my job. I thought if I could keep her safe, she'd never walk out the door and disappear. She'd always be there."

Camilla's hand came to cover his on the steering wheel and he used it to anchor him here, in the car, in the present.

"I still try to control Leah, even now. I need to know she's safe. I need to know what's happening in her life so I can protect her. I call her every day to check that she's okay."

"There's a surprise," Camilla said, and he realized that's what he'd done with her, too.

"When I became a cop I felt it was my chance to protect people. But every time I failed—every time someone got hurt on my watch—I felt I was responsible for what had happened.

"And then Sara died...." His voice broke there, and Camilla sidled closer to him, wrapped her arms around him, gave him the strength to continue.

"I thought, here I had built my life around being the Protector, the Guardian. And then I failed. So who was I? What was I?"

"You're a good guy who isn't perfect."

He turned to her then, took her in his arms. "I'm sorry, Camilla. I haven't given you room to be an adult. I haven't respected you, just like you said."

"You saved our lives."

"But I wouldn't let you do anything on your own, even deal with your own father."

"I invited you."

"To support you. Not to take over your life."

"Yeah," she said.

He looked at her, and she was smiling.

"It's a real problem," she said. "I was kind of hoping to find a guy who was perfect in every way, but I guess you'll have to do."

"Will I do?"

"Let's see."

She kissed him then, and he let her take charge, relishing the feel of this incredible woman choosing him, wanting him. Could he be the man she wanted, needed him to be? He didn't know.

But he was going to spend the rest of his life trying.

"YOU CAME BACK." OLIVER WAS SO TIRED HE COULD BARELY KEEP his eyes open, but he had waited up for her.

She hugged him there on the Serrano's living room sofa. "I gave my word."

He nodded.

"And I'll always keep my promises to you."

Ryan nodded from the doorway. "We always keep our promises in this family."

"Good," said Oliver. "I want to go home and go to bed."

She took his hand and led him to the door. "Good plan. Tomorrow we buy real beds. We'll never have to move them again."

EPILOGUE

PAJARO BAY, CALIFORNIA
Saturday, September 15, 11:45 a.m.

RYAN FINISHED TYPING UP HIS SUMMER WRAP-UP REPORT FOR THE county. The Labor Day weekend had ended with one capsized boat (no injuries), three lost kids (quickly found), about a hundred cases of sunburn among the tourists (Dr. Lil had run out of calamine lotion), and one more report of missing chickens up on Pajaro ridge. Ryan had handled the last case personally, assuring the farmer that he would get to the bottom of the crime if he had to interview every raccoon in the tri-county area.

"What are you doing here?"

He looked up to see Joe Serrano standing in the doorway, looking stiff in a gray suit with a lavender tie.

"Just finishing up paperwork."

Joe went over to the coat rack. Ryan's tie was draped over the rack, next to his khaki hat. "Where's your suit jacket?"

"On the back of my chair." He kept typing.

"Dot the last i, cross the last t, and get a move on, Captain."

Ryan stood up, still typing. "Just a little bit more."

Joe came over and pulled him away from the keyboard. "Come on. I will not hear the end of this if you're late."

Ryan took back the keyboard, hit save, then quit. "Done."

"Good. Let's go." Joe grabbed the tie off the coat rack, and shoved Ryan out the door.

It was one of those glorious fall days on the California coast where not a wisp of fog was present, the air was just slightly cool, and the sky and ocean were a heavenly clear blue.

Cliff Drive was packed with cars, pickup trucks and SUVs. Joe finally found them a parking spot in Ms. Zelda's driveway, between her ivory and gold 1954 Bentley and a pink 1968 Volkswagen Beetle. "This'll do," Joe said.

"Don't hit the Beetle," Ryan warned. "That's Windy Madrigal's car."

Joe laughed. "Yeah. Better to scratch Ms. Zelda's car than the mayor's little sister's."

When they went into the backyard of the Honeymoon Cottage, Ryan saw the yard held more people than he ever imagined it could. The DiPietros, Madrigals, Hector and his cousin, Dr. Lil, Mama Thu and Big Mel Machado. Whether you needed your car repaired or a cup of chowder, you were out of luck today.

Ryan chuckled. "I guess it's fine for both of us to be off-duty at the same time," he said to Joe. "Since there's nobody left in town right now."

Joe caught sight of Hector fumbling with the pocket of his lavender tie-dye shirt, and he quickly excused himself to go over and explain to Hector that it would be a bad idea to light up during the ceremony.

Ms. Zelda fluttered around the cottage's jam-packed back yard, her vivid yellow hat matching her yellow full-length dress and giving the impression of a very authoritative sunbeam.

"Stand still!" Ms. Zelda said, in that voice that brooked no argument.

The whole crowd in the backyard stood still and stopped talking.

"Sandy, make sure the roses on the arbor are fixed so they don't droop." Her handyman went to work on the disobedient flowers.

Ms. Zelda turned to Ryan's sister. "What is your name, young lady?"

"Leah, Ma'am."

"Well, Leah, make yourself useful and straighten up those chairs on the lawn."

Ms. Zelda turned on her next target. "Mabel, stop standing there like a fool and center the cake on the serving table, and lay out the silverware properly."

Mabel Rutherford sheepishly stopped staring and went to work.

"Young man!"

Oliver froze in his tracks. "You have a job to do. Come over here and wait by me."

Oliver ran over and took her hand.

Ms. Zelda winked at Ryan. "All it takes is a little organization."

She nodded to the string quartet set up on the brick patio where the old shed had once stood, and they began to play. The people began heading to their seats.

"Joe, see that Ryan is in his place."

"Yes, Ma'am."

Joe pushed Ryan down the aisle toward the spot by the stone wall.

Robin already waited there under the arbor along with the

minister. Robin wore a lavender skirt suit with matching fingernail polish, and she winked at him. "Ready, Ryan?"

He nodded silently.

The arbor was a riot of flowers. The florist must have plucked every bud from the garden in back of Camilla's office in Alvarado Alley. She'd be looking at bare branches for months. But it was worth it to give her this moment.

The music changed mood, and Ryan heard the brief fanfare from the violin that signaled the bride's entrance.

Everyone stopped talking.

His throat constricted. The fanfare segued into a rousing classical piece that he'd only heard fifty times as Camilla sampled mp3s and debated music choices.

Then she was there, outside the dutch door.

Her dress was a mass of snowy tulle, old fashioned looking, but somehow fitting her just the same. Her curls were loose, he was glad to see, without any fussy arrangement that took away from her natural beauty.

The sun hit her curls as she stepped out of the shadow of the cottage's peaked roof, and his breath caught. She had looked like that the first time he'd seen her, with the sun making a halo of her hair and her green eyes the color of fresh-mown grass, wide and guileless in her round face.

She didn't look nervous. Oddly, once he saw her he didn't feel nervous either. All this elaborate ceremony was just a celebration of what they already knew in their hearts.

Oliver, in his little gray suit and lavender tie, with his polished shoes already scuffed from running around, ran up beside her.

"Wait!" he said, loudly enough to be heard over the joyful chorus of the string quartet. "Don't start yet. We have to go up the aisle."

"You're supposed to march," Marisol corrected him from her position as flower girl. She walked with great dignity across the lawn between the folding chairs, throwing petals around enthusiastically as she passed through the crowd. Several people ducked as they were pelted with handfuls of flowers.

Oliver took Camilla's hand. "Okay, now, march!" He pulled her down the aisle.

All the people of the little village rose to their feet as she passed.

When she came to stand next to him under the overflowing arbor, he saw that she had lavender ribbons in her curls. She carried a bunch of flowers that she'd spent hours picking out, with lavender to go with the color theme of the wedding, green ivy to symbolize the tiles above the cottage's fireplace, and blue buds, she'd told him, to match his eyes.

This woman was really going to be his wife. She loved cinnamon in her coffee, hated grape juice, and had freckles all over. She owned eight different pink sweatshirts, could rewire a lamp in five minutes flat, and liked to kiss at the top of the roller coaster. She told Oliver the cottage had invisible fairies living in the chimney, and Ryan wasn't absolutely sure she was making it up. She was a far better person than he could ever be. But she was forcing him to be better than he'd ever been.

He'd learned to let go of responsibility for the whole world. Well, he'd let go a little. He still went over the line sometimes, but he'd learned that Camilla, and Leah, and Joe, and the rest of humanity, really could exist without his constant supervision. And when he forgot, which was still often, Camilla just crossed her arms, glared at him with those big green eyes, and said, "get over yourself, Ryan," and he did.

But he was never getting over her.

"Hey!" Oliver said at his elbow.

Oliver grabbed Ryan's hand and pressed it together with Camilla's. "I give you guys to each other to get married. Hurry up so we can eat the cake," he said, in a complete mangling of the speech Camilla had so carefully taught him.

"Thank you, Oliver," he said, finding his voice.

Camilla smiled. "Thank you, Oliver. Cake later. Wedding first."

"Hurry up then," Oliver said before Robin quickly scooted him off to the side. "I'm ready."

Ryan couldn't agree with him more.

READY FOR ANOTHER HAPPY ENDING? YOU CAN EITHER GET THE next book, Boardwalk Cottage, or save big with the discounted Box Set, each available at your favorite book retailer.

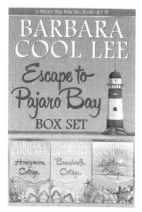

Have you been to Pajaro Bay?

THE PAJARO BAY NOVELS ARE HEARTWARMING ROMANTIC mysteries guaranteed to leave you with a happy ending. Each is a standalone story, so they can be read in any order, or you can follow along from the beginning and see how the world of Pajaro Bay develops. Collect them all:

- 1. Honeymoon Cottage
- 2. Boardwalk Cottage
- 3. Lighthouse Cottage
- 4. Little Fox Cottage
- 5. Rum Cake Cottage
- 6. Songbird Cottage
- 7. Sunshine Cottage

Pajaro Bay newsletter subscribers get so much great stuff! Sign up today for all these exclusive free stories from the world of Pajaro Bay.

http://subscribepage.com/WebBBB

CHARITIES

Ten percent of the earnings from Barb's books are donated to charity. You can learn more about the groups receiving donations at http://BarbaraCoolLee.com.

BARBARA COOL LEE IS THE AUTHOR OF THE *Pajaro Bay Mysteries*, as well as a fantasy series called *The Deeds of the Ariane*. She has three more series in the works, so stay tuned.

Right about now, you'll find her hanging out in her little cottage by the sea on the California coast. She's got a loaf of sourdough bread in the oven, a pot of veggie soup on the stove, and the fog is billowing outside the windows.

Look for her at her desk, sipping her coffee (extra cream and sugar), with her little rescue pup sitting by her side as she works on her next book.

Visit her website at http://BarbaraCoolLee.com.

Made in the USA
Middletown, DE
22 June 2018